# DOUBLE BOOKED IN CORFU

## SAMANTHA PENNINGTON

Serendipity

Serendipity, 51 Gower Street, London, WC1E 6HJ
info@serendipityfiction.com | www.serendipityfiction.com

Print ISBN 9781917163767
Ebook ISBN 9781917163774

Set in Times.
Cover design by Alice Greenway

Samantha Pennington writes light-hearted, uplifting fiction and romantic comedy. She was selected for the inaugural Kate Nash Literary Agency Mentorship program in 2020 and is a member of the Romantic Novelists Association. Sam lives in rural Essex and, when she's not writing, enjoys being first mate on her husband's tiny fishing boat and reading books for her wine club.

You can follow Samantha on social media:

Website:
www.samanthapennington.co.uk

X/Twitter handle:
@sjpenno

Instagram handle:
@sampenningtonwrites

*For Jimbob*

'It's terrible when the one who does the judging judges things all wrong.'
– *Sophocles*.

# PROLOGUE

## CORFU, DAY FIVE

It's been on my mind all day.

As I traipsed half-heartedly around the labyrinthine streets of Corfu Old Town in the blazing heat. As a tour guide gave a potted history of the grand Venetian fortress. As I sipped an Aperol spritz under the shade of a street cafe. Even as I fingered the soft leather of a beautiful red tote, before concluding perhaps I owned enough bags (a sure sign I'm distracted). In short, my sightseeing day has been accompanied by a fizz of nervous excitement that keeps catching me unawares. It is the tell-tale anticipation of pre-date nerves, and yet... we've never met.

Finally, I step from the air-conditioned coach after an excruciatingly long bus ride back to the resort, into the now gentler warmth of early evening. Most holidaymakers out at this time of day are families heading for dinner, or the last of the sun worshippers ambling lazily back to their hotels after a day spent at the beach. It's just that bit too early for the multitudinous couples who flood the streets with their giddy handholding and their freshly washed, bronzed skin. A thrill buzzes through me at the notion that tonight, I might be one of them – dining with company, instead of myself. Unless you counted the needy cats, whose scrawny skeletons I've been trying to flesh out with pickings from my plate.

I walk quickly, having grown used to the steep gradient after days of traversing this hill. I desperately want a shower, but first I head across the track that snakes past my villa and towards the swimming pool of Hotel Electra. The pool is empty but for a long shadow cast from a lone palm tree basking in the setting sun. The sun loungers are finally free of towels and the small bar that serves everything from coffees to cocktails is closed up for the night.

My destination is the small, covered area next to the bar where a small wicker shelving unit houses a chess board, games and books. Three entire shelves are dedicated to Richard & Judy picks of summers past, the former bestsellers and prescribed beach reads often purchased at airports for exactly this destiny; to be left behind.

I'd brought along plenty of books of my own, of course; I could easily read a book in a day. But something I cannot do, *ever*, is pass by a bookshelf without stopping to browse. It's a weakness of mine.

What draws me to this shelf is more obsession than weakness. I need to find out who he is. The writer of all those messages. Messages for me.

At first it had seemed corny, a recently dated platitude left in a second-hand paperback, addressed to the next anonymous reader. A reader who happened to be me. Yet I hadn't been able to resist responding to the message with one of my own, nor checking whether it had been seen.

It had.

Countless messages later and there's barely any blank space left in the book – we've filled every margin.

Which is why I've done a brave, or possibly stupid thing. This morning I left a postcard tucked inside, inviting my correspondent to meet me for a drink… tonight.

He could be an axe-murderer, the pot-bellied guy from around the pool, or even the Greek kid who cleans the pool and collects glasses. But something about this mystery man draws me back every time.

I *have* to know who he is.

I kneel by the bottom shelf, locate *The Girl on The Train* at the far end and I reach behind to the hidden place, to where our book should be.

Only, it isn't.

Feeling the first flush of panic, I pull out the books to either side, then remove them all from the shelf entirely. I move up, systematically removing each book from each shelf until every single paperback is piled in heaps around me.

Our book has gone.

# CHAPTER 1

## ESSEX

### (Six Weeks Earlier)

'Operation Slingshot is underway,' hisses Jess, bobbing in and out of shot as the camera pans around to reveal her location.

Howard leans across me and squints so hard at the strange-looking woman on my phone screen that not only do his eyeballs vanish into slits, but his considerable excess of chins contract to form one giant, formless face.

I'd warned Jess about facetiming me whilst I was at work. Anyone might see. My boss had now seen. Fortunately, Howard is unphased.

'Is that Jess?' he asks, unnecessarily; who else would it be?

Familiar dark oak shelving comes into view as she moves further into the shop. Shelves stacked with neatly displayed paperbacks. Shelves the same as ours.

'Oh God, she's not at it again?'

'Hey Howard,' grins Jess, bumping past a table of celebrity chef hardbacks. Wearing an unconvincing brown wig and oversized spectacles, she bears more than a passing resemblance to Velma from Scooby Doo. 'Just checking in. See you at lunchtime, Annie?'

'Uh-huh,' I reply, before ending the call.

'She really took this whole thing to heart, didn't she?' remarks Howard.

He picks up a stack of books and heads over to the shelves.

'What can I say? I have loyal friends.' I smile and shrug.

'You mean crazy ones,' mutters Howard.

He isn't wrong. Jess and Vikram are quite possibly the daftest people I've ever met. But they are my people. My gang. My cheerleading Davids who are quite willing to take on a literal giant just to help me keep my job.

Strictly speaking, if the Goliath in question, Franklyn's Bookshops, had even the slightest inkling I was behind the prolonged and childish campaign to disrupt business at their Chelmsford City Centre branch, I would likely never work in a bookshop ever again. There may even be a blacklist somewhere for bookshop saboteurs.

'You know it won't work, don't you?' calls Howard over his shoulder. 'The powers that be will have made their minds up long ago. The writing's on the wall, Annie, my love.' He points to the wording above his head. 'That will be us, by Christmas.'

He is, of course, referring to the sign above the tiny section, in this equally tiny, small-town branch of Franklyn's: HISTORY.

The quaint market town of Langtree, my home for over half my life, was the kind of place where you would expect to find: a delicatessen, an antique shop, literally dozens of tearooms, bistros and cafes, an obligatory boutique targeting customers of a Jacques Vert persuasion and without question – a bookshop. It was written in law. Probably.

It was a sad truth that I'd dreamed since girlhood of one day running my own old-fashioned bookshop – the kind with a sliding ladder to reach the top shelves and where I'd be a metaphorical Hugh Grant meeting his Julia Roberts; where the future love of my life would walk through the door with a desire only I could fulfil. Tousled and serious, as I located the last surviving copy of J R Hartley's finest work, our eyes would lock across a faded dustjacket and, eternally grateful, he'd suggest dinner, then bed (the hottie in my fantasy is Mr

Hartley's grandson, in case you were wondering; I do not have a thing for long-dead octogenarians). Kind of *Notting Hill*, but also *Antiques Road Show* and with definite Hot Priest vibes.

Some of those things were at least partly true. I'd worked in a bookshop just like it, this one in fact, on Saturdays as a teenager. However, when I'd returned to my hometown after a stint in the capital, it had since turned into a branch of Franklyn's. And that's where the dream ends and reality begins. Because Franklyn's is a soulless, pound-sterling-worshipping, multinational high-street chain whose ruthless economics have cannibalised Langtree's oldest independent bookshop and then proceeded to measure its employees' worth in the bloodletting ceremony otherwise known as 'The Franks'.

Ah yes, 'The Franks'; a ghastly incentive scheme to cajole us into selling as many books as possible, dreamed up by a board of hedge-funders, in a bizarre self-styled American Dream of the bookselling world. Any one of the two hundred and thirty branches and some two thousand employees could aspire to win an accolade. Most books sold. Best-dressed-window of the year. Regional star bookseller. The list goes on and on. As does the CEO, for literally hours, when representatives of our shops are forced to attend the annual Franklyn's conference at Head Office.

I'd long since given up trying to win anything. No matter how many books I sold, or how many events we organised – author signings, talks and promotions – for the past two years the award for East of England Regional Bookseller of the Year has gone to none other than Liam-up-himself-Shaw, AKA manager of the Chelmsford City Centre shop, our geographical neighbour and contender for survival.

Because that is what we were facing, Howard, Tom, Milly and I. Survival of the fittest.

Take one small bookshop whose core customer base was encapsulated in Mrs Summers, who repeatedly asked where the medical romance section was, because 'back when Mr

Braithwaite owned the shop', as many of our customers remind us, you could find anything you wanted. Alas, our once healthy romance section has since dwindled only to offerings by Ms Austen and Ms du Maurier. Pitch it against a city centre branch with an extra seven hundred and fifty square feet of shop-floor space, add in a dash of job-loss jeopardy to really heighten the senses, then get them to battle it out until the best man wins. Because apparently, it no longer made 'financial sense' to have two outlets of Franklyn's within six easy miles of each other.

It had been three months since the announcement. Who knew how long we had left?

Now, I know what you're thinking.

How could we possibly even compete?

That would be where Vik and Jess come in.

'For what it's worth,' I call back to Howard, just as the door swings open, 'the show's not over until the er, man, has sung. That's you, Howard, you're the man and you're going to deliver on a Pavarotti scale.'

Howard is prevented from replying, by the approach of a man hand in hand with a small child.

'Excuse me,' says the blonde-haired, blue-eyed Adonis and I feel the words land in my belly. There really is something about the tenderness of a man shining with love for his child that makes you hope the mother has left him for her gym trainer.

'We were hoping to return this, please,' he says, pulling a copy of *James and the Giant Peach* from his rucksack. 'Isaac got another one for his birthday, didn't you, buddy?'

In the time it has taken for him to unzip a bag, I've transitioned from coveting him to plotting his violent murder using the only weapon at my disposal – the latest Paolo Carlotta recipe collection, *Eat Yourself Italian*.

Refunds are definitely *not* going to help us win this war.

'Of course,' I reply, taking care to fix Isaac with my brightest, sweetest smile. 'And is there another *exciting* book you'd like to exchange it for? I can show you some of the brand-new ones that have come in this week if you'd like,' I add for the benefit of his father.

'Oh, just a refund, please,' says Dad, distracted by his phone. 'He's got too many books. We're going to go and choose a toy in Tesco instead.'

And indeed, why not? It's commonly known that the social, emotional, developmental and educational benefit of a lump of imported moulded plastic far outstrips anything to be gained from the immersive experience of a story. But what would I know? I apparently only sell doorstops and dust gatherers for a living.

'Can I interest you in the latest Paolo Carlotta, sir? We're offering a promotional discount of twenty per cent and a complimentary Wispa with every copy purchased today.'

Even I want to shrivel up like a five-day-old party balloon at the sound of my limp patter.

'I like Wispas,' says Isaac, his wide-eyed face the picture of innocence.

'I like them too,' I say, conspiratorially. 'And I also *really* like pasta.' I tap the glossy hardback cover featuring an apron-clad Paolo leant against a balcony overlooking a stunning Sorrento vista – an ever-so-conveniently placed bowl of spaghetti napolitana on a table centre stage. 'Do you?'

Isaac grins. 'Yes! Cheesy pasta is my favouritest.'

And there is your argument for more reading, sir, right there.

As I scan in the Roald Dahl book and process the refund, I try not to smile at the sound of Isaac pleading with his dad for a Wispa.

'Ok, that's done,' I say, handing Isaac's dad a copy of his receipt.

'Actually, do you know what?' he adds, although it's unclear whether he is addressing me, or his son. 'Mummy likes that chef guy. Shall we get it for her birthday present?'

'The Wispa?' asks Isaac, a note of unadulterated horror having crept into his voice.

'No, silly. The book. If you're a good boy, you can have the chocolate.'

I feel like high-fiving the pair of them. One copy of this godforsaken waste of wood pulp won't cover the personal cost of providing a box of Wispas, but by Jove, my ploy is working. Even if it is in the form of infant bribery.

It's also one more copy of this week's book of the month, as dictated from upon high, that Franklyn's Chelmsford *won't* be selling. Thanks to Jess.

Two hours later, just as I'm about to pop out for lunch, I witness Howard selling the last of our stack of the Paolo Carlottas. There are another two boxes out back, but it feels like a mini win. I perform a celebratory twerk behind the customer's back, which provokes a cough of discomfort from Howard, and exit the shop into the relentless grey drizzle of spring.

Next door, in the imaginatively named Langtree Tearooms, Jess is already waiting.

Thankfully, she's ditched the wig, which had lent her an oddly demure appearance and I'm glad to have my friend back, complete with edgy undercut crop of startlingly silver hair.

'Ordered you a oasted eese and acon,' she mutters, attempting to inhale cooling air into the molten contents of her mouth. Presumably, she also ordered a toasted cheese sandwich.

'And *this* is why I love you,' I announce, flopping into a chair. 'Mine too?' I motion at the enormous cappuccino.

She nods, before swallowing her food and taking a large glug of her own coffee.

'Fuck me, that's hot,' she exclaims. 'They could use these as a method of torture.'

'Maybe give it a minute?'

Her expression has become thoughtful, as though she is genuinely picturing the practical uses of a scalding toastie.

'Anyhow,' she says, back in the room, 'mission accomplished. Twenty-seven copies of *Eat Yourself Out*, or whatever it's called, successfully redistributed to Religion, Horror, Picture Books, Computing, Parenting, Poetry and, in a moment of genius – the jigsaw section. Managed to stack quite a few of them up there.'

I can't help smirking. Even though this is wrong on all levels, it's also incredibly funny, picturing my friend slinking around the shop depositing their book of the month into places it won't be found. Not for a while anyway and Saturdays, as everyone knows, are the perennial Black Friday of the retail week.

'But Jess, what on earth were you going to say if anyone called you out?'

She makes a pff noise and picks her sandwich back up. 'Call me out on what exactly? Putting a book back in the wrong place? I didn't steal anything, or damage anything.'

'I bet you there's something they could get you on. Knowingly preventing the normal conduct of business, or something like it,' I say.

'Actually, no,' comes a third voice. 'There is no criminal offence of sabotage in UK law.'

Vikram, the third participant in our Save My Job scheme, also the second of my treasured, loyal, and much-loved friends, shakes off his rain-soaked parka and slides into the chair beside me.

'All right, Vik?' acknowledges Jess before sinking into her toastie once more.

'They could possibly cite misleading the customer under consumer protection from unfair trading regs, but only if they could link the act to you, Annie. We'll just have to hope no one from the Chelmsford shop pops in here for lunch and spots us all together.'

Jess shoots Vik one of her Medusa-inspired death stares,

but is thankfully prevented from going full-on pit bull, by the arrival of my own much-anticipated lunch.

'Ah fab, thanks Daphne.' The petite teashop owner with her pure white bob is a complete enigma to me. Impossible to guess at her age, because dyeing one's hair the colour of Daenerys Targaryen's is today's statement of fashion – take Jess as an example, and sensational she looks too. It's more that Daphne possesses the grace of a ballerina in poise and movement, yet has the gob of Peggy Mitchell. She is also the daughter of the now late Mr Braithwaite himself and landlady of this establishment, as well as Franklyn's next door.

'Usual, is it, mate?' she asks Vik, who never ceases to be mesmerised by her.

He manages a slow, adoring nod, his semi-formed legal brain already lost to us.

Vik had dutifully followed the vicarious ambitions of his father when he embarked upon a law degree twelve years ago. It took him six gruelling months of that first year to garner the courage to quit and switch to a music course. Then, having crushed his father's hopes, he decided 'in for a penny, in for a pound' and rocked up for dinner one evening with his new, white boyfriend Steve in tow. A decade later and Vik is still feeling the shockwaves from his choices that fateful year. He enjoys a good relationship with his mother and sisters, a rewarding career as a music teacher at a nearby comprehensive, and the love and support of Ash, who superseded Steve six years ago. But his father barely tolerates him and has refused to ever meet Ash. There have been many times when Jess and I have been tempted to pay Mr Shah a visit and furnish him with our opinions. It hurts to see our friend practically stoop under the weight of rejection after every encounter with his father. Fortunately, Ash is the best kind of tonic – kind, supportive and strong.

'So, did you see him?' I ask Jess, my trail of thought leading me down an alley teeming with selfish, bigoted menfolk.

She treats me to a grin. 'Oh yes. I entertained Liam Shaw

for a full half an hour. After setting my little treasure hunt, I sought him out to enquire if he stocked *Notable Toadstools of the British Isles,* whose author I couldn't quite recall, but whose work was of great import in the field of fungi, my specialist PhD subject, so if they didn't stock it, could they possibly order it in for me?'

Vik snorts and I bury my face in my hands.

'What?' asks Jess. 'Correct me if I'm wrong, but I thought the whole idea here was to stop him from taking your job, Annabel. That was half an hour of selling time he lost, thanks to me. I won't lie though; I've had worse half-hours. That man is H.O.T.'

The gleeful expression on her face only goes to prove she's had a thoroughly enjoyable morning.

'I was surprised actually,' she adds. 'He has a lot of patience for someone you've repeatedly described as an arrogant prick.'

'Speaking of arrogant pricks,' interrupts Vik, 'is there any news on the house front?'

Ah yes, chief among my foes in that grim alley of bigoted adversaries, is my ex-fiancé, Travis.

'It's going on Rightmove next week apparently.' I sigh and put the remaining corner of my toastie down, any appetite bolting from the cafe as fast as Travis had from our home after delivering the news that he was seeing someone else.

'Tosser,' remarks Jess.

'Bastard,' mutters Vik.

'At least he's letting me stay there until it's sold,' I counter, feeling I owe him a shred of loyalty, even now.

The explosive sound from Jess assures me my feelings are misplaced. 'Excuse me, Annie, but it was your home too. I still don't understand why you won't fight him for half.'

I sigh, too weary to have this conversation again. Vik offers a supportive smile. He likely knows, as do I, I'm entitled to nothing. We weren't married, my name isn't on the deeds. My paltry wages barely covered the grocery shopping let alone anything towards mortgage payments. And yet, when Travis had asked me to move in with him two years ago, I'd finally believed I might one day have all those things.

Now single, I was facing not only the loss of my job, which I loved despite everything Franklyn's stood for, but the loss of my home. Everything was falling apart, again, and I felt powerless to stop it.

'It'll all work out,' says Vik, giving my shoulder a quick squeeze.

'Hey. Maybe we can practise some of our specialist skills on potential buyers?' says Jess, suddenly perky. 'Sabotage the sale.'

'There's certainly a law against that,' says Vik.

'So, we don't get caught. Come on, that arsehole deserves it, doesn't he?'

'No,' I say, with more force than I'd intended. 'It's not a crime to break up with someone.'

Jess and Vik exchange a glance.

'Sorry.' I sigh, any buoyancy of this morning's success now dampened by the harsh reality of my life. 'Look, I'd better get back to work, whilst I still have a job.'

'Yep. Those books aren't going to sell themselves,' says Vik in his practised schoolteacher tone.

I heard the subtext: *you're never going to be a maestro, but with a bit of extra effort we can certainly get you a GCSE pass.* There's plenty you can do with that.

'Thanks guys,' I say, placing enough to cover the cost of my lunch on the table. 'I appreciate everything.'

And I absolutely do. I honestly don't know how I'd have got through the past few months without my friends. But as I walk back into the shop and clock the replenished glossy stack of Paola Carlottas, with their obscenely blue sea and sunshine yellow villas steeped into an impossibly beautiful mountainside, a thought blooms, filling the panicked space in my head.

I need to get away. I really, really want a holiday.

# CHAPTER 2

Each year, the benevolent Franklyn's gods permit the manager and one member of personnel from each of their shops to attend the annual conference. This is in no way perceived as a 'jolly'. There is nothing remotely jovial about a day of tedious teambuilding exercises, pep talks, egg sandwiches and by way of a finale, The Franks. Chuck in the personal expense of a train ticket, not to mention the irretrievable hours of your life lost forever to capitalism, and it is sadly lacking appeal.

I'd suffered this miserable fate thrice already and had begged Tom, our only other full-time member of staff, to go in my place but he'd said he'd rather eat the complete works of Tolkien. Even Milly, our part-time A-level student, had pulled a face and retorted 'sounds about as much fun as herpes'. I couldn't really argue with that.

Which is how I come to be sitting on an orange plastic chair opposite a bosomy blonde who is answering the questions I'm required to ask of her from a handout.

'Tell me about your hobbies?' I ask, with as much interest as I can muster.

Niamh, as her name badge indicates, has entirely missed the point of '*Read* Dating' because she answers in an accent borrowed from Emmerdale.

'Mostly, I wander all over t'moors, looking for my girlfriend Cathy.'

Designed as just another way in which Franklyn's could

humiliate us, the concept of this game, unlike *Speed* Dating, is to find out 'fun facts' about our colleagues, most of whom we'll never encounter again in our lives, whilst they take on the persona of a famous fictional character. Then, on their slip of paper, a guess is made as to which character is being impersonated. In the last thirty minutes I have encountered five Heathcliffs, a Cathy and three Christian Greys. Such an imaginative bunch, my colleagues. Nobody had guessed at my Edward Cullen when it had been my turn. Helen of Troy may have launched a thousand ships, but Team Edward launched one of the fastest-growing sub-genres of all time. You can keep your Heathcliffs.

I groan inwardly, wondering if Niamh will cite grave exhumation and necrophilia as her 'weak points', having already listed dark and sexy as her 'strengths', but I am saved by the loud Britain's Got Talent-style buzzer signifying participants should move on.

A cacophonous scraping of chairs ensues, and my next interviewee takes his seat.

'Hi,' says Liam Shaw, with an impish smirk.

It feels like both a greeting and a challenge.

So, he remembers me then.

Which might have *something* to do with our encounter last year.

When Liam had been announced as "Top Regional Bookseller" for the second year running, and bounded onto stage to collect the prize, I'd been so incensed with anger, I'd stood and shouted across the room, 'Excuse me, but I'm not sure that's fair. Surely the same employee shouldn't be able to win each consecutive year. Don't the rest of us deserve a chance?'

Liam had frowned, scanning the crowd until he'd spotted the source of the disruption; I was standing near the back. As he already had the microphone in hand, he replied, in a slightly bemused and vaguely transatlantic accent, 'Gosh, perhaps the lady is right? I don't want to offend anyone.'

A titter had rippled through the crowd and my cheeks burned as heads turned in my direction.

'My *name* is Annabel Baines,' I'd called back. 'I'm the *lady* that works in your closest shop. We're practically neighbours. But as there's only four of us versus your sixteen, and half the shopfloor space to sell from, you probably won't ever see us up there.'

'I should rescind this prize,' he'd said, addressing the CEO, 'perhaps she has a point – the little-store sellers should have a chance at winning too.'

*Little-store.* Seriously? And we call them shops over here, buddy, not *stores.*

I'd become aware of Howard tugging at my sleeve, but it was only when the CEO stepped forward to take the microphone from Liam that I slunk back down into my seat, muttering under my breath.

'Too much?' I'd whispered.

'You're my hero,' he'd whispered back, squeezing my knee.

'Thank you, Liam,' said the CEO, 'your prize won't be rescinded – keep up the great work – and thank you Annabel, you make a good point. Which is why we operate a pro-rata system based on number of employees per square foot when calculating our sales data. Fairness, after all, is the Franklyn's motto – It's All About the Books. And I'm sad to say, Liam, you may have to hone your talents elsewhere, as we do have a two-year rule on consecutive prize winners.'

I drag my attention back to Liam, sitting there smirking at me. Regardless of the warm sensation in my cheeks, I am prepared. One of the sole benefits of this truly awful exercise, is that I've watched him inching his way around the room. I'd made some crude calculations and hoped the lunch bell would beat him to it, but alas, it wasn't to be.

*So* typical that among the five hundred delegates at this

torturous event, we'd found ourselves in the same breakaway group.

Unsmiling, I scan my printed sheet for the most obscure question I can find and throw it at him. This self-obsessed, arrogant fly-by-night is bound to have picked a ubiquitous brooding cad. It doesn't help, of course, that he has the looks for it. Jess was right about that. Well, I'm not about to give him the satisfaction of a chance to flirt. Not with me.

'Imagine you've found an IKEA flatpack bookcase without instructions. Talk me through how you'd assemble it, please.'

Stick that up your tight-fitting Franklyn's regulation polo shirt, Liam Shaw. How's Mr Darcy going to figure that one out?

To my surprise, he crosses his legs and sits back in his chair ramrod straight, transforming in front of my eyes into something quite disturbing.

'Well now, the first thing we'll have to do is get the darned box open. I always think a task becomes so much more enjoyable when you hum a little tune, don't you?' He leans forward conspiratorially and *actually* winks.

I stare back at him, this bane of my life, whose very existence puts my job and my livelihood in jeopardy as he grins like a lunatic. He has lovely teeth, I begrudgingly note.

'And what is a bookcase, but a place to put one's books? I think I know the perfect song for that. It goes…'

I'm saved from hearing any more, but not from the growing curiosity of wondering if Liam really had intended to burst into song when the buzzer sounds again, and lunchtime is announced.

'Can't *wait* to see what you write on my card,' he says, handing me the small slip.

We are meant to hand them all in at the end, for what purpose I can't possibly fathom. After all, if the aim of the game is to get the most correct guesses, then why not simply spell out your character in idiot fashion as Niamh had done, and to hell with all the questions? I hadn't learned a thing about her, other than she probably watched all the Yorkshire-set soap operas.

'Can't *wait* until this hell-day is over,' I mutter, scrawling 'Generic Disney Heroine' on the card. I slap it down on my chair before making my way to the trestle tables that are in no way groaning under the weight of so little free food.

I wrangle my way along the queue until I fall into step beside Howard. 'Kill me now. End this misery.'

Howard passes me a paper plate.

'Don't be so melodramatic. It's not that bad, and you never know – we might actually win something this year, especially after they implemented your Secret Santa book gift idea across all shops last Christmas. It was a roaring success and I'm sure you've plenty more to pull out of your magic bag.'

'It wasn't *my* idea, Howard, there are entire mail order companies dedicated to the very concept. Blind date with a book? Mystery boxes? And as for...' But I tail off, my brain having lodged on Howard's last words.

Magic Bag. Bloody bollocks. Of course – Liam was Mary Bloody Poppins. Oh well, an incorrect guess can only be a good thing when it comes to denting an already over-inflated ego.

Howard shrugs, already lost to the mini pork pies. As much as I'm fond of the big-hearted man who has been my boss, and my friend, for the past six years, his interest in the Franklyn's chain is now solely limited to this buffet table and the four-month countdown to his retirement. Whilst I, on the other hand, had been completely focused on stepping into his shoes as manager and a modest increase in salary, right up until they'd announced that one of our shops would be closing imminently. I'd been banking on it, in fact, because renting somewhere to live by myself, on what Franklyn's currently paid me would be a non-starter.

After a tedious luncheon of curling sandwiches and a few cheesy puffs we all dutifully retake our seats, which have now been rearranged into rows as we'd munched. If I were being honest, Howard was right, the day hasn't been *quite* as tedious as expected – some of the games have been entertaining, at least. Even coming face-to-face with Liam, who had been disconcertingly nice, hadn't been the Mexican stand-off I'd anticipated. I'd almost felt a little guilty about calling him out last year. *This*, however, would be the truly brain-melting part of the day.

Regardless of any recognised geographical regions within the UK, the Franklyn's chain elects to carve up the country into roughly six areas. Our category, East of England, also comprises North London, which makes it not only a bulging portfolio for the area manager but next to impossible to achieve even moderate levels of sales success when compared to other shops within the group.

Nonetheless, after a rambling preamble, the CEO is passed a stack of silver envelopes by his PA and my heart begins to race – it's time for The Franks. And our turnover *has* increased by a third over the last three months. This much I know. Our near-constant string of author events, as well as our involvement with local schools for World Book Day and countless other promotions (not all, or even half of them, endorsed by Head Office), has got to count for something. Wouldn't it be nice to have our hard work recognised?

But as the awards for each category are read out and the recipients step up to claim their prizes, which consist, so imaginatively, of book tokens, any hopes I'd harboured ebb away under the almighty weight of boredom. After starting at the top in Scotland and working their way down the country, by the time he reaches our region, I am barely even awake.

Predictably, all the awards in our area are bestowed upon London shops and staff.

'Well, we might not have won anything, but at least Chelmsford didn't either this year,' whispers Howard.

'Amen to that.'

Finally, there is just one silver envelope left. The CEO clears his throat.

'And now we come to a brand-new award for this year – one I'm sure hereafter will become the Frank's most coveted prize. The recipient has gone above and beyond in the day job. Nominated by both employees and customers alike and applauded for their charisma, kindness, enthusiasm and – let's not forget what we're all here to do, folks – natural flair for selling books...'

The CEO pauses for a minor ripple of polite laughter. It's all *so* butt-clenchingly corny.

'...so, without further ado, let me announce that the Franklyn's Overall *National Bookseller of the Year* and deserving winner of an all-expenses paid luxury holiday for two is... Liam Shaw of the Chelmsford City Centre branch.'

An ear-splitting round of applause from somewhere over to my right ensues. It's like being transported to a Take That concert where the target audience averages at forty-seven and prefers a seated ticket, but after a few proseccos they still manage a rousing burst of lust for the original poster boy. Liam does not disappoint, pulling himself tall and taking a mock bow, before strolling unhurriedly to the stage.

Howard's hand on my arm pushes me over the edge.

'You were right, Howard,' I say in quiet fury, 'the writing was on the wall all along. We've been wasting our time.'

I push back my chair and slip out.

The Franklyn's head office is an ugly, concrete building. It occupies all four floors above their flagship shop in Bloomsbury, one floor of which has been converted into their very own conference facility complete with fully stocked bar. I descend the first flight of stairs, intending to head down onto the shop floor. It's of no matter that I spend almost every waking hour surrounded by books; there is always something new to look at, somewhere different to lose myself. Of course, what I want to do is lose myself in Bali, or the Maldives, anywhere really, but preferably somewhere hot and far from home. That's now looking about as likely as keeping my job, whilst Liam fuckface Shaw sips negronis on a hotel balcony, funded by what should have been my wages.

They may just as well have announced the closure of the Langtree bookshop live on stage. I mean – why even invite us? Why involve us in this charade of a training day when they're shutting us down?

As I reach the second-floor landing, I read the acrylic printed signs.

*2nd Floor*
*Human Resources*
*Sales and Marketing*
*Cafeteria*

I check the time. Three forty-five. This miserable day isn't scheduled to end until five o'clock, and there's another entire hour of company rhetoric to endure, none of which isn't spoon-fed to us on a daily basis through the staff email bulletin anyway. No one will even notice I've gone.

Working my way through a mental volley of insults to hurl at Liam Shaw, I traverse a bright corridor lined with open plan offices, empty of employees owing both to the fact that it's a Sunday and that any relevant personnel will be upstairs anyway. It dawns on me as I push on the double doors to the staff cafeteria that it will be empty for the same reason.

I am correct. Metal shutters declare the servery closed for business.

There's a vending machine in the corner where I can grab a potentially undrinkable coffee, but I scan the menu above the servery anyway, noting that absolutely none of the food or drink options are subsidised. A mere jacket potato will set you back the price of a sirloin steak in my local pub. Yet another way in which the Franklyn's machine is designed to screw over everyone within its reach, whilst purporting to nurture and value.

It's probably just as well I'll be looking for a new job. I'm not sure I can stomach the vitriol I feel for my employer another day longer, despite the emotional attachment I feel for my hometown bookshop, which, when I think about it, is really pure nostalgia for what it once was.

Cardboard cup of black coffee in hand, I take out my phone and begin a circuit of the large room. Jess's phone goes to voicemail.

I open my mouth to rant, about to tell her about Liam and the prize and the fact that the Langtree shop is now bound to close, that it had all been for nothing, when I remember my friend is on a spa break today. She does not need my petty, trivial nonsense putting a dampener on her relaxation.

God, I need to get a grip. Get my life back on track.

Ending the call, I stop by a large noticeboard and sip at my coffee, which is vile, as predicted, and tastes vaguely of fish.

It seems such an outdated thing, the humble noticeboard; there's little need for it now in modern society. Case in point – there's an orange flyer advertising salsa classes, offering a ten per cent discount on block bookings if used two years previously to today's date. There are countless faded takeaway menus too, rendered useless by Uber Eats and Deliveroo. I'm about to turn away when something catches my eye.

Pinned over the top of a spin class advert, is a small handwritten card.

*Greek Holiday Apartment – huge discounts for
Franklyn's staff
Contact Clare in Accounts or Richard in Fulfilment for
more details.*

An image of the hateful Paolo Carlotta hardback swims in front of my eyes.

OK, so not Italy exactly, but somewhere equally warm and blue. Aegean, or Ionian blue. God, it's been at least three years since I've had a proper holiday. One that involved getting on a plane and leaving these isles, anyway. Travis had been away plenty; his job meant he was constantly jetting off to far-flung cities. But when it came to our own holidays, we always seemed to end up visiting his parents in Devon.

Has Holly-Mae, his current paramour, been subjected to the guest room that stinks of dachshund and wet wellington boots yet? Good luck to her, she'll need it.

Bloody Travis. Sodding Liam Shaw. Fucking Franklyn's.

I raise my phone and take a picture of the advertisement. I can almost taste the calamari.

# CHAPTER 3

## CORFU, DAY ONE

### (Four Weeks Later)

Stepping from the EasyJet plane and into the warm evening air after a fortnight of sustained thirty-degree temperatures at home isn't quite the pinch-me moment I'd hoped for when I'd booked this holiday. A weekend in Reykjavik may have been more of a tonic, truth be told, although the sudden heatwave has brought some unexpected advantages.

For one, I'm already boasting what passes for the beginnings of a tan on my pale skin, though much work is to be done in the correcting of a t-shirt-shaped white patch from the rare glimpses of sun I get back home, a testament to how much time I spend at work.

Another by-product of the uncharacteristically tropical weather at home these past couple of weeks, had been the necessitation of some new summer clothes. It was amazing what four years of relative contentment could do to a body because when I dug out my old suitcase of holiday clothes, apart from a favourite pair of cut-off denims that had always been a bit loose, I had needed to replace all of it and quickly, given the heat. Funds were tight, but I'd always preferred the thrill of rummaging through charity shops anyway and by the time my holiday came around I'd amassed an eclectic new summer wardrobe and courtesy of Jess's sewing machine and selected parts of my favourite old dress, a cute hair scarf and matching beach bag.

It had taken me less than twenty-four hours after the day of the Franklyn's conference to secure a one-week rental of Villa Karina, in Kassiopi on the island of Corfu and a return flight from Stansted. It turned out that Clare in Accounts, whom I had emailed on the train home whilst Howard snored beside me, was amid a protracted and messy divorce. The villa, a jointly held asset, was being let out at a criminally low rate until such a time as it was sold, as neither party were able to contemplate holidaying there themselves. Too many memories, apparently.

Well, I for one was very much up to the challenge of making new memories. Most of which would involve me, one of the seven carefully chosen paperbacks currently weighing down my suitcase and various scenarios featuring beverages and snacks. I couldn't bloody wait.

At the bottom of the steps, I pull up the handle of my case and hurry along with my fellow passengers to cram into the bus waiting to transport us a mere thirty metres to Ioannis Kapodistrias (Corfu International Airport).

I'd been to mainland Greece once, many years before, and recognise with comforting familiarity many things I'd forgotten, like the rapid-fire Greek of tour operators loitering in Arrivals. The warnings in the lavatory not to flush toilet paper because of the narrow pipes. The feeling that you were far from home upon seeing words written in an entirely different alphabet. In France, in Spain, even Germany to a certain extent you stood a fair chance of guessing at words, even if you knew little of the language. Here, I may as well have been trying to interpret Martian and was grateful I'd had the foresight to order myself a taxi. It's late, and I'm exhausted.

'Kalispera. Taxi?' enquires the chain-smoking gentleman who bears a piece of torn cardboard with a handwritten approximation of my name upon it – at least, I presume *ANY*

*BRAINES* is close enough to Annie Baines to discount a third party.

'Kalispera,' I reply, offering him a tired smile in confirmation.

I follow him as he grinds out his cigarette on the roadside before throwing open his boot and placing my case inside. Then I take up residence in the back of the car and sit back to enjoy the one-hour complimentary theme park ride I didn't know I'd booked as an extra.

To say I see my approaching death at each cliff-edged chicane along the coastal route to the north of the island would be to put it mildly.

In the end, closing my eyes and breathing deeply seems the only option. Which is working until I'm flung forwards in my seat at the sudden braking to avert a head-on collision with a coach.

The stream of vitriol directed at the coach driver along with wildly gesticulating arm signals, cuts through any language barrier there may be, and I get the gist, 'fucking idiot' being the main one.

Eventually, when I've begun to think the English Riviera, Devon, may have been an altogether safer option, the car slows. We have been through countless beach resorts along the way, not that I've been able to see much beyond streetlamps and moonlight reflected on water, and the occasional stumbling reveller, but I have recognised the place names of Dassia and Ipsos, and seen signs for Agios Stefanos. This, however, doesn't look like a beach. This is a crossroads in the middle of a deserted strip; shops, bars and restaurants long closed and with them my hopes of food.

'Ela,' says the driver, pulling to a stop. He turns to face me and uses his fingers to make a walking action. 'You walk from here.'

'Walk? Walk where? I don't know where I'm going and it's...' I touch my phone to wake it up, 'nearly two o'clock in the morning.'

The driver shrugs and opens his door.

With no choice, I follow suit. 'Do you know where Villa Karina is?' I ask, waiting helplessly as he retrieves my case from the boot and I instantly regret having pre-paid online because now, I have no leverage.

'Up,' he says, pointing vaguely toward the shadow of a looming hillside. 'Go up. Car cannot go.'

'Right,' I say, weakly, taking the handle of my case. 'Up.'

As the taxi roars away, I calculate the likelihood of Clare from Accounts still being awake. At midnight UK time, on a Tuesday, it's possible. Less likely that she'll be in front of her work email, which, I belatedly realise, is the only contact information I hold for her.

'Any problems at all, call Maria,' she'd written in our last exchange, along with a mobile number for the local housekeeper they employed to clean and prepare the villa between stays. I very much doubt Maria will appreciate being disturbed either. I will just have to use my initiative and attempt to find the villa, in pitch darkness, with no street name or directions other than 'up'.

With an attempt to shake off the disappointment, compounded by discovering I had no phone signal, I concentrate instead on my surroundings. My limited research into the small but trendy resort of Kassiopi had prepared me for a hilly terrain, but this is something else. There is one tiny lane that I can see, branching off from the main road towards where the driver indicated I go and vertical would be a more appropriate adjective than steep. I take in a great lungful of the warm, vaguely citrusy night air and set off, my suitcase wheels trolleying loudly behind me as they bash upon the rough ground. It quickly becomes apparent why cars can go no further.

It's always disorientating arriving on holiday in the dead of night and I'm perfectly aware that what currently seems a daunting task would have been fun in the daylight hours; that exciting first glimpse of sea and discovering the area, street by street. But I would give anything right now for a bottle of water and a bed. To hell with the rest of it.

Sweat trickles down my back, pooling in my waistband as I puff my way uphill past hotels and terraced houses – why the hell had I worn trousers for the flight? It seems ridiculous now, when even Vik, who normally avoids exposing his spindly, hairy legs at any cost, had worn shorts to drive me to the airport. Clumps of my long wavy hair escape my messy bun and plaster themselves to my face and mouth as I climb, pausing every now and then to catch my breath and squint at tiny, illegible signs and house names.

I try to recall anything Clare has told me about Villa Karina. She said it had a partial sea view (which probably means if you perform a plank on the balcony ledge and crane your neck you can glimpse a triangle of blue). And that it was pink. That's not a particularly helpful fact right now under an inky sky when everywhere looks the same shadowy shade of dark, with the occasional white painted balustrade catching the moonlight.

Breathless, I stop at the top of a slope and look about. I seem to have reached the top. Or as near the top as the buildings go, for beyond is only the dense blackness of trees. In a moment of idiocy, I let go of my case to wipe the sweat from my face and watch in dismay as it rolls backwards, picking up speed so suddenly I can't reach out to stop it. There in the thick quiet of night, punctuated only by the gentle chirping of cicadas and the humming of air conditioning units, the rolling, bumping and eventual crashing of my tatty purple hard-shell case sounds like an explosion.

I stand, frozen to the spot, a wave of panic swelling within me.

A dog starts barking.

Another one joins in.

Then, a heated volley of voices call out into the night, before a door slams and the dog's yapping quietens to a pathetic whimper.

This is becoming a nightmare. I should have known better than to book the last flight of the day, but it was all I could afford. My paltry savings had just about covered the cost of the flights and the villa, then Howard had let me commandeer the rota for the past month so that by the time I came to order my currency, I'd worked enough extra hours to give me a modest amount. I was going to live on a diet of bread, olives and cheap local wine and couldn't be happier. Except now I'm wondering if I've made a mistake coming at all. Maybe what I should have been doing was saving my money for the new home I would be needing imminently and using my annual leave to find a new job.

Exasperated, I cross the lane to sit against a wall and catch my breath before having to descend the hill to retrieve my case and haul it back up again. I pull out my phone, hoping for enough phone signal to bring up Google maps. There is nothing, not even one bar. I can't even message Jess or Vik, even though I feel mean enough to wake them up.

Desperately, I stand, raise my phone above my head in case one more foot of altitude might do it and it's then, in the dim glow of my phone screen, I see the small sign:

*Villa Karina*

I shine my phone around to see a row of similar little signs and an arrow pointing to the right. Relief floods through me, bringing with it a galvanising thirst and radical change in mood.

Perhaps Maria will have left a bottle of water. Better yet, would it be too much to hope Clare had instructed her to provide a complimentary bottle of wine or a packet of biscuits? We were colleagues after all, and perhaps after this, I might even suggest we meet up, and lend her a friendly ear as she battles with her ex over alimony.

Buzzing with renewed energy, I bound back down the lane and find my case where it had come to rest against a metal fence, and then retrace my steps to the top.

Red-faced, panting and now bursting for a wee, I follow

the arrow and round a corner onto a crazy paved patio and stand back to take it in. It is a row of five or six villas, divided into lower and upper storeys. I already know Villa Karina is a first-floor property with a balcony, so I head for the tiled stairs leading to the upstairs apartments and follow the corridor of creamy stone, each doorway lit from above with the glow of an orangey lamp.

Villa Karina is right at the end and is just as Clare had described, with a small grey lock box beside the front door. I pull the piece of paper from my pocket, having not trusted my phone battery to last, and punch in the six-digit code, a grin spreading across my face when it opens to reveal a small bunch of keys attached to a keyring the shape of a starfish.

'Hi Honey, I'm ho-me!' I can't help singing out to myself as the door swings wide open, such is my elation. Then, realising I'm being rudely loud at this ungodly hour, I shush myself like a naughty child. I think the stress has made me delirious.

I feel along the wall for the light switch and snap it on, excited to see my home for the week.

I am in the kitchen. Whitewashed walls and terracotta floor tiles, with wooden shutters at the windows and a freestanding fridge humming away in the corner. It is all typically Greek. The air is cool on my skin, and I realise with gratitude Maria has been in and put the air conditioning on. Clapping eyes on the dining table, I also spy with relish that the saintly woman has provided a litre bottle of water.

Dropping my case, I cross the room and grab it. I'm so parched I'd probably have drunk straight from the tap, then regretted it for the remainder of my holiday. It isn't a new bottle, which seems odd. Around a quarter of it is missing. Perhaps it's simply been refilled from a larger container, I reason, necking the contents in one long slug.

Belching loudly then giggling at myself, I wander into the hallway to explore, and then stop dead.

Halfway between the kitchen and what I presume to

be the lounge, though difficult to tell in the gloom, is the unmistakable shape of a rucksack lying open on the floor, its contents spilling out like a disembowelled beast.

An icy thought shudders through me. Am I in the right apartment?

I must be. I have the key and the code.

Has Clare's husband come here without her knowing? Is there someone in here right now?

At that very moment a toilet flushes, and I watch in petrified horror as a door to my right flings open and a man emerges, naked, but for an eye mask dangling from his neck.

# CHAPTER 4

It isn't clear who screams first, me or him.

Milliseconds before he tugs the bathroom light cord off, my brain registers that the genitalia swinging in my peripheral vision is attached to a familiar shape.

He registers, too, that there is a person standing in his hallway. Scrub that – *my* hallway. This is enough to rouse me from my fugue state.

'What the fuck?' I yell.

Simultaneously, Liam Shaw yanks the light back on, with one hand covering his privates and roars, 'Don't move a muscle. I'm armed and trained to kill!'

My eyes drift helplessly to the weapon in his hand. Not the hand covering his doodah, but the other one, which wields presumably the only object within easy arm's reach, which happens to be a loofah.

'What the hell?' His voice completes a key change, as recognition sinks in. 'Annabel Baines? What on God's earth are you doing here?' He drops the loofah and removes ear plugs from his ears, which explains the element of surprise.

'What am *I* doing here? Is this some kind of sick joke?'

Liam stares back at me blankly before seeming to register his state of undress. He steps backwards, muttering 'just a sec,' as he pushes the door half closed, then re-emerges with a towel wrapped around his waist.

'Clearly,' he says, folding his arms across his chest, 'there has been some kind of mix-up. Unless, of course, you *have* been sent here to kill me?' He raises an eyebrow. 'Have you?'

The *arrogance!* Words (almost) fail me, but I manage to angrily spit out, 'The jury's out. But believe me, mate, if I had – then a loofah most certainly wouldn't have stopped me.'

He gives a small laugh. 'Don't they always say to make yourself scary and big when faced with danger? You know, bears and stuff.'

'Right. Get many bears on Corfu, do you?' I scoff. 'And also, trust me, if *big* was what you were going for,' I waggle my finger in admonishment, 'epic fail.'

To his credit, Liam doesn't bite, just shakes his head in bewilderment.

'Come through,' he sighs, rubbing his eyes and leading the way. Realising the eye mask is still hanging around his neck, he pulls it over his head and tosses it onto a console table.

As lights are switched on, it becomes apparent the apartment is narrow but long, the kitchen giving way to a corridor with two doors leading off it and eventually through to a lounge which houses a sofa, an easy chair and not much else, apart from the odd scattered personal effect: a book, a bottle of sun lotion, a pair of flip-flops. Large, shuttered doors at the end of the room indicate a balcony.

'I got here yesterday afternoon. This afternoon,' he corrects himself, 'I don't even know what time it is.'

'Stupid o'clock in the morning, which considering I'm normally in bed by ten is really bloody late.' I blow out a long, frustrated breath. 'Look, I don't know what's going on here, but clearly it's a bit late to be phoning home to sort it out now. So, if you could pack your stuff up as quickly as possible, I'd appreciate it. I'm shattered.'

Liam frowns, looking genuinely puzzled. 'Pack my stuff up?'

'Er yes,' I reply with impatience. Is this bloke thick? 'I've paid to rent this apartment for one week, starting from today, the 28th of June, or yesterday, depending on how you look at it. Forgive me, but whatever cock-up you've made is absolutely nothing to do with me. Take it up with Clare.'

'Clare? And... who is Clare?'

'Clare in Accounts? You must have booked this through her? Or her husband? Works at Franklyn's too, can't think of his name. This is their apartment.'

Liam looks blank.

'Sorry, I've no idea who Clare or her husband are. But I'm afraid it must be you who's made the cock-up. I won this holiday in the Franks, remember?'

I blink as I process what he is saying.

He gives a sarcastic laugh. 'Turns out my "all-expenses-paid luxury holiday" only extended to an EasyJet flight, a self-catering rental, which according to you is owned by a member of staff, and two hundred and fifty euros towards food. But I guess it could have been worse. It could have been a caravan park in Margate.'

'What's wrong with Margate? My grandparents live in Margate,' I snap. 'I'm so very sorry our seaside towns don't measure up to what you're used to in the U.S.'

'Nothing wrong with Margate at all,' he says, eyeballing me with caution. 'I merely meant *this*' he gestures to the room we stand in, 'isn't exactly what I'd call a "luxury" vacation. Not that I'm complaining, it's perfectly fine. And for what it's worth, I only lived in the States for the first eighteen years of my life, the UK is what I'm *used* to.'

'Sounds like you are to me.'

'What?'

'Complaining. Sounds like they should have awarded the prize to someone a little more grateful.'

Liam's brow creases and he looks unsure what to say next, but I most certainly do.

'Look, why don't we get a few hours' sleep. Then we can call Head Office and sort this all out in the morning. I'm sure once they're made aware of the error, they'll book you into a hotel or whatever and we can both just get on with our holidays.'

Liam nods slowly, then scratches his head.

'OK, OK, you're right. That sounds like the best plan, there's bound to be an explanation. The only problem is this is a one-bedroom apartment,' he points to the sofa, 'but I think that turns into a bed.'

'Excellent. Well, I'll leave you to it then.'

I turn on my heel to locate the bedroom.

'Wait a minute,' calls Liam. 'I've just been sleeping in that bed, that's my bed.'

At this I stop and turn around. Seriously? The guy who can apparently do no wrong, who has been lauded for his – what was it? 'Charisma, kindness and enthusiasm', *that* guy is going to fight like a five-year old over a bed because he was there first? I give a bitter little laugh at the irony of it all.

'Right. Of course. This will do me fine. I presume there is some spare bedding somewhere. Can you check?' I level him with a look I hope says *just do as I ask, you enormous fuckwit*, rather than *if you don't leave the room right now, I'm going to burst into tears.*

To his credit, Liam walks away.

I hear doors and cupboards opening as I go about retrieving my case from the kitchen and wheeling it into the lounge. I don't look up when I hear him approach.

'There's two sheets and a pillow. I couldn't find a blanket but turn off the air con if you get cold, the controller's over there.'

I don't respond, instead busy myself with pulling out the sofa bed, which looks about as comfortable as a recently tarmacked road.

'Let me help you with—'

'I'm fine,' I snap.

'For what it's worth, I meant surely you wouldn't want to sleep in the bed I've been sleeping in naked for the past few hours. I mean, I showered, but…' He tails off. 'TMI?'

'U-huh.'

Although let's face it, I've already seen what he sleeps in. Finally, I look up.

He is standing there slightly awkwardly, his arms laden with the bedding, which he puts down on the arm of the chair.

'I'll leave you to it then. Night.' He turns to walk away.

'Thanks,' I say sulkily, watching the muscles in his ridiculously broad back flex as he reaches up to rub his neck.

This *cannot* be happening.

# CHAPTER 5

## CORFU, DAY TWO

The sofa bed, whilst free of stains and unpleasant smells, had made for a torturous slumber. I wake, groggy, disorientated and mentally formulating a detailed Trip Advisor review on the sleep quality of the mattress, until I remember where I am, and more pressingly, with whom.

I sit bolt upright.

The shutters have kept the room in semi-darkness, but there are slivers of bright white light where they meet the tiled floor. I shiver and clutch my ineffectual sheet to me. Why is it so cold? This is Greece for heaven's sake, why the devil am I cold?

I wrap the sheet around me and slide from the bed, hunting around until I locate the tiny remote control for the air conditioning and turn the blessed thing off. Then, in one smooth action, I release the bolt securing the shutters and fling them open. Brilliant sunshine floods the room.

This, I decide, unlocking the glazed French doors and stepping out onto the balcony, this is what I've needed. Not the heat, we've had plenty of that for a change, although this is an entirely different kind – not the oxygen clogging, mind-slogging burden accompanying an English heatwave. Where you still have to work and live in houses equipped with thick carpets and fabric sofas instead of cooling stone and marble; endure festering black bins for a fortnight and fight over the last iceberg lettuce in Tesco, attempting to sleep with a damp flannel and a fan. *This* is a hazy sky and a cobalt sea, rippling like silk – Clare had actually undersold the view – and a deliciously warm breeze whispering against my skin. The small terrace boasts a stylish wrought iron bistro set, a potted olive tree and a giant urn spilling eye-popping hot pink bougainvillea over the side of the balcony.

Everything about it is perfect.

*Almost* everything is perfect, I grimace on hearing the front door slam shut.

'Do you want tea or coffee?' calls a voice from inside the apartment, 'I got both, also sugar, milk and some pastries for breakfast.'

Because there was still the small matter of finding my holiday apartment occupied by my least favourite person in the world. Well, within the county of Essex at least. OK, *perhaps* he tied for that place with Travis. But at least I had quite liked my ex-fiancé, once upon a time. I think.

'I'm going to take a shower,' I reply in answer to his question, exiting the balcony and coming face to face with him where he stands in the lounge, wearing faded blue chino shorts and a crumpled white t-shirt, munching on a deliciously sticky syrup-soaked pastry. He nods towards a bulging paper bag on the coffee table where I can see more baked goods. Why is he being so nice, damn him?

'Then I have to make some calls. But no. Thank you.'

'Suit yourself,' he says.

As I move towards him the assault on my senses is immediate. I'd kill for a sugar hit. I'd kill for a coffee. What I must try hard not do, I tell myself, somehow managing to shimmy past him, my white sheet trailing behind me like a Poundland wedding dress, is kill my work colleague.

The bathroom, which I'd visited last night once certain Liam was safely back in his room, like the rest of the apartment, is devoid of the personal touches that make a place a home. Perhaps Clare and Richard have already stripped it of anything personal in readiness for sale.

There is a plain black washbag on a glass shelf above the sink which I presume to be Liam's along with various travel-sized bottles, tubs and tubes scattered around the floor of the shower cubicle. I kick them into a corner in irritation, making a mental note to ask Maria to come and give the place another once-over when Liam's moved out.

The shower is blissful, not too hot, not too weak, but it's only after I've submerged myself beneath it, I realise I've come in here without a towel or any of my own toiletries. I bend down to take a closer look at Liam's array of man-stuff, all carefully decanted into colour-coded plastic containers. I open a few and sniff them, selecting a purple one that smells the least like Johnny Depp digging a hole in the desert. I'm pleasantly surprised by the crisp linen scent and use all the lovely froth to wash the rest of my body.

Afterwards, I have no choice but to wrap myself back up in my bedsheet, and ease the door open, hoping Liam has taken the hint and buggered off.

No such luck. He is sipping coffee on the balcony, the double doors flung open.

'Would you mind giving me some privacy?' I ask pointedly, as though me standing there dripping next to my open suitcase isn't enough of a hint.

'Sorry. Sure.' He jumps up from his seat and files past me. 'I'll be in my room.'

'*Whatever,*' I mutter under my breath, bending down to rifle through my case for something to wear.

'Oh, by the way,' he says, doubling back.

I stand upright with a cute little white dress in my hand (strapless, so I can get straight to work on evening out my tan).

'I made you this anyway.'

'What?' I ask, spinning around impatiently.

'Ahhh, shit!'

I stare down at the coffee-drenched garment in my hand, at the rich dark liquid running off my wrists and dripping down onto the tiled floor where it pools in the grouting.

'Sorry!' says Liam, jogging into the kitchen for a tea towel, 'I took a punt on espresso. You seem like the kind of woman who runs on espresso.'

I love espresso, just not all over my favourite dress. And I'm not sure I like his inference about my personality. Did he mean in a good way, like how espresso is strong and feisty, if a bit small? Or as essential fuel for an otherwise slow brain to reach even half capacity?

'Here give that to me.' He pulls it from my wet hands, swapping it with the tea towel. 'I'll put it straight in to soak.'

I mop up the mess as best I can, thankful it hadn't taken out the entire contents of my suitcase.

Liam calls out from the bathroom, 'I'll give it a quick wash and hang it out to dry.'

'It's fine, I can do it,' I snap, then feeling bad, add, 'but thank you.'

A few minutes later, I'm dressed in a vest top and shorts but already feeling hot and sweaty. I yank a brush through my fresh-smelling but tangled hair, which is in serious need of conditioning and wander out to the hallway where Liam is emerging from the bathroom with my dress.

'I think it all came out,' he says, cautiously. 'But I'll buy you another if not.'

'Don't worry about it, it was only from a charity shop, but thanks.' I take it from him and head to the balcony to hang it up.

As I shake out the dress, a powerful and familiar scent fills the still air and I'm seized with a horrifying thought. Fearfully, I sniff at the dress, and then at my long, damp hair.

Shite.

'Liam?' I call, hurrying back through the apartment.

'In here,' he calls.

I pop my head around the bedroom door. The room is

nicely decorated in eye-catching white and blue, although I couldn't care less about that right now.

'Can you come here a sec?'

He frowns but follows me to the bathroom.

I'm getting itchy now, can feel my breathing quicken.

*It's all right, it'll be all right. Calm down.*

I clear my throat. 'What did you use to wash my dress?'

He picks up the small purple container from the side and grins. 'Persil. I always bring laundry liquid, so I can travel light and just wash stuff out. Don't you?'

I want to say, *No, Liam! I bring enough clothing for the whole of my holiday, you absolute weirdo*, but instead, in a carefully controlled, non-panicky tone, I ask, 'Um, what kind of Persil?'

He makes a face. 'Uh, the regular, washing your clothes kind? Smells nice, gets stuff clean?'

'But non-biological, right?'

It's no good, my skin already feels as though it's being pricked by a thousand angry porcupines.

Liam shrugs, 'I don't think so.'

Then he seems to register something in my expression, or perhaps it's because if my face looks as red as it feels, it must be blinding the poor guy.

'Wait a minute, are you allergic?'

'U-huh,' I say, already pulling my shorts down.

'But you haven't even worn the dress yet.'

I yank the vest over my head. I'm wearing a bikini beneath but Liam's eyes bulge as he predicts where this is going, and he bolts from the room.

'Are you OK?' he shouts through the gap in the door. 'Do you need anything?'

When I don't reply because I'm frantically hosing every inch of my body with the shower head, rinsing and dousing and douching, he finally says, 'I'll leave you to it then.'

A full thirty minutes later, long after the water has gone

cold, I finally step from the shower, and see Liam has wedged a clean towel in the gap of the open door.

He sucks in a breath as I walk back into the lounge. 'Jeez. You must have a really bad allergy.'

I am radioactively hot and could be easily mistaken for Deadpool, but on the plus side, you can't see my white patches anymore.

'Just extremely sensitive skin, actually. I always use non-bio, so my clothes don't make me itch...' It's no good, I can't keep the annoyance at bay. 'But then again, Liam, I don't *normally* wash MY ENTIRE FACE, BODY AND HAIR IN BLOODY PERSIL. I mean, what moron keeps their laundry detergent with their shampoo? Let alone bring it all the way to Greece?'

'Hang on a minute,' Liam bites back. 'I never asked you to go snooping through my personal stuff and using my toiletries. Bit rude, don't you think? Particularly as you're hoping to turf me out of my own vacation rental.'

'Too right I am. Just watch me.'

I grab a fresh bikini and a loose kaftan, pop back to the bathroom to tug them on, then I slip on my sandals and sunglasses, grab my keys from the kitchen table and slam the door on my way out. I try to ignore the niggling voice in my head – which sounds suspiciously like my mother's – expressing disappointment at my unquestionably rude behaviour. This man brings out the worst in me.

How did he even get in for goodness' sake? The keys were in the lock safe. I'll ask him about that later, but for now, I just want to call Clare and sort this whole ridiculous situation out before any more of my holiday is ruined.

Outside in the mid-morning sun, it feels like someone has turned a flame thrower on me. I see, by the light of day, that the small track I'd ascended last night sweeps around past several apartment blocks, before descending again at a gentler gradient, down towards the harbour. If I'd kept walking straight through the resort last night, I would have hit the seafront eventually and found a slightly less energetic route upwards. My attention is caught by the sound of splashing, and I remember Clare writing that the apartments have use of a neighbouring hotel pool.

I follow the sound across the track and through the open gates of a pale pink complex, signposted as Hotel Electra, to where a beautiful infinity pool falls away into the hazy sky. There are sunbathers dotted around the pool, where a woman performs a gentle breaststroke, and another swimmer eases himself up the steps. A family of four sip ice-cold drinks on high stools beside a bar.

I'm hot and thirsty, so I head straight for it.

'Good morning,' says the young woman serving behind the bar. 'English?'

'How can you tell?' I ask, surprised.

'You Brits never wear enough suncream,' she says, laughing.

'Ah,' I say, embarrassed. 'That's probably true. But in this case, I'm blaming it on an idiot with OCD. Can I get a coke, please? Actually, screw it, I need a beer. Is it too early for beer?'

'Of course not.' The woman smiles, and retrieves a bottle from the fridge. 'You're on holiday. It's never too early.'

'Do you have Wi-Fi?' I ask.

'Yes,' she says, her Greek accent soft and melodic. 'The code is up there on the wall.'

'Thanks,' I say, taking the chilled bottle and heading over to a table by the pool.

I make quick work of joining Hotel Electra's Wi-Fi, ignoring all the notifications and messages popping in, and find the number for Franklyn's Head Office.

'Clare in Accounts please,' I tell the receptionist and wait impatiently for my call to be transferred.

After listening to an instrumental version of Adele's Someone Like You on a loop for several minutes, a voice comes to the phone.

'H-h-hello,' she sniffs, her voice thick and high-pitched.
'Clare?'

'M-hmm,' she clears her throat. 'Clare Morris speaking,' another sniff, 'how can I help?'

'Clare,' I say assertively, holding the bottle of Mythos against my burning face, 'this is Annabel Baines.'

'Oh!' A strangled sob ensues, followed by more sniffing. 'I'm – so – sorry.' The woman is now audibly crying. 'I can't believe he did this to me.'

'Sorry? Who did what?'

'Richard. HR just called; apparently Richard rented the apartment out to Franklyn's this week. They've told me to make you leave.' She stops to catch her breath. 'I'm so sorry, Annabel, he didn't tell me about the booking. I think he did it on purpose, to get at me, you know?'

I place my beer down on the table and get up from my chair. 'I'm sorry, are you telling me your husband renting this place out, when you've already rented it to me, has nothing to do with you and you're the victim here?'

I'd begun pacing next to the pool and watched as the lone swimmer doubled her efforts to put more distance between us.

'I know how it sounds but that's about the size of it. He's just become so damned cruel; I don't even recognise him anymore. But I'll make sure you get a refund, of course. I'll transfer the money back to your account now.'

'Woah, hold up.' I stop pacing. 'Do you seriously think I can rent somewhere else out here at the last minute for what I paid you? It won't even cover one night in a hotel.'

Clare's whimpering stops, and an edge enters her voice. 'Like I said, Annabel, I'm sorry, truly. But it's been made extremely clear to me by our employer, that their booking was made first. They have it in writing.'

I can't stop the vicious laugh that escapes me. '*I* have it in writing, Clare. And you can tell our employer, I'm not going anywhere!' I end the call.

The swimmer has reached the end of the pool and remains

there, bobbing gently against the side, presumably waiting for the ranting, red woman to leave and for serenity to be restored. She needn't worry, I'm done with raging. I am going back into that apartment, telling Liam I'm not budging, then I'm going to grab a book and come right back here, to begin the holiday I paid for.

'Right,' I call out, letting myself back into the apartment. 'We need to talk.'

'Good, you're back,' says Liam, closing the fridge door. 'Look, I've spoken with Head Office, and they've explained what happened.'

'Really? Did they explain that Richard is a gigantic arsehole who had no business renting out this apartment without first checking with his wife?'

Liam coughs. 'They explained that Richard's wife has been going out of her way to make life difficult for him, something to do with a messy divorce and the fact he won't let her keep this place. But I'm afraid to say, Annabel, it does all seem above board. They have it in writing that Richard rented this to the company – I mean, they're bloody cheapskates, I've seen what they paid for it, but hey-ho, that's Franklyn's for you. I'm afraid you'll have to find somewhere else.'

He shrugs and opens his palms, as if to say, *hard luck baby, all's fair in love and testosterone-fuelled corporate bullshit.*

He smiles sweetly.

I smile back.

'Darling, I'm not going anywhere. You could offer to fund me a penthouse suite in the most expensive hotel on the island from your own goddamn pocket, but I like *this* apartment. The apartment I rented, also in writing, from one of its joint owners. So, if you're not planning on leaving, I'm afraid you'll just have to put up with me.'

Liam gawps, open-mouthed, as I sashay through to the lounge. I think I sashay, but the overall effect is possibly ruined by the fact I'm trying to avoid thigh-rub and any potential loss of skin.

'Oh, and another thing,' I add, pulling my books from my case and pretending to choose between them. 'If we are going to be sharing, then we'll need some boundaries.'

Liam seems to be stuck for words because he just stands there, hands thrust deep into his pockets.

'Don't panic, I'm not a complete cow. If you're having the bedroom, then I'm taking over the lounge. Now, where shall I put my stuff?' I ponder, looking about.

'Um, over there?' He points limply to an empty corner, even though I wasn't asking his advice.

'Fine.' I haul my case over and stack my books in a pile, then I pull out all my sandals, flip-flops and espadrilles and line them up against the wall.

'So many shoes,' he says wearily. 'Well, I'm going to head out. See you later, I guess.'

I turn to face him. 'Let me make something crystal clear, Liam. I don't want to know your movements; I most certainly won't be detailing mine. I don't want to be sharing my holiday with you any more than you want to be sharing it with me, so let's just do our best to stay out of each other's way, OK?'

His eyes, a deep velvety green, now I'm close enough to notice them, darken in response.

'That's perfectly fine with me.'

# CHAPTER 6

The minute the door closes, I shudder a sigh of relief.

Toughness does not come naturally to me, but, for a while, it was the only way to survive.

Here's the thing about me. I may have always wanted to build a life around books, but once, I'd believed the best way to do that was to be in the business of making them. Well, not books exactly, but magazines. The great 'publishing' dream – the city, a graduate internship scheme which turned out to be selling advertising space in a Sunday paper lifestyle mag and, something I *hadn't* banked on, a level of backstabbing and trampling underfoot that made *The Devil Wears Prada* look like an episode of *Friends*. Miranda Priestly, I could have coped with. But the forty-nine-year-old son of a peer with very particular ideas about career progression and how he could help me with it? A different beast entirely.

I managed three years of it before I found my breaking point. We all have them; it's just preferable not to let it get to the stage that almost leaves you split in two.

Turns out though, six years later, I can still call on that other half of me when I need to, but the effort has left me with shaky hands as I fold away the sofa bed and pack a beach bag, pretending I'm ok with this shitshow.

From my pile of books, I select this year's most hotly anticipated comedy debut, *Not My Life*, one woman's account of living as a ghost in her home whilst her family tries to move on. The blurb assures me it's an uplifting read, but I have to say I'm dubious. My only points of reference at this point are *City of Angels*, *The Lovely Bones* and *Ghost* none of which lifted anything other than my hanky to my face.

Just as I'm about to leave the apartment, there is a loud and sustained hammering at the door, followed by the sound of a key in the lock.

My jaw sets rigid. If he's going to behave like a spoilt, belligerent teenager all week, someone needs to tell him to grow up.

I lunge for the door and yank it open, expecting Liam, but am instead flung backwards in the air as a woman bowls straight into me.

'Lypámai polý!'

The woman regains her balance, whilst I lay flat on my back on the kitchen tiles.

'Lypámai polý! Sorry! Sorry!' she repeats. I think she's offering a hand to pull me up and go to take it, but instead she retrieves a broom from the floor.

She brandishes the broom with wild eyes. 'Clean. Yes?'

I gaze up at her, bewildered, then spot the mop and bucket in the open doorway and put two and two plus a bruised backside together.

'Maria?'

'Nai,'

'No? You're not Maria?'

'Nai, Maria,' she nods, pointing at her chest.

I shift my bottom, then pull myself to standing. At this rate, my poor afflicted body will be considerably worse off for this 'holiday' than if I'd never come at all.

'Hello Maria,' I say, holding out a hand. 'I'm Annie. I've rented this apartment from Clare.'

'Clare, yes. I clean now?'

She is smiling widely, her tanned, weathered skin crinkling at the corners of her eyes and around the edges of her mouth. A small crescent-shaped mole at the top of her cheek lends her a mischievous look and I have no doubt this woman with her salt and peppered hair, woven into a tight plait, would have been a dazzling beauty in her youth.

'Yes please.' I return her smile. 'I've just got here, and it doesn't really need cleaning yet, but, well, there's a man staying here too, and, well, he's a man, so he's bound to be gross.'

I'll admit I was using my experience of living with Travis as a template for this sweeping statement, and that despite his best efforts, his marsupial-like torso had shed like a bitch; in the shower, in the sink, on the toilet seat, around the toilet seat, in the bed. I'm perhaps doing Liam a disservice, because from the glimpse I got of his torso last night, it appeared remarkably smooth and also, rather toned.

Maria nods enthusiastically, then fetches her mop and bucket of cleaning supplies.

'OK, I'm going down to the pool, so I'll see you later, Maria, and thank you.'

'Kanéna próvlima, Clare. I discreet, always,' beams Maria, before turning back to her work.

I don't bother to correct her. Perhaps she thinks I'm also called Clare. Clearly English isn't her strong suit, so I'm mighty glad I didn't call her in the middle of the night asking for directions.

I've barely been gone an hour, but back at the pool, every sunbed is now taken, although half are empty of anything but towels, likely because it's lunchtime.

My skin has calmed down, thank God, and could now be a case of mild sunburn, rather than the pox. I strip to my bikini, place my clothes on top of my bag, then slip one delightful inch at a time into the soothing water.

In just a few lazy strokes, I feel the weight of the last few hours unshackle themselves from my body. It's peaceful bobbing there, the gentle notes of something ambient drifting over from the bar area and the occasional giggle from a toddler in armbands, enraptured by the joy of splashing. I smile at the child's mother, who is patiently playing with her in the shallow end, whilst aware this same congenial child will likely throw a screaming fit at some point and shatter my serene thoughts. It is no accident I'm holidaying strategically before most schools break for summer.

Eventually, coaxed by my rumbling tummy, I pull myself from the pool, dab my tender skin dry and tug the kaftan over my head, before heading to the bar and grabbing a menu.

The same bartender from earlier asks without even turning around, 'Mythos?'

'Better not. I haven't eaten yet. Can I grab a tuna salad and a coke please?'

'Sure.'

I watch thirstily as she pours my drink.

'You are staying here at the hotel?' she asks.

'No, actually I'm renting Villa Karina across the way.'

'Ah!' she says, as though I've given her the clue to a quiz question. 'You are with Liam.'

How on earth, in the mercifully few hours Liam and I have cohabited, has he found the time to meet, and get to know on first name terms, the server at this bar?

'Erm, well I'm not with Liam. I just happen to have the misfortune of sharing my apartment with him.'

The server laughs. 'Yes, he said. He's a nice guy, good-looking too. I think it could be worse, no?'

'Hmph, can I come back to you on that?'

'Well, I am always here and here there is always ouzo.' She grins, adding, 'I'm Greta.'

'Annie,' I offer back.

'I hope you enjoy your holiday, Annie.'

I drift away from the bar with my coke and wander into the adjoined covered area where rattan sofas and low tables provide respite from the midday sun, deciding I'd better keep my sore skin out of the sun until at the very least I've slathered myself in factor fifty.

I place my drink down and gravitate towards a shelving

unit in the corner. Never expect a bookworm, especially a bookseller, to resist a bookshelf. I love the smell of a brand-new paperback, fresh from the printers without a crease in sight – brimming with possibility. It's like being on the cusp of an adventure; just you and its crisp, clean pages. But a *second-hand* book, is a different beast entirely. Each wrinkle in its cover, each splodge, speck and stain tell of a journey already taken and there's something about that I love. As though simply by handling a used book, you are connecting with another person.

I don't *need* another book, I've brought seven with me already, but as I trail my fingers along the crumpled spines, my eyes alight on a title: *My Family and Other Animals* by Gerald Durrell.

A smile tugs at my lips. A memory. Sunday evenings curled up on the sofa with Mum, watching *The Durrells* on TV. It was her favourite show, probably still is. And in a world where chemo and steroids, appointments, doctors, and depressed fathers dominated – Keeley Hawes and her chaotic on-screen family were pure medicine.

We'd swoon longingly over the impossibly blue ocean and delight at the madcap characters, picking their way through life as English newcomers in the nineteen thirties on the island of Corfu. I'd completely forgotten about it when booking this trip, which is testament to Mum's recovery.

I select the book and pop it into my bag. I'll replace it with another later.

'Tuna salad?' calls out a gangly young lad with bleached spiky hair, who barely looks sixteen.

'Yes, thank you,' I say, leaving the bookcase and returning to my table.

The salad looks mouth-wateringly fresh, huge slices of deep-red juicy tomato and kalamata olives, chunks of cucumber and flakes of golden tuna drizzled in olive oil. I might well be in heaven, I muse, picking up my fork.

After lunch, I say goodbye to Greta and pop back to the apartment for my forgotten suncream, feeling ready to explore.

As I let myself in, I notice there is a clean folded tea towel lying on the drainer and our coffee cups from this morning have been washed and put away. Maria shouldn't be cleaning up after us, and I feel a pang of guilt – a feeling that is replaced with alarm when I wander through to the lounge, where my case and belongings should be, and see they are missing.

'What the...?'

I turn on the spot, scanning the room, seized by panic as I remember my spending money was still in the bag I'd used to travel and which I'd tucked it into my case last night. It was literally all the money I had left in the world.

Oh my God. I shouldn't have left her alone. Who's to say that woman was even Maria? Now I think of it, she just repeated my own words back at me. She could have been anyone.

Anxious, I race to Liam's bedroom, less concerned currently about my own stuff than how I would explain to this man I barely know that everything he owns has been stolen by someone I let into the apartment.

Without stopping to knock or check if he's in his room, I fling the door wide open.

Thankfully, Liam is not there.

And I seriously hope he doesn't come back anytime soon.

The double bed has been remade with crisp white sheets upon which sits an approximation of two entwined swans hewn from fluffy white towels, surrounded by a scattering of sex-red rose petals. As I draw closer, I'm further mortified to spot that my Minnie Mouse pyjama shorts set has been folded and placed on one pillow, whilst in what looks to be a blatant statement of disgust, Liam's eye mask is placed on the other.

My eyes flick to the louvre doors of the double wardrobe and before I even pull them open, I know that is where I will find my clothes.

Sure enough, every last garment from my suitcase has been

carefully hung or folded. Even my knickers, I see with a flush of embarrassment, have been decanted onto a shelf next to Liam's own startlingly white jersey boxers.

The suitcase itself is stashed in the bottom of the wardrobe, and inside I find my purse, cash duly intact. I'm equal parts touched and infuriated by Maria's imposition upon my personal belongings. Even my shoes are neatly arranged – all eight pairs – because every woman alive knows even if you wear a singular pair of flip-flops for the entire holiday, there will be a time when you wish you'd brought others. And with no man to comment otherwise, that is exactly what I had done.

Except now there *is* a man, and he has already commented.

This thought alone is enough to have me grabbing wildly at clothes hangers and stuffing everything back into my case. Imagine if he came back right now and thought I had done this; he'd think I bloody fancied him. I scoop up my shoes and sandals, lob them in the case on top of crumpled skirts and tops, grab my pjs from the pillow and my make-up bag from the dressing table. I'm about to fetch a bowl to scoop the petals into, when I hear a key in the lock.

*Shit.*

Frantically, I sweep the petals onto the floor and kick them under the bed. With no time to do anything else, I grab one of the towels, leaving the remaining swan to nosedive, and flee the room with my case.

I make it into the lounge just as Liam is padding through the kitchen.

'Oh,' he says, as I stand there with my case in hand. 'Did you find somewhere else to stay?'

I can't decide from the tone of his voice whether he is surprised, disappointed or triumphant.

'You should be so lucky,' I reply as breezily as I can, wheeling it back into my corner. 'The housekeeper came, so I tidied my stuff away.'

He looks vaguely surprised. 'I didn't know there was a cleaner. That was thoughtful of you. I hate when people deliberately leave their hotel rooms in a mess, expecting the maid to sort it out. As if their jobs aren't hard enough.'

And then there's those who merrily seek out extra work, I think to myself.

I delve into my case for my suncream, aware of Liam's critical gaze upon the carnage within.

'If that's your idea of tidy, I'd hate to see your mess,' he quips. 'You know, there's plenty of space in the wardrobe if you want to hang anything up?'

'Why would I want to hang anything up? I plan to spend the week on the beach and forgive me if I'm mistaken, but I wasn't aware of any formal dress code for that.'

He holds up his hands in surrender, as if I might be a little unhinged. 'Your vacation, your prerogative. Look, I'm going for a nap, but if you change your mind, the offer's there.'

Liam disappears into his room and shuts the door, leaving me feeling like a stroppy teenager.

It is so tempting to leave this place and find a cheap hotel for the remainder of the week, even a hostel would be preferable, but the thought of giving in to him – of giving in to the bullying tactics of Franklyn's, I can't and won't do that ever again.

And where the hell is my suncream?

Exasperated, and having pulled everything out of my case, I kick it all into the corner. I know I packed it, and remember it not fitting into my toiletry bag. It's likely rolling around in the bottom of Liam's wardrobe, so I guess I'll be buying another one.

# CHAPTER 7

Kassiopi, by the glorious light of day, is spectacular.

The compact marina is home to visiting yachts, catamarans and working fishing trawlers alike, as well as motorboats for hire and a passenger ferry chugging away from the jetty.

Cafes, bars and restaurants decorate the sweep of the harbour, so there will be no shortage of beauty spots for the odd sundowner, or three. Instinctively, I follow the harbour wall and trace a path alongside the perfect blue sea, unable to tear my eyes from it as a gentle incline takes me higher and higher atop rocky, rugged cliffs.

The images I'd ogled online in no way prepare me for the panoramic vista as I round a corner to see the twin crescent coves of Paralia Mpataria and Paralia Pipitos flanking the headland ahead. Their bleached-white pebbled beaches are dotted with royal blue umbrellas, the turquoise water so transparent, I can see swimmers, in detail from here.

The smaller beach, Pipitos, looks to be the quieter of the two, so that is where I choose to head, descending the crude rocky steps that have been fashioned into the steep hillside. Within nanoseconds, I've dumped my belongings and flicked off my flip-flops to sprint eagerly into the delicious warmth of the crystal-clear water, that is right until I yelp pathetically at the pounding of a thousand marbles against the balls of my feet and slip into an undignified, splashing, bottom-flop.

Tomorrow, I decide, watching enviably as a sure-footed

woman in a one piece and sturdy neoprene swimming shoes traverses the beach in confidence, I will procure some of those. A small sartorial price to pay for water filtered to such mirror-clear clarity by the beautiful, smooth stones that I can see tiny, colourful fish weaving in and out of my legs.

I've never been on holiday alone before, and I experience a sudden burst of freedom that reminds me of the old, independent me. All I must do is avoid Liam as much as possible and this will do me the world of good. Equip me for returning home and starting a new chapter. New job, new home. A life reboot.

After a brief, heavenly swim, I hobble from the water, lurching wildly like an orangutan as I try to keep my footing, and take up residence on my towel. There seems little point in paying for use of a sunbed this late in the day. Reaching into my bag, I pull out *Not My Life* and stare at the cover illustration, which features a family sitting on a sofa, with a ghostly silhouetted female figure standing behind.

Here on the beach, where lush olive trees overhang from plateaus of rock above and the distant shape of the Albanian mountains loom through a heat haze, this domestic scene jars. A couple meander past me hand in hand and barefoot along the water's edge. They must have soles like baking trays, I muse. No, I don't fancy reading about dead mothers right now, no matter how funny the writing. This doesn't feel like a beach read.

I stuff it back into my bag and my fingers close around the book from the hotel pool area, *My Family and Other Animals*. A book written about this very island. Could it be more apt?

I open the battered front cover, surprised to find a handwritten inscription on the first page. The looping letters are gently slanting, neat but full of purpose.

It reads:

*To the next reader of this enchanting book, may your own adventure on Corfu be filled with sunshine, laughter and joy.*

The paragraph is dated with yesterday's date.

As a self-confessed bibliophile, I have an uneasy relationship with the annotation of books. Dedications and personal notes within a gifted book – highly acceptable, encouraged, even. But underlines, highlights, and marginal notes, uh-uh. Folded down corners – punishable by death. If you really must have a literal conversation with yourself whilst reading, use a bloody Post-it note.

Cynically flicking through the pages to spot signs of a serial offender, I'm satisfied to find none and hereby deem this scribe to be an agreeable 'gifter'.

Within the first few pages, I am chuckling away; Gerald Durrell's childhood recollections of exploring the island's wildlife, whilst hampered by the bizarre and ridiculous antics of his family are just the tonic I need.

By page one hundred and two I look up and notice the sun is beginning a slow descent and I am alone on the beach. The sea is a moody blue and the sky is streaked with pink. One evening I'll come and sit right here to watch a full sunset, I decide. But for now, my rumbling tummy informs me I need to eat, which is no surprise when I check the time and see its way past seven o 'clock.

In fact, I calculate, dragging myself to my feet and pulling my kaftan over my head, I've been on this island nearly twenty-four hours and all I've had is a tuna salad. I need greasy food; chips ideally, and I need wine.

After a slow stroll back to the harbour, I'm too tired to contemplate returning to the apartment, showering, and coming back out, so I pop into a small supermarket and buy a bottle of white wine and then I queue for gyros. Although I'd intended to save it until back at the villa, the aroma's too good to resist, so I perch on a bench overlooking the peaceful harbour and devour the tasty pork souvlaki, all wrapped up with onions, tomatoes and fresh tzatziki and the tastiest seasoned fries in a soft folded pitta. It is pure indulgent heaven and vastly superior to those I'd previously enjoyed from pop-up stalls in London's markets, no matter how authentic their claim.

Flushed from the sun, the earlier allergic reaction, and the effort of hiking back up to the villa, I enter the apartment with trepidation. If Liam is here, that might be enough to force me back out.

But I'm in luck. There is no sign of Liam at all. Even his bedroom door is ajar, allowing me to check he's not in there either. No doubt he's off spending some of his Franklyn's euros on a slap-up meal whilst I'm likely to be living on gyros for the entire week. Not that I'm complaining.

The kitchen cupboards, I discover, contain very little. Either Clare and Richard have already cleared them out, or they have zero interest in the self-catering element of a self-catering apartment, something they should perhaps have addressed before letting it out as such.

If I want to knock up any grub, I'll be restricted to whatever can be conjured up within one saucepan. As far as I can tell, there are four plates, four bowls, three forks, two knives, one spoon and a cheese knife. I'm reminded of little Isaac with his *James and The Giant Peach* book – cheesy pasta, such a fine culinary choice, is about the limit of what can be cooked here.

In the absence of any glassware, I grab a mug, my bottle of wine and take my book to read on the balcony.

I'm a fast reader but, fortunately, a slow drinker, because by the time I hear the front door closing, I'm on the last page of my book and must have been reading for hours in the lamplight.

'What ya reading?' comes a soft voice at the balcony door.

Liam blinks furiously as though he's having to concentrate hard on standing still.

'You're drunk,' I say.

'First night,' he states in reply. 'Vacation law.'

I counter, 'Yesterday was the first night.'

His mouth twists as he tries and fails to formulate a reply.

I get up and drain the rest of my wine.

'Time for bed, I think.'

'What? What's the problem? You're drinking too,' he says, like a child arguing with his mother.

'Oh, that old chestnut, what is it with guys? Newsflash – did you know, you can enjoy a glass of wine or two without getting wasted, or is that some kind of witchcraft to you?'

Liam pulls a 'what's up with you face' and stumbles backwards as I manoeuvre past him.

'You know what, Annabel?'

In his semi-American accent, every syllable of my name sounds drawn out.

'Enlighten me, Liam?' I reply, crossing my arms.

'For someone on *vacation*,' he just about resists air quotes, but imbues the word with sufficient sarcasm, 'you're really uptight. You need to chill out. And I don't get why you have such a problem with me.'

My instinct is to list in detail the many reasons I have a problem with him. Starting with the clear favouritism bestowed upon him and his branch by our bosses and ending with the fact we are battling for our jobs. I could add that I find him cocksure and possessed of the kind of arrogant charm that would doubtless always ensure his survival.

Instead, I turn away and begin pulling out the sofa bed again. Fortunately, despite Maria's efficiency, my bedding is where I left it, folded and stacked on an armchair. What did she think was going on? A lover's tiff? A mysterious third occupant?

'I'm going to bed, Liam,' is all I say.

It's obvious he wants to say more, and he scrunches his face with the effort of respecting my lack of desire to engage in a bit of friendly, tipsy banter. But I busy myself, making my bed and ignoring the fact he's still standing there.

Eventually he lets out a breath in a long, melodic whistle and saunters away to his room.

As I slip between the sheets, I can't help smirking. It's rather fun, being a pain in someone else's arse for a change.

And really, no matter what Liam might think, I'm not even particularly annoyed anymore, such is the power of a beautiful location.

Before I turn off the light, I reach across for my book, undoubtedly another prime reason for my cordial mood this evening. It had been a joy to read from cover to cover and I'm now possessed of a similar sentiment to the mystery scribe. I scrabble around in my bag for a pen, hotching upright in the bed of persecution and open the front cover.

I chew the end of my pen in deliberation, then scrawl my own message beneath the original:

*Dear previous reader, how right you were. What a joyful book! And what a special place. I can't wait to explore. Is it even Corfu, until you've seen two jousting tortoises attempting to win their lady? All other romantic tropes are ruined for me – I hadn't honestly thought the fight scene in Bridget Jones could be bettered, but there you have it.*

I date the passage, then add a smiley face for good measure. My words will mean nothing to anyone who hasn't read the book but refer to a passage that made me laugh aloud as a young Gerry received his sex education, courtesy of the animal kingdom.

There, I've done it. Graffitied a paperback and I didn't die. Still smiling, I turn off the light and settle down to dream of sandy beaches and boats called Bumtrinket. If you know, you know.

Seconds later, the overhead light is snapped on, blinding me momentarily, and Liam is standing at the end of my bed, his face aghast.

'What now? I was almost asleep.'

Liam pulls a face like he's just discovered his face flannel was used to clean the toilet.

'I think someone's been in here. Whilst we were out. And whoever they are, they're one sick motherfucker.'

'What?' I scrunch my face against the harsh light. 'Of course nobody's been in, go back to bed.'

'No, I'm serious. Come and see.'

Eventually, the sheer disgust on his face galvanises me from my bed and I have to admit to being curious.

I follow after him as he pads through the hallway to his bedroom. Everything looks exactly as it did when I saw the room earlier.

'What? I can't see anything weird.'

'Well,' begins Liam, pacing over to the open wardrobe and wildly flinging rattling garments on hangers apart. 'First off, my lucky Hawaiian shirt is missing, and I *never* go anywhere without it.'

I shake my head, already turning on my heel. 'Seriously? You turf me out of bed because you can't find your shirt? You probably forgot it, Liam. Perhaps it's actually your *unlucky* shirt, after all – you ended up stuck here with me.'

'Trust me,' he says abruptly. 'I brought it.'

I turn away, hands on hips, rapidly losing my good mood.

'There's more!' he announces, flinging back the bedsheets.

I wince at the sight of several splodges and streaks of red, before realising the unsightly stains aren't in fact blood, as they appear to be, but the result of a few errant flower petals having been squashed into the bedding.

Before I can formulate an explanation for this occurrence, Liam goes on.

'And there's this too, I mean who would do such a thing? They weren't there last night.' He yanks out the drawer of the nightstand and points down into it purposefully.

I have to physically force my legs to move, my skin creeping ever so slightly with dread as to what I'll see.

'Do you think this is someone from Franklyn's idea of a sick joke? Or how about this Clare woman, how well do you know her?'

I peer into the drawer and swallow down a tight ball of cringe. Rolling to a halt inside is my missing bottle of suncream. But also – a transparent plastic case containing a duo of pink vibrators and a tube of hypoallergenic lube, items that to this point I *hadn't* noticed were missing, having had neither opportunity nor inclination to look for them in my case.

This would of course be the moment to hold my hands up and explain the mix-up with Maria earlier, but of course, I do not do that.

'I don't know Clare at all,' I say with caution. 'Other than to arrange this booking, which was all via email. This morning was the first time I've ever spoken to her. I mean, she was a bit upset, but…'

'Well, that's it. I'm phoning the office first thing tomorrow. I mean who else has keys to this place? You let the cleaner in, right? But you were here. It can't have been her.'

Technically, that was true, I did let her in. Before I left her to her own devices to create a scene fit for *Fifty Shades Freed*. I'm surprised she didn't leave her feather duster behind for a bit of light spanking.

'Er, yeah. But look, that – um, stuff, probably just belongs to Clare, you must have been mistaken.'

Liam looks me in the eye with an intensity that sucks the breath out of me. As though he can see all the way to my innermost secrets. My cheeks flame.

'Trust me. I checked the drawers last night. I was looking for somewhere to hide my cash.'

'Hide it from who? From me? What are you trying to say?'

Liam sighs and rubs his forehead, sobering up by the minute. 'I'm saying you should go and check your stuff too, Annabel. See if anything is missing. This is exactly why I hide my cash, which is thankfully all still there.'

'Oh, right, yep,' I say, willingly obliging and fleeing the room before my flushed face can give me away.

Shit, shit, shit.

I should have just told him about Maria unpacking my stuff in the first place, but I didn't and now if I do, I'll look like a moron for letting him think somebody has soiled his bed and put sex toys in his drawer. But that is preferable, right now, to confessing them to be *my* sex toys.

'Anything?' he calls out from his room, the sound of doors banging and drawers clanging as he completes his search for evidence.

My case is open on the floor, and I make a quick show of rummaging through it as I hear footsteps in the hallway. Then I spot the disturbingly unfamiliar pattern of a violently colourful piece of fabric nestled among my clothing and quickly stuff it towards the back.

'All present and correct,' I say, spinning around and flashing Liam a rare smile. 'I say we sleep on it. I'm sure there's a perfectly reasonable explanation.'

'I don't really care about an explanation; I just want my shirt, that's all.'

He looks suddenly rather vulnerable, his eyes glistening, and his jaw set rigid. Though I've no desire to fess up, I'm strangely torn between wanting to comfort him and ask why a ghastly Hawaiian shirt is so important to him.

But mercifully, he shrugs and goes back to his room, leaving me alone to work out what on earth to do with an accidentally pilfered lucky shirt.

# CHAPTER 8

## CORFU, DAY THREE

When I slip from the apartment, there has been no sign of Liam all morning.

Presumably he's sleeping off a hangover.

This has been fortuitous, because I was able to stow away his hideous Hawaiian shirt into my beach bag, whence it will be accompanying me on a day of exploration.

First stop though, is the book exchange by the pool, where I call a hello to Greta behind the bar before returning *My Family and Other Animals* to the shelf ready for its next custodian.

'Good morning, Annie,' she calls back cheerfully, drying glasses with a towel.

Lucky cow, living here. Although, realistically, what's to stop me from living somewhere like this? Nothing, really. Mum is better now, they don't need me anymore, not like they did. Dad still struggles, he tries to hide it, but I see him watching her. He's terrified it will come back. Ironically, the same terror prevents him from fully appreciating the time they do have together, just another of life's sad ironies.

'I'll be back later for a swim,' I say on my way past, 'I want to pick your brains on the best places to eat.'

She grins back. 'There are no bad places here, only good ones.'

I laugh. 'I can well believe it.'

This time when I reach the harbour, I follow the lane up into the village, passing the takeaway I visited last night, bars, restaurants and countless souvenir kiosks, their wares spilling out onto the street. I wander in and out of the shops and pass a delightful morning browsing traditional handmade lace, products crafted from olive wood, crystal bracelets, and other trinkets aimed at tourists. Eventually, I spot a rack of snorkels and masks and find exactly what I'm after, a pair of Velcro swim shoes.

After a brief but necessary stop at a gelateria, I pause outside a tourist booking centre to peruse the advertisement boards whilst enjoying my mint choc-chip, when something catches my eye:

CRUISE THE EAST COAST AND VISIT THE HOME OF THE DURRELLS

Oh hello, could be fun. I read on...

*Take a relaxing one-day cruise along the spectacular east coast to Kalami, home of the famous Durrells.*

*Spot dolphins at the Blue Caves and dive for champagne. Lunch and drinks included.*

*Trip runs every Friday and Tuesday. BOOK NOW.*

I do a quick calculation. Tomorrow is Friday and I fly home Tuesday. It would have to be tomorrow.

Of course, the price isn't advertised. Classic sales technique.

Just as I stuff the last of my ice-cream cone into my mouth, a woman with burnished gold hair fastened into a chignon appears at my side.

'Kalimera, can I help? Is there something that takes your interest, Madam?'

'Hmm, mm, mm,' I say, or something like it, whilst rotating my hands like helicopter blades to speed up the swallowing process.

She flashes me a patient smile. She has all day. She's a

saleswoman. She'd probably purchase me another ice cream if it meant she would get a sale.

'Um, I was thinking about the Durrells trip, can you tell me how much it is?'

She nods knowingly. 'Our most popular trip. When were you thinking of going?'

'Tomorrow?'

Now she is shaking her head, with a look of complete insincerity. 'Sadly, tomorrow is fully booked, Madam. But we have space on Tuesday.'

'What a shame. I'm going home on Tuesday. Never mind.' I make to leave.

'Perhaps I can interest you in another of our special trips? How about Paxos and Anti-paxos? Or a day in Albania?'

'I don't think…'

'Corfu Town?'

'Sorry, I've already planned a trip to Corfu Town.' This was partly true, in as much as I'd grabbed a bus timetable earlier.

'Are you travelling alone?'

I confirm that I am, then instantly regret it.

'Ela. I know the perfect trip for you – our *Sunset Cruise*. We have one scheduled for tomorrow, leaving the harbour at 4pm; a gentle cruise along the coast, a swimming stop, supper, cocktails and of course, a magnificent Corfiot sunset. Who knows, maybe you will meet the man, or woman,' she hastens to add, 'of your dreams onboard.'

I'm about to protest that my wildest dreams currently include finding a place to live and a new job, that crowbarring a love interest into the picture would be like asking me to prepare for a marathon. I've neither the stamina, nor the inclination. Before I can say as much, she adds:

'I can do special price for you, only a few places left, come with me.'

Ten minutes later, I'm leaving the shop with a ticket for tomorrow's sunset cruise at a price so reasonable I couldn't refuse. Even if it had become apparent within the short time I was there, 'no' wasn't a word the Greek woman understood.

Later that afternoon, hot and sticky from climbing up to see the ruins of a Byzantine castle perched high above the village, I seek refuge in the famous Church of the Panagia Kassopitra. I'd read in my guidebook of the importance of the church, which stands on the site of a fifth century temple and is considered by the many who pilgrimage there to be a place of miracles. Stepping into the blessedly cool foyer of the church, I'm approached by a woman who gestures I should cover my shoulders.

I rummage in my bag for a sarong, but haven't brought one with me, so I'm offered a shawl from a basket. I drape it across my shoulders and enter the stony silence of the holy building.

Awestruck, I take in the ancient frescoes and Catholic icons of the sacred space. Several worshippers sit in pews, their veiled heads bent in prayer and an elderly gentleman is lighting a candle. My interest is primarily with the history of the building, being predisposed to agnosticism, but a shiver runs down my spine as my eyes briefly lock with the dominant edifice of the Virgin Mary. Perhaps it's my guilty conscience, as I stand before her with stolen goods secreted away in my beach bag, but I decide I've seen enough.

As I'm queuing to exit the building, a couple of waiting tourists with nothing to cover themselves with are also directed to the basket, where they take a garment each, and it gives me a brainwave. I pull out the cool cotton fabric of the gaudy Hawaiian shirt, noting the familiar scent of Liam, vaguely spicy with an undertone of Persil, and as I pass by, I let it slip from my fingers into the basket. I briefly stoop to bury it beneath shawls and veils, consoling myself that whilst Liam will never see his lucky shirt again, it will continue to fulfil its destiny by bringing good fortune to ill-equipped tourists.

After a busy morning of sightseeing, I decide to treat myself to a late lunch of calamari at Niko's Bar, overlooking the harbour.

'Oh my God, I would die to be you right now. Look at that view.'

I've caught Jess on her lunch break and she's hunkering in the doorway of Daphne's tearooms whilst the reliable UK rain batters her from all angles.

'What happened to wishing you lived in a Swedish valley, snowed in for winter with no one but a husky and Alexander Skarsgård for company?'

'That was during the heatwave, Annie. Now, it's just as shit as it normally is in this country in summer. One week you can't plan a BBQ because the thought of being outside makes you want to unzip your own skin, the next – you can't plan a BBQ because it never. Stops. Raining.'

I acknowledge the truth of her words and noisily slurp at my drink. 'That's too bad. You know what you need, don't you? A holiday.'

She sticks her middle finger up at me. Jess and her boyfriend Stu have been planning their 'trip of a lifetime' for what very much feels like a lifetime. I'd been receiving email links to impossibly stunning and prohibitively expensive destinations for nigh on a calendar year, until finally it was booked; a month-long extravaganza taking in Thailand, Singapore and Sri Lanka before spending Christmas at a beach house in the Maldives. Potentially, I still have another four months of Google images to endure.

'Anyway,' I continue, 'nothing is ever as good as it seems, Jess. Did you not get my message? About whom I'm having to share this little patch of paradise with? It's a complete nightmare and I haven't even told you the dildo story yet.'

'Your calamari, Madam?' comes a voice to my left and I look up to see a tanned, gorgeous waiter, his thick dark hair scraped back into a manbun.

Jess, where she is propped against the salt and pepper pots, audibly snorts like a snuffling pig. 'God, I can't wait – I hope it involves him!'

I shoot her a glare, as my food is placed before me.

'Thank you so much,' I say, grimacing and avoiding eye contact with the waiter.

'You are welcome. Can I get you anything else?'

'Oh yes *please*,' purrs Jess and I reach across to end the call, just catching sight of her bending double and guffawing with laughter before I do.

Sighing, I glance up at the waiter who is barely supressing a grin. 'Please ignore my friend. She's not even my friend really, just some random woman I can't seem to shake off. Like a feral cat.'

'Ah,' he says. 'We have many of those, as you see.'

He gestures behind him to where a cardboard box against a stone wall offers a makeshift shelter to a selection of skinny, balding felines. One particularly flea-ridden soul appears to be sunning itself on top, whilst others slumber in various patches of shade. A metal water bowl indicates a human hand in the arrangement.

'You feed them?' I ask, recognising compassion in his honey-skinned, congenial face.

He shrugs. 'Sometimes. They are not all homeless, even though they do not look as healthy as the cats you are used to. They adapt to the heat here, and they know where they will get fed. We try to look out for them. There are many.'

I recall, as he says this, that I've been spotting cats all day. Slinking around gardens, sitting under cars, lying in the shade on steps.

'Your English is brilliant,' I say, feeling ashamed my Greek is limited to a few carefully curated food and beverage requirements.

He gives a small laugh. 'I worked in London for a while, before coming here to open my own bar.'

'This is your place? It's an amazing spot.'

'Thank you. And now I must leave you to enjoy your food

and your peace. Enjoy,' he says with a smile. "I'm Niko, by the way,' he adds, before turning to take another customer's order.

For the next half hour or so, as I sip at my drink and watch speedboats darting around the bay, I am aware of Niko and the effortless way he moves between customers, chatting amiably, presenting his food with pride. I see him top up the cat bowl with ice-cold water from a bottle and it makes me smile.

'Thank you,' I call out as I push back my chair to go. I've left my payment in a dish, along with a small tip.

'Goodbye, lady of the strawberry hair. I hope to see you again soon.'

Perhaps you might, I think to myself, throwing my beach bag over my shoulder. Perhaps you might.

# CHAPTER 9

'Don't you ever take time off?' I ask Greta, between sips of a deliciously icy San Pellegrino.

I've been for a quick swim before heading back to the apartment and I'm perched on a bar stool, enjoying the warmth on my rapidly drying skin.

'Yes, of course, I have Mondays off,' she replies. 'On Mondays I take my mother to Roda to do her big shopping, isn't that what you call it?'

I laugh. 'Yeah, apparently. Although my idea of a big shop these days is not one, but two baskets filled with pizza, ice-cream and cereal, maybe a bunch of bananas to keep me regular.'

'Regular?' she enquires, a bushy eyebrow cocked.

'Don't worry, not something you have to worry about here, I'd imagine. Not with a never-ending supply of sun-ripened fruits and vegetables. Do you know, I could play billiards with the tomatoes I buy in Asda and still they wouldn't burst.'

Greta shakes her head. 'You Brits are crazy. I have absolutely no idea what you're talking about. This morning, your guy asked me how well I knew Clare and Richard, and did they seem a bit kinky? Like I would know every British person who visits Corfu and their bedroom habits!'

I'm not sure which part of this statement to process first.

'Greta, Liam isn't "my guy". He's not my boyfriend. He's just someone who works for the same company as me and, well," I nurse my glass, realising I can't even be bothered to go into it, 'it's all got a bit complicated.'

She pauses in wiping down the bar to shoot me a look that could unnerve Tommy Shelby.

'Oh. Believe me. If I were going to have a holiday romance, it wouldn't be with him.'

Niko, with his kind, yet mildly suggestive eyes, floats briefly through my mind, before I shove the image back towards a mental cupboard marked 'no men allowed' and lock it firmly away.

'You are on holiday. Anything could happen,' says Greta devilishly. 'So where are you going to dine this evening, have you decided?'

I'm grateful for the change of subject. 'I passed a really cute taverna in the village today. I can't remember what it was called. It had yellow tablecloths and tonnes of olive trees on the terrace.'

'Ah, The Olive Grove. Yes, is a good choice. Their kleftiko is excellent.'

'Fab,' I say, jumping down from my stool. Then, before I even register what I'm doing, I find myself heading towards the bookshelves in the corner.

My fingers graze along the shelf, bumping over the spines of books I've read, books I have no desire to read, and some I'm not in the mood for, until I arrive at the now familiar copy of *My Family and Other Animals*.

I can't resist pulling it from the shelf and opening the cover, just in case, and there, almost startling me when I see it, is another scrawling message in the original scribe's handwriting.

*A quick reader. A fellow bookworm? One that re-visits books?*

I have the sudden and irrational fear I'm being watched and glance out across the pool. There are a couple of sunbathers dotted around; a man and woman in their sixties, I'd hazard. Him dozing under the umbrella, his tattooed fingers laced across a protruding beer belly, her behind a hardback autobiography, written by a celebrity who almost certainly never wrote, let alone read, her own work.

The young family with the toddler from yesterday are packing up their stuff and a slim, bronzed twenty-something is pulling her long limbs from the pool.

None of them look likely candidates as the author of these messages, if I was going to be judgemental.

There is an arrow to suggest the message continues overleaf. I turn the page.

*Sometimes I'm in a post-book haze for a while and can't read anything else. Like when your favourite TV show ends and nothing else seems as good.*

*Other times, I love nothing more than slipping back into a book I've already read and greeting the characters like old friends. I've read Catcher in the Rye five times.*

*Travelling is a bit like that too. Isn't the thrill of exploring a new place only a temporary thing? Don't you find yourself returning to some destinations year after year? Same bars, same restaurants, until you're on first name terms with the owners and they know to mix your martini exactly the way you like it? Isn't it those details that give the experience permanence?*

*People, too. The more you get to know them, the more you analyse them, fill in the blanks. It's human nature, we can't help it and before you know it, you no longer remember the first impression they made, because that space has since been occupied.*

The neat writing flows horizontally across the white space in the top margin of the page then picks back up at the bottom. Another arrow suggests it goes on.

I pause reading, glance up again. Nobody is looking my way, even Greta is wiping down tables and collecting menus. Nobody notices as I sink down into the rattan sofa. Somehow, this complete stranger has articulated exactly how I feel about Travis.

It's been bothering me lately, how remarkably unaffected I am by his desertion and how for the life of me I can barely recall what attracted me to him.

When I think of him now, it's not as the smartly dressed, softly spoken man who blinked back at me as I scrabbled around on the pavement outside the bookshop picking up the scattered paperwork that I'd knocked clean from his hands, before crouching to assist. I knew I'd viewed him as a gentle, considerate man, a safe option. A low-risk date proposal that I'd accepted, the first in a long time.

The gaping hole in my life now isn't down to his absence, it's the absence of who I thought he could help me to become.

*All of that said, as much as I enjoyed this book, it's the first in a trilogy so there's more to come. Besides, I've no desire to read it again, it wasn't that great. So, what's your excuse?*

This time, a smiling face, from him.

*P.S. I'm sure on an island as beautiful as this, romantic gestures abound. Absolutely no need to bring randy reptiles into the equation, or Hugh and Colin, for that matter.*

That makes me giggle. Is this man flirting? Impossible, how does he know I'm not a pensioner with calves like elephant legs, or a pub landlord from Coventry? I mean, I'm assuming he's a he. Perhaps he's hoping *I* am a he.

'Greta?' I ask, strolling over to the bar. 'Have you seen anyone using the book exchange today?'

Greta shrugs. 'At lunchtimes we're very busy. People come and go. Why?'

Now I feel foolish – of course she's not going to notice the movements of every customer, a large percentage of them with books.

'No reason. Have you got a pen I can borrow?'

She plucks one from a pint pot, looking bemused. 'Everything OK?'

'Everything's fine.' I smile and return to the sofa.

I sit and ponder, watching as a pink flamingo lilo drifts past.

*I can proudly say I've never holidayed anywhere twice.*
*Unless you count spells at my ex prospective in-laws place*
*in Devon, which I can assure you, does not a holiday make.*

*The world, much like the world of books, to my mind is*
*far too vast to dither around in the same old places. I haven't*
*travelled much, but if time and money were of no object then*
*I'd have a list as long as my arm, which thinking about it, isn't*
*actually all that long, so I'll change that for a list as long as*
*the combined length of an arm and a leg.*

*Books, on the other hand, are limitless. They are*
*affordable, nay free, if you're lucky enough to have a local*
*library that hasn't been decimated by the council. They take*
*you everywhere, anywhere and to all the impossible places*
*in between. I consume them as though they are oxygen and*
*rarely revisit them, unless I have reason to.*

*Take 'The Great Gatsby' as a case in point. A work of*
*genius and an important social satire, but in my own opinion,*
*best as a one-time experience. Let's be honest, if you scrub a*
*bath tap enough, you take the shine off – why do that to one*
*of literature's finest enigmas? Jay Gatsby may be beguiling,*
*but he doesn't fare well under scrutiny.*

*I've known a few chrome-plated men, as it goes. Better*
*left well alone.*

*No amorous animals spotted so far, just me, the sea and*
*some extremely good calamari. But there's always time, I*
*guess...*

Oof, a little suggestive there, Annie. I click the ballpoint
pen off and slot the book back on the shelf with a smug grin.
Then, reconsidering, I move the book to the bottom shelf
where it has less chance of being spotted by someone who
isn't looking for it.

'See you tomorrow,' I call out to Greta as I gather up my
bag.

'Have a lovely evening Annie and remember – the kleftiko
in The Olive Grove...' She throws me a chef's kiss and my
tummy rumbles at the thought.

As I turn to leave, I think of something.

'Greta, do you know how many rooms Hotel Electra has, by any chance? I'm doing a bit of research for a friend who's thinking of getting married on the island.'

This of course is an outright lie as I have no friends with impending plans of matrimony. I deserve to be struck down by a vengeful Titan immediately.

Greta's eyes roll skyward as she thinks.

'Thirty-two I think, plus the seven self-contained villas up the hill.'

She points beyond my own villa, to a small steep track I hadn't even noticed before.

Excellent. So that's potentially near on a hundred hotel residents, plus staff and private renters who all have access to the pool. The chances of running into my new pen pal seem rather remote.

As I let myself in to the apartment, I remember the lost shirt and the found vibrators and brace myself for either rampant lies or mortification, depending on Liam's conviction to unearth the truth. Neither are required, it seems, because I have the apartment to myself.

In the middle of the dining table, there is a note scrawled in shouty block capitals on the back of a receipt.

WAITED FOR CLEANER, NO SIGN TODAY. STAY VIGILANT.

WTF? Is Liam seriously sacrificing entire days of his holiday to stake out the cleaner? All because he can't find one pretty horrible shirt?

There is no blank space on the receipt, so I rummage in my bag for another scrap of paper and add my reply.

YOU NEED TO LET IT GO.

Irritated by Liam's dogged determination to get to the bottom of the mystery, yet also feeling guilty at my hand in the matter, I go to take a shower.

When I leave the apartment and set off down the hill, my hair feels clean and silky, swishing loose around my bare shoulders. I rarely wear it down but took some time to untangle my locks from their trademark messy bun after an excruciatingly lengthy process of rinsing out the conditioner in Corfu's ultra-soft water. Unlike many holidaymakers, saltwater does not enhance my hair, it turns it into a scratchy bird's nest that looks to have been constructed from shredded wheat.

I'm wearing my favourite peacock-blue maxi dress which would have looked fab with the white wedge sandals, but predictably, I opted for the same pair of flip-flops I've worn since arriving on the island. And as I meander down the hill towards the harbour in the gentle warmth of evening, I'm again feeling something I've not felt in many months: optimism.

It doesn't matter what happens with the bookshop. It doesn't really matter where I live. Nothing is permanent, everything changes. The only thing that matters is health and happiness. And if there's one thing I've learned, the implied loss of either is the only thing big enough to derail a family.

The softly lit harbour is humming with activity; from hungry diners loitering to look at restaurant menus, to those enjoying a drink and watching the world go by from cane settees on verandas. A family sit on the deck of their boat playing card games and eating crisps, whilst aboard another, a fisherman spools rope and tidies nets. It's a peaceful, beautiful resort and I'm reminded how lucky I was to stumble across the villa advertisement, even if I have been forced to share it.

I stroll through the main village, enjoying the powerful scent of eucalyptus and citrus trees that bedeck the pavements, patios and gardens. The island residents are resourceful – every patch of arid ground is turned over to grapevines, beans grown on canes, misshapen cucumbers and ripe tomatoes. I drink in every detail until I arrive at The Olive Grove, with its whitewashed walls and lemon-yellow gingham covered tables, the entire terrace crammed with so many terracotta pots and trees it feels like a tropical oasis.

'Kalispera,' says a mature gentleman, red-cheeked and

sweating, in shirt and trousers. 'Welcome to The Olive Grove. You eat?'

The man's face is tanned and weathered like a walnut and his thick crop of hair is gunmetal grey, but he has the twinkling eyes of a man thirty years younger. I like him instantly.

Once seated, and in possession of both a jug of iced water and a glass of house wine, I relax and take in my surroundings. A tealight gently flickers on the table and traditional Greek music filters through from inside. It would never even occur to me to go out for a meal alone back home. I couldn't afford it for one, but here, it feels like the most natural thing in the world, and I'm not the only one. The table in front is also laid for one, with a freshly poured glass of wine from a small carafe and a book. I crane my neck to see which book – another by-product of my vocation – I can't even sit on a train without jumping to ludicrous assumptions about my fellow passengers based solely on their reading material, but I can't comment as to this punter's taste because their napkin is obscuring it. If it's a novel it's a slim one, a novella perhaps.

A scraggy feline edges closer to my table, as though aware of imminent food, and when I hear footsteps approaching from behind, I lay my napkin in my lap, belly rumbling. I'm *so* ready for this.

What I'm not ready for is the sight of Liam taking his place at the table opposite and saluting me with his wine glass.

'Kleftiko, Madam,' announces the restaurant owner, swooping in with a plate containing an open parchment parcel and the intoxicating aroma of slow roasted lamb.

'A great choice. I had it last night,' calls Liam.

I detect a twittering from somewhere over to my left and glance up to see a couple smiling at me. The woman winks and darts her eyebrows towards Liam in the most un-subtle display of matchmaking I've ever encountered. Fortunately, I don't catch the whispered words between them, but I certainly register the tone.

I want to shake my head, tell them this man is not, as

they believe, flirting with me. He is taunting me. Ruining my dinner and my good mood, again.

'It was recommended,' I reply through gritted teeth.

I guess there was always a chance our paths would collide. Kassiopi isn't large, but from what I've seen there are upwards of twenty dining options. Perhaps I should have taken a taxi to a neighbouring resort. The only thing that could make this worse right now is if he starts blathering on about his shirt again.

After the first mouthful of fiercely resentful chomping, and no further comment from Liam, I try to relax. The kleftiko, as promised by Greta, is sensational. Sweet lamb and zingy fresh oregano, exquisite cubes of waxy potato that melt in the mouth. I take my time, wanting to savour every mouthful but what with the mangy cat circling my feet, and the silent but intensely felt presence of Liam in front, it's quite a stressful dining experience.

Liam must have already eaten, because no food is delivered to his table. He works his way slowly through his half-carafe, whilst making occasional notes in what I now see is a notebook, and pauses to chat with the waiter whenever he passes his table. He doesn't look directly at me again or make any further comment. It's as though we are complete strangers.

Appetite diminished and no longer quite as confident in my own company, I feed the remnants of a bread roll to the cat and visualise how the evening might go if Liam was to look up and say, *Hey, doesn't it seem a bit silly, sitting separately like this. Shall we order dessert and another carafe of wine?*

Surprisingly, now I've grown used to it, the idea doesn't horrify me. In fact, it might even be pleasant. Perhaps my good sense has been dulled by the wine, or perhaps, I wonder, looking out to where the street beyond throngs with couples, there's something to be said for sharing. Would it be so dreadful if just for one evening I forgot Liam represents everything I loathe and simply enjoyed a chat?

I don't have a problem with men. I consider myself a moderate feminist, though I draw the line at putting up shelves when there's a perfectly serviceable chap with a drill about. I *do* have a problem with charming men though. Speaking from experience, charming men always prosper at the expense of someone else.

And of course, there's still the small matter of him ridiculing me in front of five hundred people. Although, perhaps, if I were being honest, I might have asked for it, a bit.

I clear my throat and set my cutlery down on the empty plate with a loud chink, hoping to catch his eye, but instead, Liam puts his notebook down, extracts some notes from his wallet and places them on the table. He pushes his chair back and thanks the restaurateur, who is now shaking his hand as though they are old pals.

Almost as an afterthought, Liam nods in my direction.

'Enjoy the rest of your evening, Annabel.'

He throws me a parting smile and there's something hesitant about it. As though it almost pained him to do it.

It is the very opposite of charm.

# CHAPTER 10

## CORFU, DAY FOUR

In a perfect example of redundant traditions, I picked up a postcard today from a souvenir shop to send to my parents, then realising I would arrive back in Langtree long before it did, I took a photo of it and sent it instead via WhatsApp with the following message:

*Hello from the land of The Durrells! Wish you were here x*

I did briefly wish they were here when I saw a large family on the beach earlier, three generations all playing frisbee, picnicking and holidaying together. But the whimsy quickly passed when I remembered a family holiday to Portugal and my father's repeated requests for steak and kidney pie at every restaurant in the Algarve. He's a simple man, my dad, with everything he'd ever wanted or needed met in my mother. I wonder if she'll convince him to take a holiday now, or whether his insistence she remain wrapped in cotton wool will push them further apart.

All in all, it's been a most relaxing day. I've swum in the sea, a much easier experience with my new swim shoes, read a little and stopped off at Niko's bar for a coffee.

I was served today by a strikingly beautiful young woman in jeans so tight it made my eyes sweat just thinking about wearing them in this heat – no sign of Niko, but I guess everyone deserves time off. As I'd sat there, my thoughts had wandered back to the book. Not the one I'd just been reading, but *the* book, from the book exchange. What he'd said, whoever the writer is, about first impressions had really struck a chord with me.

Take Liam, for example. My overriding first impression of him had been one of vanity, swagger, and overconfidence. The basis for these sweeping accusations were looks (he has them in abundance) and an award-winning track record in salesmanship (untrustworthy, likely to flog his own grandmother for praise).

My spidey senses were honed with hard-won first-hand experience and I'm a little peeved to find them letting me down. So far, Liam isn't fitting into the mould I'd made for him.

If anything, he's been reserved. Quiet and even aloof.

And as for the writer of those messages, what's my first impression of him?

Hmm. Someone with a sense of adventure. Someone who's travelled the world. Sensitive, but friendly. Why else would you write anonymously to strangers? Perhaps he does this with every book he reads? Perhaps he's one of those people who leave books on benches and trains for others to find. Perhaps this is how he meets people, rather than using cheesy pick-up lines in bars. He sounds like my perfect guy.

I'm disturbed from my reverie by a notification on my phone.

It's a message from Mum.

*How lovely dear, we're so pleased you're having a nice time. I popped into the bookshop today for a present for Gran, thought she'd like the new Alan Titchmarsh. Howard behaved very peculiarly, couldn't get a word out of him. Perhaps he'd had bad news. Lots of love, Mum.*

Oh.

It had always been a gamble, encouraging mum to use social media. On the one hand it was great to stay connected, but on the other she couldn't quite grasp that her message was uniquely attached to her name and that she needn't sign off as though it were a telegram. Nor had she considered I might not want updates from the shop. If Howard had learned the shop was to close, it would be just like him to keep it from me until I returned home. Pity my mother couldn't think to do the same. I forward the message to Jess and Vik on our group chat, followed by a deflated emoji. Then, because I feel bad about offloading on them again, follow it up with the middle finger, a fist bump and three cocktails.

Well, there's nothing I can do about it now. Besides, I have a cruise to go on and just enough time to go back and freshen up first.

No sooner have I come through the door than Liam appears, rubbing at his hair with a towel.

'Hey,' he says, dropping the towel, his hair sticking up at right angles in an oddly vulnerable way. 'I thought we should swap rooms, as it doesn't seem fair that you spend the whole week on the sofa bed. I've packed up all my stuff so move in there whenever you're ready.'

'Oh,' I say, taken slightly aback at the gesture. 'OK, if you're sure?'

He nods. 'I found some clean sheets, so you won't have to sleep in – whatever that was.'

'Right. Thanks.'

Liam disappears into the bathroom, and I see his rucksack is parked in the corner of the lounge, a few of his belongings beside it, his own soiled sheets folded on the arm of the sofa in readiness.

I make quick work of gathering my stuff together, bundling it all back into my case and shunting it through to the bedroom. Then, because I want to change, I empty the whole lot onto the floor to find my top. I'll sort it all out later, the cruise leaves in half an hour and there's something I want to do first.

'See you later,' I say, passing Liam in the kitchen as he's washing up a plate. 'Have a good evening.'

'You too,' he replies.

Goodness, we're in danger of becoming almost civil.

I hurry across to Hotel Electra. Fortunately, Greta is occupied, as I don't have time to stop and chat. In a matter of moments, I have the book in my hands, and I hastily flick through to find my last message.

Excitement blooms in my belly when I see a new reply.

*I think we probably have much in common, mysterious holidaymaker. 'The Great Gatsby' is my favourite book of all time. And I'm sorry you've had such bad experiences of men, truly, but Gatsby is a fascinating character; even beguiling people make mistakes, it's what makes them interesting.*

*Tell me, what is so awful about Devon, besides ex-prospective in-laws? Perhaps seeing as they are now ex-prospective, it had more to do with the prospect?*

Arrows indicate the messages continue, but I don't have time to read on. There is something so bizarre about this method of communication between us, two total strangers, that it feels a little special. There are only ten minutes until the boat leaves so I drop the book into my bag, because let's face it, no one in their right mind would want to read the book now. It's ruined, with our scrawling handwriting flowing across the margins of the pages. As I head to the harbour, I fight the urge to bring it back out and read on.

I strongly suspect the Sunflower to have seen better days; the blue and yellow paintwork is flaking and faded but its jolly presence dominates the jetty and I join the tail end of the last few people queuing to board. A bearded man with a clipboard counts us on as we show our booking receipts and I make my way up to the open-top deck, to bag a good viewing spot.

As I take in the demographic of my fellow cruisers, I note with sinking predictability they are nearly all couples, but I find an entire vacant bench near the back and settle down as the boat begins to move.

A deafening white noise startles me half to standing and a crackling voice booms from a speaker right above my head.

It's so loud, my ear drums are clattering like tambourines, and I only manage to pick out the words; 'dolphin', 'cock' and 'snacks'. What any of that has to do with a sunset cruise is anyone's guess but I sincerely hope it isn't a summary of what's for supper.

When the orator switches off his microphone, I breathe a sigh of relief and glance fruitlessly about for a different seat.

The couple across from me pout sympathetically.

'We sat there first, didn't we, Marvin?' says the woman in khaki shorts and a straining peach vest top.

'Happen we did, Sue,' replies Marvin, in equally broad Yorkshire tones. 'Near blew us heads off.'

Marvin, whose top half is respectably clothed in a short-sleeved linen shirt, has made an unfortunate choice of shorts. At least I'd like to believe he's oblivious that his sandy-coloured safaris encase his meat and veg so prominently and compactly that two suet dumplings and a pig in blanket can clearly be detected. He can't possibly be wearing underpants. The look is further enhanced by a roadmap of varicose veins on legs that end in unwieldy, yellow-horned toes squeezed into walking sandals.

Some things are simply not fit for public viewing and this, I gather, is to be my view for this romantic sunset cruise.

I smile good naturedly. 'Never mind, I'm used to the cheap seats. But I didn't catch what he said, something about dolph—' My words are swallowed whole by the violent eruption of the speaker again, as it begins blaring an instrumental arrangement of Celine Dion's *My Heart Will Go On*. Quite aside from the wildly inappropriate reference to perishing at sea, I fear that my own death will arise as a result of cochlea combustion.

Sue must take pity on me, because I see her nudging Marvin, who eventually takes the hint and shuffles along before patting at the one-buttock-sized gap that has been created. It is the work of a nanosecond to calculate that spooning myself into the space beside Marvin will be preferable to gazing upon him.

'Dolphins,' he bellows in my ringing ear. 'Captain reckons if we're lucky, we'll spot dolphins off coast.'

'Ah,' I say, trying to look thrilled.

'And,' adds Sue, leaning across Marvin, 'we'll be stopping for a swim before sunset, followed by cocktails and a selection of both sweet *and* savoury snacks.'

'I hope they've got some of that balaclava,' adds Marvin. 'We tried it last night, didn't we, Sue? It were alright, that.'

It's unclear whether Marvin's malapropism is unintended, or whether he simply fancies himself as a regular Peter Kay and does in fact know the difference between a burglar's disguise and a traditional Greek syrupy filo pastry.

I'm dying to return to the book and read more of the messages, but Marvin would have an unrestricted view and as I'm unwilling to share the experience, I turn my attention instead to the vista on my left. The rocky coastline grows ever distant as we track a path alongside it and the ocean gradually darkens to deepest Cadbury purple in the low afternoon sun. Even with the questionable music in the background, I must have drifted off, because it's only when the crackling tannoy roars back into life that I startle awake and realise I've slumped right onto Marvin's cushiony shoulder.

'Gosh! I'm ever so sorry,' I begin, but Marvin quietens me with a hand to his ear, as both he and Sue strain to hear what the captain is saying.

Afterwards, I'm furnished with a translation.

'We can go off and swim or snorkel if we want,' says Sue.

She points to a bay and an outcrop of small rocky islands. We bob gently as passengers begin to move about.

'Going for a swim, love?' asks Marvin.

'Not sure,' I reply. 'I think I'll go for a walk about though. Sorry for snoozing on you.'

'Oh, don't apologise, I was rather enjoying it, until you started dribbling.'

'Teck no notice of the silly old fool. You go on and enjoy yourself love,' says Sue, giving Marvin a playful poke.

Levering myself up, I run a hand over my chin to check for drool, then make for the stairs.

Down on deck, there is a flurry of activity as passengers either dive or jump into the sea. A dozen or so bodies float happily on their backs, basking in the low sun, whilst others entwine in lustful displays of synchronised swooning. I lean over the railings at the front of the boat, contemplating a dip, before sitting instead with my book and returning to the last message.

*I'll let you into a secret. This is my first holiday in four years. For reasons I won't go into, I find them difficult, although this one is turning out better than expected. It's my first time visiting Corfu, and it won't be my last. Apologies in advance for future dithering in this particular corner of the planet. I know how much this offends you.*

*Yes, the calamari is good, but have you ever tried rigorous debate with a complete stranger within the margins of a book? You really should try it.*

A smile cracks on my lips and I'm almost compelled to hug the book to me. Impossibly, I'm here alone on an actual love boat, surrounded by couples and I don't feel lonely at all.

I pull out my pen and begin to write.

*See, now you've gone and made me feel insecure. Are you cheating on me? Are there more books? More strangers? And there was I believing this meant something.*

*I'll let you into a secret too. I've stolen this book (temporarily), and I've taken it on a trip. We're somewhere beautiful, at sundown, surrounded by amorous animals, but I find myself thinking about you. Wondering what sort of a person you are, what you might look like. What might make you dread something most people long for. A holiday can be many things, a break from day-to-day life, a trip that isn't*

*business, a celebration, a commiseration, a reward, or a*
*dream. But it normally has good connotations (unless you find*
*yourself on an extended trip to one of His Majesty's pleasure*
*hotels). I guess if you were agoraphobic, a spell away from*
*home would be a penance. God, that's not it, is it?*

*I LOVE holidays. I love everything about them, choosing*
*them, planning them, counting down the days and hours until*
*them. But I also love going home. Usually.*

The tannoy erupts again, but from this spot I can also see
the captain as he speaks, from behind the glass-fronted cabin.

'Ladies and gentlemen, please make your way back to The
Sunflower. Refreshments will soon be served.'

*Time for me to go. I feel a bit guilty about defacing this*
*book (I hold you entirely responsible, by the way), so I propose*
*concealing the crime. How about the bottom shelf, behind the*
*last book on the right?*

Smirking to myself, I shove the book back inside my bag
and look up to see – none other than Liam Shaw hauling
himself onto the boat.

Even as the smile drops from my face at discovering him
here on this trip with me, I find my eyes roaming the firm,
toned contours of his body as he climbs aboard with ease.

Since meeting him naked on the day I arrived in Corfu, I
haven't again witnessed him in a state of undress. He doesn't
swan around the apartment in his boxers, as I might have
expected; even on the balcony in the heat of day, he's always
respectfully clothed. I can't even say I registered much on
that first day either, other than extreme shock, so I hadn't
appreciated how remarkably well built he is. Broad-shouldered
and lean, with visibly defined stomach muscles that tense as
he moves, tanned skin glistening with water droplets.

To my embarrassment, as my gaze travels up his chest, I
see he's looking right at me. It's too late to pretend I haven't
noticed him, and as the corners of his mouth tug upward, I
remember my mother's text. In all likelihood, since we've
been here, Franklyn's have announced the closure of the

Langtree shop. Something I'm suddenly certain he already knows about. The pretence at chivalry in offering up his room today now makes so much more sense, and probably eased his conscience enough to look me in the eye. Before he can make more than a step towards me, I rise and turn my back, then head inside the cabin where a questionable-looking drink is thrust into my hand.

'Punch,' says the woman, when I look at it for a beat too long.

'Ah,' I say, as though enlightened. But really, it could be methylated spirits, given my need for immediate inebriation, so I neck the contents of the plastic tumbler in one gulp and hold my hand out for another.

'Annabel.' I hear my name and turn.

Liam has pulled on a loosely buttoned shirt, its hem dampened by the spreading moisture from his dark blue swimmers.

'Everything OK?' He frowns, as though I've offended him in some way.

'Everything's fine, why wouldn't it be?' *Other than the fact I can't seem to go anywhere on this planet, without bumping into you, of course*, I think to myself.

He shrugs. 'I fancied a boat trip; this was the only one they had left. Look, I'm sorry if my being here has spoiled that for you, although I'm truly baffled as to what I've ever done to upset you so much. I just don't understand.'

So, we're doing this then, are we?

I down my second drink and metaphorically roll up my sleeves.

'Well, you wouldn't, would you?'

'Er no, that's what I just said.'

Just as I'm about to start listing 'Reasons to Dislike Liam', I'm interrupted by the arrival of Marvin, whose wet shorts are now adhering to his silhouette in an even more X-rated way, thanks to a dip in the sea.

'Would you look at that. You found each other. I were only

saying to young Liam just now, whilst we were enjoying a mutual appreciation of the *scenery*,' he winks and indicates a woman in a skimpy yellow two-piece draped across the lap of her lover, leaving me in no doubt of the scenery in question, 'that there were a nice young lady aboard, who happened to be on 'er own.'

'Yep. We found each other,' I reply tersely.

Liam misses my barb, because his attention is still caught by the canoodling couple, which is just as well, because Marvin, it seems, as he launches into a comparative monologue of boat trips past, has plenty to say for the both of us.

'Excuse me a moment, would you,' says Liam, leaving me and Marvin staring after him as he strides purposefully towards the woman in the yellow bikini.

Except, it's not the woman in the bikini he approaches. It's her boyfriend, a man who looks to be in his twenties, dark and tanned, his oiled torso showcased through an open shirt. A shirt, I'm realising in sinking dismay, that looks horribly familiar.

'Excuse me,' he says, addressing the man, his voice cool and even. 'Where did you get your shirt?'

Bikini-babe casts a quick appreciate look over Liam that I catch even from here, before dismounting her boyfriend and treating us all to far more gusset than we wished to see when bending to retrieve her sarong.

'Quoi?' asks the man, irked at the interruption. 'De quoi parles-tu?'

'French,' interprets Marvin helpfully for my benefit, 'haven't come across many of them so far on this trip. Plenty of Italians, Germans too, but no French, as yet.'

'The shirt?' repeats Liam, folding his arms across his chest. 'Where did you get it? Because I think you'll find that shirt belongs to me.'

Oh. My. God. Please don't let this be happening. How the *fuck* has this guy got hold of Liam's shirt? Of all the garish, hideous Hawaiian shirts in the world, why did it have to be this one?

'What are you talking about, you crazy Brit?' snaps the Frenchman. 'I think the sea air has got to your head, no?' He taps his temple aggressively as though it will aid in Liam's understanding of his accent.

Marvin sucks in a breath beside me. Others turn to look.

'I'd watch who you're calling crazy, fella, and I'd appreciate it if you would answer the question. That is my shirt, it was stolen from my apartment. So, I'd very much like to know how it came to be in your possession.'

Christ, Liam is *fierce*. But, in a weirdly attractive way – and this comes from someone who can sniff out an alpha male at a distance of three football pitches and usually runs in the opposite direction. However, the other guy doesn't look too pleased either. I glance about, grasping for a way to defuse this situation before it becomes fisticuffs at sea.

The man takes a step towards Liam, fury radiating from his balled-up shoulders.

Liam merely tilts his head in invitation.

I think I might be sick.

'Luca? Laisse-le, ça ne vaut pas le coup,' interjects Bikini-babe, slipping an arm through her boyfriend's.

There is uncertainty in her expression, and I couldn't say why, but I really don't like the way she is appraising Liam, huge eyelash extensions fluttering like spiders' legs as she rakes her gaze over him. She turns to her man and mutters something in his ear, which I can't catch, even if I could speak fluent French.

Then she faces Liam and speaks slowly, enunciating each word, 'I bought this shirt for Luca. Sorry, but you are mistaken.'

She holds his gaze, defiant. Challenging him to accuse her of lying.

I hold my breath, torn as to whether I should intervene, to tell the truth and admit my part, even though I have no idea why this man is wearing a garment that should be buried in the bottom of a headscarf basket in the Church of the Panagia Kassopitra.

But it seems no action is necessary, because Liam holds up his hands in a gesture of surrender.

'Well then, it appears I *have* been mistaken. Please accept my apologies.'

The Frenchman looks like he'd still prefer to bop Liam on the nose, but his girlfriend is running a soothing hand up his arm, which eventually quietens his rage and instead, he lets out a huff and turns his back, muttering under his breath.

Liam comes back over, his face a mask of polite indifference. But I can tell he's fuming; I can see it in the flexing of his fingers.

'Sorry, guys,' he says with a wince, then lets out a tight laugh, 'didn't think it was possible anyone had such terrible taste in clothing as me, but there you have it.'

As Sue arrives at Marvin's side, the tension is swiftly broken by the couple's ability to talk for all of England, but I'm still left with the unpleasant taste of guilt in my mouth.

# CHAPTER 11

When the Sunflower finally sails back into Kassiopi Harbour, I almost jump overboard in a bid to reach shore first.

My decent upbringing prevails however, and I remain sandwiched between Sue and Liam. I've been obliged to hear in detail of her recent gastric band procedure whilst also being acutely aware of Liam's firm, warm thigh alongside mine as he and Marvin, on his other side, discuss the highs and lows of *Frasier*. I grudgingly admit Jess was right, his patience and ability to listen abound, whilst I fear my own resting bitch face has rather given me away.

Eventually, the boat docks. Like that poxy necklace in *Titanic*, my heart plummets to new depths when the other passengers disembark as though we're aboard a plane, ensuring every last soul reaches dry land before us, despite the fact we're sitting next to the gangplank, or whatever freedom is called.

This gives Marvin more than enough time to hatch a torturous plan.

'Well, t' night's young, kids, what do you all say to a nightcap?' he asks, slapping his thighs for effect. He is not aware of Liam's and my prior acquaintance, but if his plan had been to play Cupid, he's absolutely rubbish at it.

Spying the end of the queue approach, I seize my opportunity and spring to my feet, saying, 'That sounds lovely, but I've got a bit of a headache.' Then I add sweetly, 'But you must go Liam, don't let me spoil everyone's fun.'

Liam merely smiles back at me, his polite expression impossible to read, although I'm sure he's subjecting my mental effigy to unspeakable acts of violence.

He pulls himself to his feet, then turns back to Marvin and Sue. 'Do you know what? A nightcap sounds wonderful. Have you tried that cocktail bar in the square?'

I do some swift goodbyes, nice to meet yous, perhaps we'll bump into each other agains, then beat a hasty retreat uphill. But why does the parting image of Liam chuckling away with Marvin as they head off towards the village keep niggling at me? It couldn't be 'Fear of Missing Out'. Absolutely not. I'm bloody glad to get away from the lot of them.

Before returning to the apartment, I make a quick detour to replace the book at the pool, mindful not to leave it in an obvious place. I wonder how long I will have to wait for a reply. I've no idea how long is left of my correspondent's holiday, nor if he even *is* on holiday. It could all be utter bollocks. Of course, there's nothing to stop me spending a day by the pool and staking out the bookshelf, if I really want to catch him red-handed. Maybe I should.

No. That way madness lies, and I've a date with Corfu Town tomorrow.

Even though it's only just gone nine, I decide an early night is in order, especially, I remember with glee, because tonight I get to sleep in a proper bed.

Giddy with anticipation, I grab the packet of biscuits I bought at the supermarket yesterday and a bottle of water from the fridge and head straight for the bedroom.

My suitcase is not where I left it by the bed. My belongings are not where I left them, in a heap on the floor by the bed.

With a growing sense of déjà-vu, I approach the wardrobe and fling it open to find, once more, both Liam's and my clothing all neatly hung and folded.

'Oh Maria. Maria, Maria, Maria,' I sing out, feeling

exasperated and possibly slightly unhinged. 'I've just met a maid named Maria...'

I don't remember the next lyrics of the song, but I somehow doubt I'm sharing the same heart-struck sentiment as poor tragic Tony from *West Side Story*, as this situation is more 'Same Old Story'. I can't even begin to fathom Maria's reasoning – surely it is quite apparent there are two separate rooms in operation. Perhaps this is simply good sport, to be shared with other housekeepers on a WhatsApp group named 'How to Fuck with Tourists'.

Whilst there are no towel sculptures or scattered petals this time – they were presumably a once-a-holiday treat – I do now have the unfortunate predicament of needing to repack Liam's rucksack. And whilst I don't know him well, I'm taking a stab in the dark there would have been method to his packing. Or at the very least, an element of folding, unlike my stuff-it-shove-it-cram-it technique.

And if I don't restore his belongings to exactly as he left them and instead explain about Maria's diligent housekeeping, he will know that the mysterious vanishing and subsequent reappearance of his lucky shirt upon the body of a Frenchman was entirely down to me. A garment no longer within my possession, nor power to return. And that's not even to mention the contents of his bedside drawer. Speaking of which, I cross the room and open the drawer with trepidation. Along with my personal items, which are safely still within, there is the disturbing addition of several loose packets of condoms. At least, I trust they are condoms; they are the right size and shape, but rather than any reputable or recognisable brand, they feature illustrations of Greek gods and goddesses in compromising positions, and the slogan 'Best Lover in Corfu'. A souvenir gift shop purchase, I suspect, and questionably fit for purpose. The thought of Liam buying these fills me with strangely conflicting feelings. Would he seriously have considered bringing someone back here with me in the room next door? Would *I* bring someone back here, to this bedroom, knowing Liam was in the lounge?

Perhaps Liam didn't even buy them. Perhaps the provision of contraceptives forms part of Maria's very personal service. However they got here, the reality is I'll have to decide whether to repack these into Liam's rucksack too.

Various options swim through my mind as I return to the wardrobe.

Perhaps I could simply remove every garment from the villa, including my own, claim burglary and spend the rest of the trip in this one bikini and dungaree shorts. Although a burglar would have been far more interested in passports and money than my second-hand high-street wardrobe. Mind you, some of Liam's shirts do feel of particularly high quality, I acknowledge, fingering the soft fabric of a blue linen number I've yet to see him wear. It has Liam's signature scent – bergamot, I think, combined with eau de Persil.

I drop my hand and shake my head. Terrible idea. Some of my clothes are vintage, and where would I get another BHS blouse?

Then, it comes to me in a white-light flash of inspiration. I'm a genius.

Hurriedly, I remove all of Liam's clothes and pull out his rucksack from the bottom of the wardrobe, where it had been stowed next to my suitcase, then I stuff it all in any old how, adding any of his personal effects I find in drawers and on surfaces. My hand hovers over the condoms, before scooping them up too – but instead of adding them to the bag, I slip them into my suitcase. Best the evidence is hidden, for now, until I work out what to do with them.

Next, I race to the kitchen and fling open the fridge door. I need to find something horribly wet and stinky to feasibly be carrying through the lounge, when I accidentally trip and douse poor Liam's rucksack. With saintly levels of concern for his belongings, I will then have a valid excuse to pull it all out haphazardly onto the floor.

There is an opened packet of salami that Liam must have bought. I haven't done much shopping myself, having abandoned all notion of catering in this ill-equipped kitchen, and there's only a teaspoon left of milk – this is a shame because nothing soils quite like milk. On the other hand, I would have to move out immediately because of the rancid smell. Other than the salami, there is one bottle of beer, an unopened packet of feta cheese and a solitary tomato. None of these items are remotely up to the task.

What I need is a nice big bottle of full-bodied red wine. A few glugs of it before it meets its demise wouldn't go amiss either.

I check the time.

It's been half an hour since we parted ways at the harbour, but if I've got even half the measure of Marvin and Sue, Liam will be a while yet. Enough time, I'm certain, to run down to the little shop at the bottom of the hill.

As a precaution, I dump the rucksack in roughly the position it was when I saw it earlier, then I grab my purse and flee the apartment.

It is something of a challenge to attempt the steep slope at speed in flip-flops, but after a few near tumbles, and with screaming calf muscles, I finally arrive at the shop, procure the booze, then wearily retrace my steps.

Sweating, I trudge the last few steps to our floor and round the corner, just in time to see Liam slotting his key in the lock of our front door.

'Liam,' I call, my voice coming out an octave higher than usual, 'you're back already.'

He looks up, raises his eyebrows and continues to let himself in. 'Gatecrashing a party for one, am I? Thought you had a headache.'

Blindsided by this comment, and ever so slightly horrified about the idea of him reaching his rucksack first, I offer a morsel of honesty.

'I don't really have a headache, and I did fancy a drink...'

I follow him in and then snake around him, blocking his path.

'Just not with those people.'

Liam's eyes darken and he tilts his head slightly, as though trying to decode what I said. Then, his gaze drops to my hands, where I've been nervously passing my right hand up and down the shaft of the bottle my left hand is holding.

Mortified by what I've just insinuated, I'm transported to a moment six years ago. To the memory of biting the inside of my cheek so hard, I taste blood. Anything to distract from Garrett Delaney closing the blinds on the window into the open-plan offices and asking if I feel OK, if I'd like to sit down. I'm focusing on the urgent page proofs in my hand, as though they contain the answer to eternal life, assuring him I'm quite well and suggesting he take a look. He says he's already looking, that he really likes what he sees, can't I tell?

Beneath Liam's quizzical gaze, my hands begin to shake. Abruptly, I turn on my heel, undoing the screwcap as I go and taking a long swig. Thank goodness for cheap wine. I doubt there's a corkscrew in the kitchen and I may have been forced to smash off the neck in desperation.

A hand lands on my arm.

'Annabel.'

'What?' I snap, spinning round.

Liam is standing there, arms folded across his broad chest, a frown burrowed into his forehead.

'You know, I thought it was just me. That for some irrational reason you'd decided you hated me, though for the life of me I don't know what I've done, besides win this prize – which I had zero control over, by the way. But then I witnessed how rude you were back there, and now I see that for whatever reason, you're bitter at everyone and everything.'

'I beg your pardon?'

'Marvin and Sue. They're nice people, they were just being friendly, there was no need to scurry off as though they had something highly infectious. Did you know this is their first vacation since losing their grandson in a motorcycle accident three years ago? They're quite determined to enjoy every single minute of it and bloody well done to them.'

I open my mouth to say something but close it again when no words come out.

'You do know vacations are meant to be fun, right? Isn't it exhausting being mad all the time?'

He's looking at me as though I'm a genuine enigma, and then suddenly, the absurdity of this whole situation hits me in the gut and an uncontrollable fit of hysterics bursts out of me. My job is likely gone, my home will soon be gone, he's wrecked the holiday which cost all my savings by refusing to leave the villa I booked, turns up everywhere I go, threatens a stranger aboard our boat and somehow – *I'm* the bad guy?

'Oh, you're a fine one to talk Mr Always-Pack-Laundry-Liquid in case your clothes need washing. You eat at the same restaurant every night and have a full-on meltdown because you lost a stupid shirt. And yes, I can see you're cramming as much unadulterated hedonism as possible into each minute of your stay.'

For a moment I think he's going to shout at me. He stands there, eyes flashing with anger and something else. Hurt.

I've upset him. Good.

I'm beyond caring about the stupid rucksack now. Let him work it out. What does it even matter? I never have to see him again after this anyway. In fact, I might see if I can find a hotel for the next couple of nights and stick it on a credit card, salvage what I can of this shitshow excuse for a holiday, hang the expense.

'I'm going to take a shower,' he grunts, before turning and walking away.

'Mind you don't have too much fun in there,' I call after him childishly.

He stops, turns and strides purposefully towards me, his jaw set rigid and whilst I don't flinch, an unexpected surge of electricity travels along my arm as he brushes past me and makes straight for his rucksack.

OK, so perhaps I do care, a little.

My stomach buckles as he unzips it, but then to my surprise he picks the whole thing up and upends its contents onto the floor. If he notices everything land in an unorganised crumple, he doesn't show it. Instead, he rifles through until he finds I presume clean boxers and a t-shirt and then he heads back to the bathroom.

I'm left standing there with a bottle of wine I no longer need, not for its intended purpose anyway, but I take it with me to the bedroom and gently close the door, before slipping between the fresh new sheets.

# CHAPTER 12

## CORFU, DAY FIVE

*I like that you have been wondering about me. I wonder about you too. About what sort of a woman comes to Corfu on holiday alone, not that there's anything wrong with that as I'm also holidaying alone. It's much better than I thought it would be.*

*I'm jumping to scandalous conclusions of course; you haven't told me you're alone. Call me jealous, but if you took our book on a trip, I'd like to think it was just the two of you.*

*What can I tell you about me? Well, I'm the full cliché; an unpublished writer, chasing a childhood dream. The rest of its all just detail, I'm not that complicated. Give me a good book, a nice view and somewhere to jot down my thoughts and there's little else I need.*

*How about you? What makes for your perfect day? What makes you tick, mysterious holidaymaker?*

I sit back on the sun lounger, holding the book away from me to stop it from getting wet. It's early, and I'm thankful I fell asleep last night before I could drink too much wine. It's refreshing to be up early enough for a swim before the sun heats up and before I get the bus into Corfu Town for a day of sightseeing. I also managed to avoid Liam, which was a bonus.

I'm considering my reply as I lay there, watching as one by one, guests appear, drape their towels across loungers, then disappear again. Behaviour I'll never understand.

I didn't expect a reply this soon; after all, I only returned the book late last night. It makes me suspect my mystery scribe is as curious about me as I am about him and that, I can't deny, is flattering. Not only that, but the book was waiting in my suggested hiding spot, on the bottom shelf at the far end, behind *The Girl on The Train*. There were three other copies much nearer the top, so it seemed as safe a place as any.

The pitying way in which Liam had looked at me last night replays in my mind, along with his words: *You do know vacations are meant to be fun, right?*

The bloody cheek. I know how to have fun; I have a lot of fun. I *am* fun. Ask Jess and Vik. It's a ridiculous dialogue to have with myself, as if I care what he thinks of me. He knows nothing about me.

An idea begins to take root. A recklessness. Or a reckoning.

I reach into my bag and pull out the postcard I'd intended to mail to Mum but sent via WhatsApp instead. Turning it over, I write quickly.

*We are running out of space in this book, but it's ok, I have a solution…*

*Meet me tonight. Eight o clock? Do you know Niko's Bar on the harbour front?*

Then, before I can change my mind, I slide the postcard inside the book and take it back to the shelves, taking care to replace it exactly where I found it.

As I return to the poolside, Greta is opening up the bar.

'Annie,' she calls out cheerfully, 'I haven't seen you for a while. Are you having a nice holiday?'

'Wonderful,' I lie, pulling my cotton dress over my head and slipping into the silver sandals I'd chosen today for their comfort. 'I'm just off to catch the bus to Corfu Town.'

'Ah, you will love it, it's a beautiful town. Here, take this.' She hands me a small, printed business card that reads *Taverna*

*Diana, Agioi Nikolaoi, Corfu*. 'It is my cousin's restaurant, you show this and mention me, and you will get big discount.'

'Oh, thank you, I'll look out for it.'

I tuck it into my purse, whilst Greta draws an imaginary map of the old town on the bar with her finger, using the serviette holder to denote the Byzantine Museum and a plastic straw to mark out the street. She seems exceptionally keen on my grasp of the restaurant's co-ordinates, so I duly assure her I'll seek it out before heading off for the bus.

The bustling streets of Corfu Town are a world apart from the sleepy village of Kassiopi. The old part of the town, tucked away from the modern glazed bus station, high-end clothes shops and recognisable brands of the west, is a maze of cobbled lanes and alleys flanked with stunning Venetian buildings. It is a riot of colour; four-storey buildings painted in rich shades of peach, terracotta and marigold, balconies hung with washing and strewn with flora. Awnings overhead provide respite from the sun to those who languish below, watching the trail of tourists wind its way along the myriad of gift shops, jewellers, delicatessens and bars.

I could spend hours here, mooching around shops strung with traditional Greek lace, minded by elderly women dressed in black, fanning themselves in the shade, shops laden with leather products – bags, belts, shoes, wallets. I stop to finger the soft, buttery leather of a beautiful red tote bag before concluding I own enough bags and tearing myself away. Ordinarily this would be my idea of heaven, sniffing out unique gifts for my friends, soaking up the eclectic mix of new and old, traditional and tacky, but my heart doesn't seem in it. Instead, it is languishing somewhere up near my increasingly parched throat, wondering if the postcard has been seen yet and if there is a reply.

I pass a cafe occupying a corner spot, making the most of its prime pavement space with a pergola draped in deep purple bougainvillea, and spotting a vacant table, divert to it at speed.

Aperol spritz in hand, I flick through the pamphlets I picked up at the bus station, deciding where to go next. I visited the old fortress this morning, though took in little of what the tour guide was saying, but the views from the grounds were incredible and I took a few pictures, which I attach to a message on the WhatsApp group I have with Jess and Vik.

Both ticks turn blue immediately, so it's no surprise when I see Jess already typing a reply.

Jess: *Nice pics. Bonked the hot dude yet?*

It takes my brain far too long to realise she's referring to Niko, and not Liam, or the anonymous stranger I have apparently asked out on a date, whose hotness I can't yet attest to.

Annie*: No... But don't rule out my Shirley Valentine moment just yet.*

Vik: *Wait – what hot dude?*

Jess: *Vikram, it's Greece, all the dudes are hot. But anyhoo, its Saturday, so guess what that means?*

Annie: *Ant and Dec and a bowl of toffee popcorn?*

Jess: *I'm that predictable? Probably tbh, but before that @Vik — fancy a bit of fun in a certain Chelmsford bookshop? I'm ready and raring to go.*

Two seconds later a selfie of Jess in a Cyndi Lauper wig, complete with electric blue eyeshadow comes through, which I recognise to be part of the fancy dress outfit she wore at our local pub's eighties night last year.

Annie: *Bit extra for a shopping trip, isn't it? Look, as much as I appreciate the gesture, I really don't think there's any point anymore.*

Jess: *There's every point. Besides, it's too good an opportunity to miss, seeing as Liam's over there with you.*

Vik: *Count me in. Ash is rehearsing his lines and if I hear the words AC12, OCG and Document Pi54b again I might be forced to make a citizen's arrest.*

At this I chuckle aloud. Ash is an actor, whose credits to

date have included breakfast cereal commercials, walk-on parts in *Hollyoaks* and a stint in local panto. His speaking part in the much-anticipated new *Line of Duty* special has elevated his status to that of a local celeb.

Annie: *Liam's not with me. I just have the misfortune to be inhabiting the same lump of rock as him right now.*

Jess: *Well, make the most of it, it's pissing down here. Toodle-pip, mischief to make. @Vik, I'll pick you up in ten.*

The idea of Jess and Vik creating havoc in Liam's shop whilst he languishes blissfully unaware on a beach has me sniggering into my glass as I drain it and get up to leave. I think I'll simply spend the rest of the afternoon wandering and soaking it all in, visit one of the many impressive Greek Orthodox churches before getting a bite to eat. I don't have the required concentration today for any more museums and palaces.

A couple of hours later, hot, sweaty and dreaming of the pool back at the villa, I finally locate Taverna Diana, which is in reality quite substantially further than the distance between a serviette holder and a plastic straw to the museum where I began searching for it. I've passed countless inviting eateries on my travels, all of them promising ice-cold beers, fresh sardines, traditional bigos, stuffed peppers and any number of other delectable authentic dishes. But out of some odd sense of duty, I bypassed them all and instead ended up here, down a side street in front of a plain, peeling building with green shutters. It's only because the faded sign above the door is painted in identical lettering to the card in my hand, that I determine this to be Greta's cousin's restaurant.

Once inside, I'm pleasantly reassured by the considerable number of diners. The décor is simple, unfussy and unquestionably Greek, as are most of the patrons, which I deduce by listening to them speak, hopefully a sign the food will be good.

I'm led to a small table and am about to order a glass of

water, when I spot someone extremely familiar across the room. *You have got to be kidding me.*

'Excuse me,' I say, as politely as I can through gritted teeth. 'I'll be right back.'

The server shrugs her shoulders and instead clears someone's plates whilst I take three purposeful strides to the table where Liam is sitting, tucking into what looks like moussaka in a brown stoneware dish.

'If you think this is funny, I can assure you it is not,' I say in a tone loud enough to draw the attention of several other diners.

Liam looks up in surprise.

'Annabel?'

'Don't give me that. What are you doing here, Liam?'

He puts his fork down and wipes his lips on a linen napkin. 'I'd have thought that was obvious. I'm eating.'

'Right, and you're telling me the fact I travelled an hour and a half by bus to come to this fairly large town, to this pretty innocuous restaurant,' I hear a titter from behind, but ignore it, 'is entirely coincidental when you have done exactly the same?' I give a nasty little cackle. 'I don't think so.'

'Well, yes, that's exactly it. I didn't know you were coming into town too – how could I? You barely give me the time of day.'

'You tell me. You're the one who seems to magically appear everywhere I go: apartments, restaurants, boat trips. What exactly is it you're hoping to achieve? Isn't screwing up my work-life enough for you?' I cross my arms and tilt my head, letting him know in no uncertain terms I'm on to him and I don't care who witnesses it.

'Well, at a guess, Greta also gave you one of these?' he says, pulling the small card out of his pocket.

I narrow my eyes.

'What are you trying to say? That she's matchmaking us?' I give a derisive snort. 'She's barking up the wrong tree there.'

Liam sighs and puts the card down.

'No, Annabel, but she's a friendly woman whom I've chatted with a fair bit, plus she makes commission on every customer she sends to this lovely restaurant that makes absolutely stunning moussaka, so if you don't mind, I'd quite like to eat it whilst it's still hot.'

He looks up at me patiently and I feel my cheeks flood with heat.

'Sit down, order something. I promise you it's good.'

'I – uh,' I stutter, unable to think of a suitable response and aware of how much I've humiliated myself, even if Liam does manage to easily brush my rudeness off. 'I need to get back. I, um... Enjoy your food.'

With that, I turn on my heel, conscious of every set of curious eyes tracking me as I go, until I burst from the restaurant and back out into the stifling heat of late afternoon.

It's only once I'm safely installed on the air-conditioned green bus, part of the public transport network serving the island, that my thoughts turn back to my potential date this evening. I've been on edge all day, veering between panic and nervous anticipation that he might have said yes.

If anything, I should be grateful for encountering Liam in Taverna Diana, because if I'd stayed and dined, I wouldn't have made it back in time – apparently the 18.05 and the 18.40 have been cancelled due to driver sickness, so this, the 17.40, is the last bus arriving back into Kassiopi until nearly nine o clock tonight.

After I'd got over the shock of seeing Liam sitting there and properly thought about it, it wasn't that weird after all. Of course Greta was going to give him the same sales pitch she'd given me, of course she wanted to help boost her cousin's business and if she was even half as friendly with Liam each time he went for a swim as she was with me, then it made perfect sense. Although I strongly suspect Greta rather enjoys her tête-à-têtes with Liam, given how often she's quizzed me on our status quo and commented on his good looks.

What made no sense was my reaction.

I know, deep down, my paranoia has nothing to do with Liam and everything to do with the manipulative agenda of Garrett Delaney, Editor in Chief of *Sunday Living*.

Liam has done nothing, when I think about it, to indicate he is anything other than courteous, respectful and fair. I'll have to apologise, I suppose. It'll kill me, but I'll do it.

In the meantime, I'm going to spend the remainder of this journey mentally cataloguing my wardrobe for a suitable 'first date' outfit.

But as it turns out, I needn't have bothered.

After I disembark from the air-conditioned coach and hike up the steep hill, I make a beeline for Hotel Electra and the bookshelves beside the pool.

I kneel by the bottom shelf and reach past the rest of the books to where our book should be.

Only, it isn't.

I pull out each and every paperback until I'm looking at empty shelves.

Our book has gone.

# CHAPTER 13

Donna Summer blares from my phone on the bed, whilst I run a mascara wand across my lashes for the first time this holiday and stretch my lips to apply pale pink gloss. My hair is all wavy after being left to dry in a messy bun after my swim this morning, so I tease it through with my fingers and let it hang loose on my shoulders, quite liking the tangled effect. I'm wearing a knee-length floral silk dress with a cute sweetheart neckline and spaghetti straps. It has tiny pearlescent buttons running all the way through and was my ultimate charity shop star buy – a vintage Max Mara.

Potentially, the book has been borrowed by an unsuspecting reader; if so, they're in for a surprise. There is also the possibility my correspondent has removed the book but not yet returned it.

Either way, I don't know if my invitation has been seen, whether there has been a reply, or if there ever will be. But I've decided, regardless, to go out tonight and have me some fun. I take another swig of yesterday's cheap red wine and try to ignore my rumbling tummy. There wasn't time to eat, having left Taverna Diana without tasting so much as an olive, but I'll grab a gyros later. It's Saturday night on the island of Corfu and there is partying to be done.

As the clock strikes eight pm, I muster an air of confidence, aided by the remaining wine, which I'd necked from the bottle along the way, then deposited into a glass recycling bin, and stroll towards Niko's bar.

The terrace looks beautiful at night, comfortable sofas and bistro tables lit from above by fairy lights strung from trees, transforming the lunchtime spot into a romantic grotto. I scan the waterfront tables, looking for a lone male, but seeing only couples, groups of friends, and the occasional family. There is a woman sitting alone, though; older than me and stylishly dressed in wide-legged trousers and heeled, strappy sandals with an arm full of bohemian silver bangles.

Did my correspondent ever *specifically* state he was a man? I try to think back over our messages. Perhaps I just assumed. God, now I don't know.

A man in a cream linen suit and leather flip-flops saunters over to her, replacing his wallet in his trouser pocket as he goes. I watch as he holds out his hand, which she takes as she rises. Hand in hand, they walk away, and I'm left feeling oddly alone. The advances of a literary lesbian would have been flattering, even if not reciprocated.

'Lady of the strawberry hair,' comes an exotic voice behind me, and I turn to see Niko leaning against a pillar, an empty tray dangling from his hand.

'Are you just here to admire the view, or can I get you a drink?' he asks.

'It *is* a lovely view' I reply, looking to the still water in the bay, nightfall darkening the horizon, where tiny lights illuminate the vessels at sea. 'One that might be enhanced by a drink, I'll admit.'

'Then take a seat. What can I get you?'

I glance again at the waterfront, at the many couples, and hesitate.

Perhaps he notices my reticence, because he says 'come,' and jerks his thumb towards a couple of high stools inside, near the bar.

Above the ambient background music, I detect quickfire

Greek drifting from the kitchen. A customer wanders through, and heads towards the toilet facilities signposted at the back.

'Is it normally this quiet in here?' I ask, as Niko circles behind the bar.

'At this time, people are mostly out for dinner. Later, after approximately ten o' clock, it gets busier. Now, what would you like to drink?'

I chew my mouth. Not wine – I've had enough of that.

'Surprise me?' I say, surprising myself in the process.

Niko smiles, his handsome face lighting up as though I've given him a gift, then he nods knowingly and reaches for a cocktail shaker.

I watch him as he works, enjoying the way he takes such care to get every detail right; from the way he mixes, then pours the liquid at height into a highball glass of crushed ice, to the way he deftly slices a slither of watermelon and places it onto the rim. I can't say I'm disappointed either when he reaches up above his head to pick fresh mint from a hanging planter and I'm treated to a flash of smooth, browned skin.

Eventually, he hands me the glass with a wink, before heading back outside.

I've no idea what's in this elegant, colourful concoction, but I take a cautious sip through the straw.

It tastes good. Deliciously sweet, yet sharp. Fruity, yet spicy. Heck, I could guzzle this down in one long gulp.

I force myself to sip slowly, glancing around as I do. My eyes connect with a row of mirrored tiles behind the bar, and when I catch sight of myself, my eyes widen in horror.

The straw slips from my lips.

For fuck's sake.

The solid purple stain lifting at the edges of my lips would give Joaquin Phoenix a run for his money. I look like the Joker in a party dress.

Mortified, I slide from the stool to head for the toilets, pausing momentarily – my drink will be left unattended – something I would never have done in the city. But then again, a stranger has served me something I don't even know the name of, which I've been merrily chucking back, so I think I'll take my chances.

When I return to my seat, nose, mouth and chin chafed, sore and pink from scrubbing with a rough paper towel, Niko is back behind the bar.

'Everything all right?' he asks, glancing up briefly as he works.

'Fine,' I say, from behind my hand.

'Is your drink all right? I can make you something else if you prefer?' He slides two open bottles of beer and a lemonade onto a tray and drums his hands on the bar to signal for a server.

'No,' I say, hurriedly. 'I like it, thank you.'

The server appears and takes the tray. I recognise her from yesterday.

'What is it anyway?' I ask, twiddling with my straw, avoiding looking directly at Niko. I suspect I looked better with a merlot moustache than with a scarlet face rash.

'I've no idea,' he says, a smile in his voice. 'I just made it up. There is rum, a little mint, watermelon, a splash of tequila, strawberry, of course, for the lady with the strawberry hair. A cross between a sour margherita and a sweet daquiri.' He grins, then adds, 'You could say I was hedging my bets.'

'Ah,' I say, nodding along, 'I see what you did there. Truthfully, I'm a fan of neither, but this,' I say holding my glass aloft, 'you might be onto something.'

Niko raises a beer bottle from the other side of the bar and chinks my glass.

'Yamas! Cheers!'

I toast him back and take another sip of my drink, darting a glance outside in case any single, intrepid males have arrived, looking for their date.

'Can I ask you something?' asks Niko, dragging my attention back to him.

'Mmm.'

'Are you allergic to anything in that drink? Because your face is really red and I'm getting kind of worried you'll go into anaphylactic shock and I must be honest, that scares me a bit.'

Maybe it's all the alcohol working its way into my bloodstream, or maybe it's the crazy day I've had, but the look of genuine concern on Niko's face right now pushes me into a fit of giggles.

'Ah Niko, bless you. No, I am not allergic to your wonderful concoction. In fact – I desire another.' I push the glass towards him.

'Shall I tell you why my face looks like a baboon's arse? It's because when I walked in here tonight, I was meant to be meeting someone and I was a teensy bit nervous, so I drank half a bottle of some truly shit wine from the shop at the bottom of the hill which, as you will no doubt have noticed, stained my mouth the colour of red cabbage. I used one of those scratchy blue hand towels in the loo to clean it off and I have, like, *really* sensitive skin, so I'll look like this until next Wednesday, but do you know what? Fuck it, because he didn't even show up.'

Niko, without even breaking eye contact, calls out something in rapid Greek.

Fabulous, he's probably having me ejected now for being drunk and dermatologically repulsive.

Instead, a young employee emerges from out back and steps behind the bar, seamlessly taking over the drinks order just presented to Niko.

Niko fixes me another drink, snaps the cap off another bottle of beer, then to my surprise, comes around to my side of the bar and lowers himself onto the stool beside me.

'I think I'll take a break. And so, this guy,' he begins cautiously, 'it was like a date?'

'No,' I say, far too quickly.

'U-huh.' Niko seems unconvinced.

I let out a long sigh, suddenly feeling an overwhelming desire to tell someone about it. I haven't even mentioned the messages to Jess or Vik. Maybe because it all felt rather silly. But more likely because it felt exciting; a secret between two strangers.

'It wasn't a date,' I explain, 'it was more like meeting a pen pal really. Someone I've been chatting to but haven't actually met. He probably took one look at me, decided I was a wino and made a quick exit.'

'Ahh, so you've been chatting to him on Tinder? You do know that counts as dating, right?'

'Not Tinder. Though that looks like my fate for the future. No, this has been a rather more primitive method of communication.'

Niko tilts his head slightly, conveying his confusion.

'Primitive? Er, old-fashioned. Basic.'

Niko nods knowingly. 'I pick up words like spag bol and holibobs in the UK, but sadly not enough of the useful ones.'

'I wouldn't say spag bol was useless, far from it. It's my favourite comfort food as it goes, and has far too many syllables anyway. To be honest, I usually just call it bol.'

Niko smiles. 'Then you must have tried pastitsada, yes?'

I shake my head.

'It's a Corfiot pasta dish handed down from the Venetians, so not a million miles away from your bolognese, but far, far superior.'

'Well, you would say that, wouldn't you? But OK, I'm sold. Do you have it on the menu?'

Niko holds his hands up in apology. 'Alas, no. My apologies, we only serve food at lunchtime.'

'Oh, well. I guess I'll have to get my calories from more of your delicious cocktails then. Do you think we should give it a name? How about *Jilted Wineface*? I think that's got legs.'

A curious smile plays on his lips. He really is extremely good-looking. Wisps of chocolatey dark hair are escaping his trendy man bun and there is at least a couple of days' stubble on a face otherwise olive-smooth.

'What is your name, strawberry hair?' he asks, watching me intently.

'Annabel. But everyone calls me Annie, not really a name you want as a kid, to be honest, especially when you're a *ginger*. It's a hard-knock life, but at least I had parents, so that was something.'

'I have absolutely no idea what you're talking about, Annie, but wait there,' he says, sliding from his stool. 'Don't go anywhere.'

'Oh, I'm not going anywhere,' I purr as he walks away. Gosh, perhaps I should slow down on the old *Jilted Winefaces*. I'm starting to feel distinctly tipsy.

Night has fallen fast since I've been sitting here, and flickering tealights now decorate the tables outside. It's got busier too, and customers are spilling from the terrace into the bar, the sounds of merriment increasing in volume, music growing louder, and I can feel the beat working its way through the chrome bar stool and into the sandals on my feet, compelling me to get up and dance.

As I'm contemplating doing just that, Niko reappears and places something extremely exciting on the bar in front of me.

'I thought you said you weren't doing food,' I gasp, in awe of the golden waffles stacked on top of one another, smothered with generous scoops of ice cream, strawberries, kiwi and blueberries. A generous sprinkling of crushed pistachio nuts completes the dish and has me salivating where I sit.

'Technically, we're not,' he says, passing me a spoon. 'But I am the owner so I can bend the rules.'

'This is amazing,' I gush, shovelling in a mouthful of the sugary dessert.

'Well, I figured if you intend to keep making me fix you cocktails, you'd better eat.'

'I thought you were on your break. Surely, *technically*, that means I can't make you fix me cocktails.'

He smiles, a hint of mischief reaching his dark eyes. 'It means, you can try.'

'Do you know what, Niko?' I say, between mouthfuls. 'I think this holiday might be looking up. Shame it's already halfway over.' I sigh at the thought of returning to Langtree and all that will entail.

He frowns. 'You have not enjoyed your time in Corfu?'

'Oh, don't get me wrong. I *love* Corfu, I love Kassiopi too, and I've had a great time. Mostly. *If* I put aside the fact that I've been forced to share my holiday apartment with a virtual stranger because the incompetent owners double booked it. And if I try not to mind that said stranger is the reason I've probably lost my job. Oh, and I got stood up tonight. But apart from that, it's been wonderful. I love the beach, the food, the people and the laid-back atmosphere. It's such a chilled out pace of life, nothing like home at all. I can't say I *particularly* loved my time aboard the Sunflower, which involved a loudspeaker in my ear for much of the cruise, some dubious refreshments and a man from Leeds with very tight shorts, but I'm sure that was just bad luck. What I'd really wanted was to go on the cruise to Kalami and see the Durrells' house, but that trip was fully booked.'

Niko shrugs. 'I'm sorry to hear that. But you know, maybe I can help with something.'

'What?' I ask.

What on earth could this handsome Greek possibly help with, other than taking my mind off things for one deliciously boozy night?

'I have a boat,' he says matter-of-factly. 'I could take you to Kalami, if you want? Are you free tomorrow?'

*Am* I free? I ask myself. Of course I am! I'm on holiday, answerable to nobody and with no place to be.

'You don't have to work?' I ask, remembering this gorgeous man is not, like me, on holiday.

'On Sundays, no. On Sundays I like to fish. Ever tried it?'

'I like to *eat* fish. Does that count?'

Niko laughs, then reaches forward and strokes a gentle

thumb across the side of my mouth, bringing away a waffle crumb.

'Annie, you are funny. I think we could have a nice time tomorrow. Will you come?'

The surprise of his touch on my skin heightens my senses and whilst the room isn't exactly spinning, I become hyper aware of the music, the background noise and the heat. Those cocktails must be superstrong. I need to get some air.

'Thank you, I'd love to come on a boat ride tomorrow.'

Niko smiles, his eyes lighting up his face. 'That's sorted then. Another?' He gestures at my empty glass.

'You know, I don't think I can manage another, the waffles have done me in. So, if that was a cunning ploy to make me buy more drinks, I'm sorry to say it failed.'

He shrugs. 'You were hungry and it pleased me to make you happy.'

'Trust me, I'm happy. What do I owe you for the drinks?'

He shakes his head in reply. 'I'll pick you up from the jetty. Is eight o' clock too early for you?'

I feign horror, then, because I'm emboldened with booze, I lean in and kiss him lightly on the cheek.

'See you tomorrow.'

He remains there on his bar stool, beer in hand as I walk away, and I can almost feel the heat from his eyes burning a hole in the back of my dress. I make sure to add a little sway to my hips for good measure. It feels good to be desired, on my terms.

As I walk from the bar out into the street, I cast a happy gaze over the many revellers, no longer sad my date didn't show, because tomorrow promises adventure! My eyes snag on two familiar figures lounging on a sofa beside the harbour wall and as their eyes meet mine, they give me a little wave. It's Marvin and Sue from the Sunflower. Then I spot who is sitting opposite, managing the smallest of nods in my direction, before turning back to their conversation. Liam.

# CHAPTER 14

## CORFU, DAY SIX

I fling an arm out to silence the obnoxious noise coming from my phone, desperate to return to my prone position upon a lounger, enjoying the cooling breeze of the Ionian Sea as the oiled, muscular man before me labours on deck. But it doesn't matter how hard I squeeze my eyelids, the spell is broken, and I've been booted from Goldie Hawn's sunbed in the *Overboard* movie, where in a weird turn of events, Kurt Russell had morphed into Liam Shaw.

For some reason, I'd set an alarm on my phone last night before falling into a vivid, alcohol-induced coma, yet hadn't managed to get undressed. This was, I suppose, preferable to the alternative, which could have seen me stumbling to the bathroom for a wee in my birthday suit. Although I do owe Liam a good flash to even up the odds. I dredge my memory banks to conjure the image of him stark-bollock-naked, as I have a few times since, but it's just not there.

Then the mist of sleep lifts, and I sit bolt upright, finally remembering why I set my alarm and possibly why I dreamt of opulent yachts and hot men. Clearly my brain misfired there, because I do indeed have a date with a boat and a Greek sex god, but it most certainly isn't Liam. My brain seems to have several maladies as it goes, the main one being a stonking headache.

I groan and lever myself to the edge of the bed, legs dropping heavily over the side, feet finding the cool stone floor tiles. I've got half an hour. Enough time for a quick shower and a coffee so strong I could eat it with a spoon, the only possible way forward.

Further along the corridor the lounge remains in darkness, so I creep to the bathroom, keen to avoid a small-talk situation. Besides, Liam barely acknowledged me last night, so I hardly think pleasantries over breakfast would be high on his agenda either. I'd bet a buttered croissant he was bitching about me to Marvin and Sue, bemoaning my diva attitude and how I've ruined his holiday. Well, he doesn't get to ruin mine, not anymore.

I'm not sure what the dress code is for a day on a boat with a gorgeous Greek, but given that simply breathing and remaining upright is presenting enough of a challenge right now, I opt for the comfort of my favourite denim shorts and a crocheted halter neck top over my bikini. I chuck a large floppy hat, my suncream and a towel into a bag and leave the apartment, stumbling back against the door frame when the sunlight stabs at my eyeballs like the blades from a circus knife thrower.

I inhale deeply, which simply fills my lungs with cloying, airless heat and lower my sunglasses from my head before setting off for the harbour.

The jetty is empty for a change. There are no tourists photographing the view, or waiting to board the Sunflower, no speedboats or dinghies bombing around from the waterside hire centre, overzealous day-trippers at the helm. The only sounds are from a delivery driver unloading produce from his vehicle to the taverna behind me, stacking cases of bottled water and crates of beer onto the street, whilst a harassed woman ferries it inside. A shop owner uses a pole to hook an awning into place, then wheels a stand of merchandise out onto the street; a resort leisurely preparing itself for another spectacularly beautiful day.

A movement catches my eye and I see a small, white boat moving off its mooring over by the mouth of the bay, before embarking on a trajectory towards me.

As the shape of Niko standing at the wheel comes into focus, I see that far from the yacht in my dreams, I am in fact destined to set sail in a glorified rowing boat, albeit with an engine. No matter, the skipper is as aesthetically pleasing as ever, which more than makes up for the vessel's shortcomings.

'I'm so glad you came, Annie,' he calls out, manoeuvring the boat into position against the sea wall and threading a rope through the mooring ring, before jumping ashore. 'I wasn't sure you would.'

He looks genuinely pleased to see me, a smile lighting up his fresh, un-hungover eyes as he offers me a hand.

'I'm here,' I reply, taking his hand and stepping down into the hull whilst he steadies it. 'But it might take a bit longer for my brain to catch up, as it seems to be lagging about two hours behind. I blame you entirely, of course.'

Niko unwinds the rope and hops into the boat, revving the motor and pulling away before I've barely had chance to settle onto the hard wooden bench.

'The sea air will do you good,' he says with authority, above the engine noise. 'Today is a good day to be on the water, as it will reach thirty-seven degrees later, the hottest day of the year so far for Corfu.'

I wish I was as confident. Unfortunately, I've realised, a little too late, my stomach isn't quite up to the sensation of being in a moving bathtub.

'What on earth is that smell?' I ask, catching a whiff of something utterly repugnant.

Niko points to a bucket by his feet. 'Maybe the bait? I don't notice it anymore. I'm used to it, I suppose.'

It's then I notice three long rods tucked against the side

wall of the boat and several plastic boxes containing colourful tackle and floats. He had been deadly serious when he said he was going fishing. I have tagged along on a sea-angling trip, in a fishing boat meant for one.

'How far is it to Kalami?' I ask, heart sinking deep into my sloshing stomach.

'Not far, a couple of hours. The northern straits are great for dorado, so we'll hang there for a bit before the shipping lanes get busy, pray for a good haul, then we'll head over to the bay. There's a great taverna in Kalami – we could moor up for lunch, or, if you preferred, we could buy some food and find somewhere a little more secluded for a picnic.'

'Dorado, huh?' I reply dumbly, ignoring the not-so-subtle reference to finding a secluded spot.

Niko mistakes my response for interest and begins to reel off a litany of facts regarding the best lines for trawling, the different uses of bait depending on whether you were fishing for dorado, mackerel or tuna, and the wide and varied types of lures: glittery, luminous, rubberised, plastic. All of it is the exact opposite of alluring. All of it, and especially the putrid stench of chum wafting from his bucket, is making me feel sick.

I force myself to look out to sea, gulping down great lungfuls of fresh, briny air. We've cleared the harbour now and are motoring east, the land mass of Albania straight ahead. The wide-open water is littered with other vessels: motorboats, dinghies, the occasional fishing boat, even cruise liners can be spotted on the horizon. The sea might be as calm as a Radox bath, but our boat is small and so every time a speedboat crosses our path, the wake created by its passing has the contents of my stomach inching closer towards my mouth.

Panic seizes me. I'm going to throw up, I know it. My head is throbbing, I'm sweating and rather stupidly I didn't even bring my water bottle.

I see a bay ahead, starboard side. A beautiful crescent of white, framed with lush green.

Land.

'Niko, what is that place, over there?' I ask, a note of urgency creeping into my voice.

He looks up, frowns.

'Avlaki, nothing much to see, just a hotel.'

'But it looks like a lovely beach?'

Niko shrugs. 'It's OK, not as beautiful as Kalami.'

To my dismay, he kills the engine and reaching for one of his plastic tubs, begins rifling through his multicoloured lures, as though they're a box of Celebrations.

'I'll just put a rod out, this is a good spot,' he says, before plunging a hand into the bucket of vile slop and sprinkling something that may once have been alive overboard.

It is enough to push me over the edge and I twist in the nick of time to retch violently over the side of the boat, adding to the nutritional content of Niko's fishy food attraction.

'Eugh,' I hear him squirm.

I hug the fibreglass shell, drawing down deep breaths. Then, in the absence of tissues or wet-wipes, I scoop a palmful of sea water to rinse my face. 'Niko,' I say firmly, without looking up. 'Please could you take me to that beach. I don't think fishing's quite for me.'

An hour's walk.

That's what Niko estimated, when I asked how far we were from Kassiopi. He hadn't taken much persuading to drop me at Avlaki Beach; whatever ideas he'd had for a pit stop somewhere deserted and romantic had now lost their sheen.

I've already been walking for over an hour, although shuffling would be a better description for the lethargic, uphill struggle in the blazing heat. What a waste of a morning. Why had I thought it would be a good idea, with a hangover, to get into a stranger's boat in the first place? I could have been abducted or drowned at sea. Anything might have happened, although every instinct tells me Niko is a decent guy, whose possibly romantic intentions were not compatible with vomit.

I could lick the armpits of a sumo wrestler, I'm so thirsty right now. I almost feel delirious and possibly have sunstroke. What I should have done is hole up in that big fancy hotel by the beach and call for a taxi, then I'd already be back at the pool, guzzling ice-cold lemonade and taking a refreshing dip before settling on a lounger to snooze away this dreadful experience.

I stop to rub at my aching feet and check Google maps again. Finally, I've reached the junction with the main road. It should be downhill from here into the village.

The blare of a car horn makes me jump so hard that my phone flies out of my hand, landing on the pavement with a thwack.

'WANKER!' I shout at the driver who has stopped and begun to reverse back towards me. Then I regret it a little, in case it's a scary, angry Greek with a baseball bat.

The driver is not a scary Greek. It's Liam.

'What the fuck do you think you're doing? You scared the shit out of me,' I cry, as he winds down the passenger window.

'Sorry, it was a reaction thing. I didn't expect to see you out here. Is it broken?'

Amazingly, as I pick up my phone, I see the screen is not broken, just a small scuff to the rubber case.

'No. It's fine,' I sigh, exhausted.

'Get in,' he says, 'I'll give you a lift.'

I weight up the pros and cons of accepting help from Liam, or dragging my desiccated carcass the remaining distance to the village.

'When did you get this?' I ask, climbing into the small hatchback and closing the door.

'Just picked it up, thought it would be fun to explore a little. Hang on, I need to figure out how to…' Liam pushes a couple of buttons and then a blast of cool air hits me in the face. 'Ah, there we go.'

I lean back my head, luxuriating in the air conditioning, then slip off my flip-flops and hoick my throbbing feet up to the air vents.

'Where were you heading? It's bloody hot for walking,' asks Liam.

'Yes. I worked that out for myself after the first three miles,' I reply sarcastically.

'Here,' says Liam and I open my eyes to see he is offering me a bottle of water from a bag behind my seat. 'It's cold.'

I grab it and tear the top off as though I'm an addict being offered crack. It is the single nicest beverage to have ever passed my lips, including the ridiculously expensive bottle of vintage Cristal I once put through on Garrett Delaney's expense account before telling him to stick his job up his arse.

'Thanks,' I manage, between hiccups.

Liam taps out a rhythm on his steering wheel.

'Listen, I'm taking a drive to the other side of the island, to a place called Paleokastritsa. It's about an hour away and beautiful by all accounts. You could come with me if you want? If you don't have any other plans today, that is?'

Strange that for the first time so far on this holiday, Liam has finally been in the right place at the right time. I honestly think I might have resorted to crawling back to the apartment on my hands and knees if he hadn't have come along. My skin is slowly cooling in the frigid temperature of the car, and I can feel my shrivelled brain beginning to hydrate.

It's a silly idea. We'd probably argue the whole time and I'd wish I'd returned to the apartment for a day by myself.

But the words that come out of my mouth are, 'Yeah, OK. Sure.'

# CHAPTER 15

I open one eye, aware of two things.

One: I must have nodded off, because my headache has gone, and I feel as though I've been asleep for a week.

Two: Liam is violating one of my favourite songs of all time. *If* you could call it singing, I'd say it's more like chanting in tongues.

'Hang on a minute. *What* did you just sing?'

Liam side-eyes me before turning the volume down.

'Feeling better, sleepyhead?'

'No, no, no, you don't get away with it that easily.' I turn the volume right back up. 'Please,' I say, gesturing at the radio as the chorus comes around again, 'do continue.'

'OK, you asked for it.'

Then, with a theatrical tap on the steering wheel, Liam proceeds to fully embrace his inner Spice and belt out the chorus with abandon.

'Swinger, Shaker, Moviemaker,

How hoodwinked you are,

Just a user, groovy, groovy,

Showman, how good you are...'

Let me tell you, I am almost rendered speechless by this abomination. Almost, but not quite.

'Liam, besides the fact that you must be either partially deaf or stupid, are you seriously telling me you've never sung this at karaoke before? Because if you had ever seen the proper lyrics, you'd know Geri, the Mels, Vicky and dear sweet Emma are definitely *not* singing about showmen and movie makers. Well, not literally, anyhow. Although I guess it does make a warped sort of sense.'

Liam shrugs. 'I like my version. It adds a whole new layer, don't you think? And no, I don't do karaoke. For self-explanatory reasons. But I do like to sing in the car or the shower. I just appreciate the public at large don't generally share my passion.'

'Nobody sounds good on karaoke. That's not the point of it.'

'You sound like you're speaking from experience. I must admit that surprises me a bit.'

'It surprises you I can have fun? Or that I don't mind making a prick of myself? Funny, because I thought I'd been doing that ever since we first met.'

Liam grimaces. 'And here was I thinking it was me with the prick issue.'

'Oh, you mean that first night when I caught you coming out of the bathroom, yeah – I'd say there are some issues there.' I grin, to let him know I'm joking, 'or perhaps I shouldn't have brought *that* up. Pun absolutely intended. No, I meant before. At the Franklyn's conference last year, I acted like a dick.'

Liam's mouth opens and closes, as he obviously weighs up whether to acknowledge my ridiculing of his penis, or whether to ignore it completely.

He opts for the latter.

'You had every right to question the process. Nothing wrong with a little due diligence.'

'Liam, come on. This is a one-time offer. An admission that I might have been a sore loser. You know what? We work so hard to keep our little shop busy and we never get any acknowledgement from the management. We might not shift hundreds of copies each day, but our customers are loyal, and they value having us. Or at least they did.'

'What do you mean?' He shoots me a look.

'I'd have thought that was obvious. There's no way Langtree will stay open now, surely you must realise that.'

Liam is quiet for so long I turn my attention to the scrubby grass flashing past the window, and the occasional half-built structure awaiting completion dotting the island's landscape.

It's the first time I've mentioned Franklyn's commitment to closing down one of our shops, and I've just yanked an elephant-sized awkwardness into this tiny Fiat 500.

'I don't know what will happen, Annabel,' he says eventually. 'But I'm sorry your work hasn't been appreciated, you're clearly passionate about it.'

'Am I? How do you know that?' I ask, in surprise.

Liam grins. 'Might have something to do with the fact your head is always stuck in a book. That and the way you chew the arse off anyone who stands in your way.'

I go to protest, but Liam is smiling. Speaking from his own experience, he might have a point.

We fall silent at the blue sign announcing our arrival into Paleokastritsa, glimpsing swathes of turquoise ocean between cypress trees and palms as we wind our way down into the village.

Even though we have just come from the picturesque resort of Kassiopi, the sheer beauty of this place takes my breath away. Three perfect horseshoe bays, set together like the leaves of a clover, are framed with green tree-topped hills.

'There's a working monastery at the top of that hill apparently,' says Liam, 'if you fancy taking a look?'

I shut the car door and follow Liam's line of sight.

'If I'm climbing that hill, I'm going to need to eat something seriously calorific. The Ionian Sea is the current custodian of the only thing I've eaten in twenty-four hours.'

Liam looks blank, so I elaborate. 'Boat trip, slightly more akin to The Owl and the Pussycat's seafaring vessel than the trusty Sunflower.'

I omit Niko and his bucket of chum from the picture.

'Good call, I'm starving,' replies Liam. 'Let's go eat.'

Twenty minutes later, we are sitting in quite possibly the most stunning setting for a bowl of fries in existence. The water's edge is so close I could almost stretch out a toe and dip into it.

'Are you sure that's all you wanted?' asks Liam, motioning at my chips, as a feta salad is placed down between us, and a large platter loaded with prawns and mussels in front of him.

'Cheese, chips and full-fat coke? Believe me, I am here for this universally acknowledged hangover cure.'

Liam begins peeling a tiger prawn, taking his time. 'Quite the night, was it? I saw you were chatting with some guy in the bar.'

I might be feeling a tonne better, but I'm not sure my stomach is up to the notion of prawn heads quite yet. I look down at my own plate and spear a chip.

'Niko? He's the owner, he was just being friendly. But tell me about your evening. How come you wound up with Marvin and Sue again? Did you guys like swap numbers or something?'

Liam laughs. 'I'm not a saint, Annabel. I was taking a walk down to the beach when they collared me, insisted I joined them for a drink. I wasn't really in the mood for company, but I guess it did me good.'

I don't know why, but this unnerves me a little. Liam usually seems so even, so cordial – had I contributed to his bad mood with all my standoffish behaviour? I mean, I practically accused the guy of stalking me yesterday.

I break off a piece of the feta and stab at a tomato.

'You know, everyone calls me Annie. Nobody calls me Annabel, apart from my dad and my dental hygienist.'

'I know,' replies Liam. 'But you can never assume.'

This makes me smile with approval. One of the worst periods of my life was compounded when Garrett Delaney began calling me 'Babybel'. Perhaps I've misjudged Liam after all.

If I began today feeling as though the Foo Fighters were

thrashing out *All My Life* against my temporal lobe, this afternoon it's more like having Enya lilting softly at my shoulder. That is the analogy my weird brain comes up with as I float peacefully on my back in the soothing waters at Agios Spiridon Beach.

Turns out the Monastery of the Holy Theotokos was indeed an experience worthy of shedding several pints of sweat for; the view from the pinnacle of the hill was jaw-dropping. A three-hundred-and-sixty-degree panorama of the most devastatingly beautiful scenery I think I've ever seen was worth any climb.

The grounds of the eighteenth-century building were equally stunning, with their white stone archways and terracotta pots crowding every surface, spilling fragrant herbs and flowers in all the vibrant colours of nature's palette. A shop in the lower grounds sold local produce: honey, kumquat, wine and limoncello. When I entered the Holy Virgin Mary church, I needed to borrow a shawl and skirt to cover my skin and as I wandered the cool, quiet place of worship, I imagined all those who had walked there before me.

I reflect on the almost spiritual experience as I bob in the water. Liam has popped back to the car for something, but for once, I'm feeling grateful for his company on this holiday. If he hadn't been there, he'd never have rescued me from that gruelling walk this morning, and I would never have discovered this place. It also turns out, after spending a few hours in his company, I don't hate him at all. He's nice.

'Penny for them,' comes a distant, echoey voice at my side and I startle, surprised to see an orange plastic facemask and snorkel.

Liam tugs the snorkel from his mouth. 'Sorry, didn't mean to make you jump. Ever tried this before?'

I shake my head. 'Never been entirely comfortable with foreign objects in my mouth.'

I don't miss the twinkle in Liam's eye, even though it is hidden behind the thick plastic goggles.

'You should try it. You might even like it. There's a whole other world down there.'

I circle my arms beneath the water, treading softly. It's amazing how much more comfortable I feel *in* the water, than in a boat atop it.

'OK then. Show me what to do.'

Liam rinses out the snorkel and tugs the mask from his head. 'We'll need to adjust this to fit your head,' he says, pointing at the rubber strap, 'slip this on and I'll tighten it for you.'

I yank the mask over my head, grimacing as it catches and pulls my hair. Then I feel Liam's fingertips at the back of my head, gently pulling my ponytail through and despite the coolness of the water against my skin, a wave of warmth trickles through me.

'That's it, you're ready,' he says. 'Now float on your tummy and breathe normally. If you get any water in the snorkel, pop your head up and blow it out.'

I dip my head under and let my body float, the vivid colours of the subterranean world taking me by surprise. I'm surrounded by orange, blue, red and white striped fish, darting this way and that, like a scene from *Finding Nemo*.

Almost as interesting, is the magnified lower half of Liam as he swims alongside me. I'm mesmerised by the muscles flexing in his firm thighs below his billowing shorts.

Once satisfied I'm ok with a thumbs-up, he powers away in the water and I'm left alone, just me and this fascinating underworld. It occurs to me this is something else I'd have been missing out on, had Liam not come along. Would I ever have thought to go and buy myself a snorkel and mask, to look below the surface instead of believing what I could see on top was everything there was to see? I've a feeling I know the answer to that. I've been too caught up in writing stupid messages in books and stubbornly resenting Liam, to embrace being here properly.

A hand to my arm brings my head above water.

'You all right there?' asks Liam, looking amused. 'Had to check you hadn't fallen asleep.'

I spit the snorkel out and stretch my aching lips. I've no idea how long I've been under. It could have been ten minutes; it could have been an hour.

'I love it,' I say, meaning it. 'Can't believe I've never done this before.'

'You should try it back in Kassiopi. The pebbles make the water crystal clear.'

'I noticed that,' I say, remembering my first day at the beach and all the tiny fish I could see weaving between my legs. 'Have you been out much?'

'Every day. It's been ages since I've had the chance, but there was a time when I spent a lot of time in the water. It's made me realise how much I miss it.'

I'm acutely aware of how little I know about Liam.

'Whereabouts in the States did you grow up? You said you lived there until you were eighteen?'

'Tampa.'

'Florida?'

'U-huh.'

'Wow, that must have been cool.'

'Yeah, it was. We used to take family holidays in the Keys. So, I kinda grew up in the water, it's all part of the lifestyle when you live somewhere like that. I'm a proper water baby at heart.'

'How come you ended up in Essex then, of all places? It's hardly known for its tropical waters. You're more likely to encounter thirteen varieties of turd in one sitting than anything remotely related to marine life.'

Liam laughs. 'I've been in Essex for just over two years. Before that, it was London and Scotland before that. But you know, Essex has its attractions. I've been known to enjoy pie, mash and liquor on a bench on Walton Pier. What more could a guy want?'

'Jesus, Shaw, you need to get out more. Never done

karaoke and your idea of an English takeaway is soggy pastry and eel juice? I think I might need to take you under my wing when we get home.'

'That sounds – scary?' He grimaces. 'Talking of getting home, shall we get going? I only hired the car for the day.'

'Sure, let's go, before I turn into a raisin.'

I swim for shore and feel surprisingly self-conscious as I make my way out of the shallow water, treading carefully across sand and shingle and resisting the urge to pluck my bikini bottoms out from between my buttocks until Liam moves in front of me.

'I had a nice time today,' says Liam, drying himself with a towel. 'Thanks for coming along.'

I tug on my shorts but leave my top half to air dry in the late afternoon sun.

'I had fun too,' I say, meaning it.

As I trail along beside Liam, making our way lazily to the car, I can't help feeling a little mad at myself for wasting so much of this holiday resenting him.

'Can I ask you something?' I say, as we reach the car.

Liam pauses with his hand on the driver's door handle, waiting for me to continue.

'The prize – this holiday, it was for two. How come you never brought anyone along? I mean, I don't know if you have a wife, or girlfriend or—'

'There's no one,' he cuts in.

'A mate?'

After a beat of hesitancy, Liam shrugs. 'I fancied coming alone.'

Then I say something I should have said a while back.

'I'm sorry.'

Liam looks back at me. 'What for?'

'I've been a complete idiot about this whole situation. It wasn't your fault the apartment got double booked. I guess I didn't really stop to think about it from your side. It can't have been fun for you either, having your holiday hijacked.'

'It's had its moments,' he says, with a grin. 'But thank you, I appreciate that and for what it's worth, I'm sorry you got stuck with me too.'

Liam taps the roof of the car, then shakes his head, a smile spreading on his face.

'Hey, you know what? The car hire place doesn't close until late. Do you fancy getting dinner here? Snorkelling is hungry work.'

I study him, noting how his soft waves of blonde hair have gone all fluffy after getting wet, and the way the setting sun is casting a glow across his face and picking out flecks of gold in his green eyes.

'Sure,' I say, 'but do you know what I'd really like?'

'Go on.'

'I'd like to stay on the beach and watch the sunset, because somehow I manage to keep missing it back in Kassiopi.'

'Annie, that's a *great* idea. There's a couple of shops in the village, let's go get ourselves a sunset picnic.'

The small grocery shop that sells everything from fresh fruit to loo roll is also attached to a delicatessen, which even this late in the day is still serving delicious looking sandwiches, cakes, pastries and sweets.

Between us we amass a veritable feast of lamb and spinach pie, olives, ripe nectarines, Lays oregano crisps, sweet cherry tomatoes, baklava and various other goodies I couldn't resist. Then we find a spot on the beach and lay down our towels on the now deserted beach, slightly apart from the waterside restaurant where we'd dined at lunchtime earlier today.

'I'm going to miss this,' I say, gazing up at the burning orange globe filling our view. 'As much as I can't imagine living anywhere but Langtree, it's at times like this you're reminded there's a whole beautiful world out there and I've hardly seen any of it.'

Liam murmurs in agreement and twists the caps from two bottles of beer, then offers one to me.

'Not sure my stomach's ready for more alcohol,' I wince, 'but I'll give it a go.'

I take a tentative sip, and don't recoil.

'Hair of the dog. Always works,' supplies Liam, with a satisfied grin. 'Besides, I'm driving, so make the most of it.'

'Don't you miss living in the States?' I ask him, looking up in time to catch a flash of something pass across his face, before he quickly rallies. 'I mean, why England, why Essex?'

'My father's American, but my mother's Scottish. They divorced when I was a teenager, and Mom wanted to move back home, so we did. Mom's still there, in Scotland.'

'That will explain the accent then.'

'Yup, part American, part Scottish, with a little bit of the East End thrown in for good measure.' He adds, dramatically, 'Does it make me sound interesting?'

'It makes you sound like the love child of John Barrowman and Katherine Hepburn, if that's what you mean?'

Liam clutches at his chest in mock offence.

'Well, you must be doing something right. The Franklyn's crowd adore you. Doesn't it hurt? Carrying the weight of all that praise, I'm surprised you're not a crippled hunchback, if I'm being honest.'

In response to my jibe, a scattering of crips hits my face and lands in my lap.

'Hey! Don't waste them.' I rescue one and crunch down on it.

'Yeah, you're right,' he says, reaching across and plucking one from my bare thigh, 'they're frigging great chips.'

'Crisps,' I helpfully correct. 'I had chips for lunch. *These* are crisps.'

Liam smiles, shaking his head. 'You know, I wish we'd done this sooner.'

'What? Have a food fight on the beach? You should have told me. I am here for this, but you should know, I play dirty, and it won't be dried goods next.'

'Oh, I can believe it. But, no, I mean *this*, getting along. Maybe we could have made the best of a bad situation.'

He takes a swig of his beer and I watch his Adam's apple bob in his throat, a day's worth of golden stubble glinting in the sunlight.

'Yeah, well that was my fault, and I'm sorry for it now. I had this idea in my head of how my holiday would be and it just felt like another way in which life was serving me up a plate stacked high with shit sandwiches.'

He looks at me, kindness reflected back in gold-flecked eyes. 'I'm guessing the reason you chose to holiday alone too means there is no one back home?'

I pop an olive in my mouth. 'Nope. That ship sailed away into the arms of Holly-Mae six months ago, shortly to be followed by my home which, although technically is all his on paper, was added to Rightmove days before I got here.'

Liam nods in understanding.

'That's tough.'

I sigh. 'If I'm being brutally honest, Liam, we weren't great together. He worked in agricultural insurance of all things and was also a little bit boring, which at that point in my life was exactly what I thought I needed.'

Even though I can sense Liam watching me, I don't look at him, instead fixing my gaze on the tangerine horizon before us.

'Turns out even the safe option was the wrong choice. All those business trips to meet clients were actually overnight stays at the country pile owned by Holly-Mae's dad, who was, admittedly, one of Travis's clients. Funny, I never would have imagined tractor insurance to come with compulsory cock.'

Liam doesn't say anything. But after a few minutes, I feel his arm snake around my shoulders, where it settles just long enough for me to both notice and enjoy the sensation of his warm skin upon mine, before he gives me a light squeeze and drops it, resting back on his elbows.

'Sounds like he did you a favour, Annie. Life is far, far too short to spend it simply existing. I haven't known you long, but I can tell you're a strong woman. You have fire in your belly, opinions, often terrible ones – believe me, I've seen your book choices – but you know what you want. You just have to be brave enough to grab it.'

'Oi!' I cry, smacking him on the leg. 'How dare you diss my book choices. I'll have you know I read very widely. Besides, as booksellers, shouldn't we know the products we're selling?'

'True,' he agrees. 'But I'm afraid to admit I usually only read the books I want to read. And they're rarely those on Franklyn's agenda.'

'Now isn't that an irony,' I sigh, though any resentment I felt towards Liam has long since gone. 'And I'm the hopeless bibliophile who has literally surrounded herself with books all her life. The Langtree bookshop has existed, in some guise or other, since before I was even born and now it will likely become a charity shop, or a bookies – isn't that the fate of all empty high-street premises? Well, that's the corporate machine for you. A group of white, middle-aged men with beach houses and Botox-pumped wives will keep on getting richer, whilst a small town like Langtree loses not only its library owing to local council cutbacks, but now it's only physical bookshop.'

Liam shifts beside me and sits up, his strong profile now a defined silhouette against a purple sky.

'Well, the sun's gone down. Are you OK to head back yet?' he asks, and I kick myself for killing the mood.

'Yeah, sure.'

I gather up the empty packages and wrappers, stuffing them into a plastic bag and look up to see Liam holding out a hand. I take it and he clamps his other hand on top of mine in a wrist wrap and pulls me to standing, warm palms lingering a beat too long, before he takes the rubbish bag from me and heads for a nearby bin.

It's a tiny gesture, little more than good manners, but for some reason my heart is racing.

# CHAPTER 16

We pull out of the car park and begin to make our way back to Kassiopi, an easy silence settling over us as we listen to the incoherent ranting of a local radio host, followed by the familiar strains of Fleetwood Mac.

Feeling an urge for something sweet, I reach down into the small bag of goodies I purchased from the delicatessen in the village earlier.

'Bloody hell. This is amazing, you've got to try some.' I offer the paper package containing a chunk of traditional Greek orange pie, which bears no resemblance to pie and is more like a dense, syrup-soaked sponge oozing orange loveliness.

Liam glances at it. 'Can you break a bit off?'

I attempt to do this, but in passing it across to his waiting hand, it slides from my fingers and lands in a sticky dollop on his lap.

'Oops.'

Liam reaches down to retrieve what he can in the darkness of the car, stuffs it into his mouth and licks his fingers.

'You joked before,' he says, then points at himself 'but at least I have the resources to wash my clothes. Just as well, seeing as I keep on losing them; somehow, I managed to lose another shirt in Corfu town yesterday, left it on the harbour wall when I took a dip after dinner, came back and it was gone. I had to buy an 'I love Greece' t-shirt to ride the bus home.'

I laugh but am brutally aware of Stevie Nicks in the background, daring me to continue with my sweet little lies. Something has changed in the last day or two and I no longer want to lie to Liam. Besides, there's every chance we'll arrive back at the apartment together to discover Maria has employed some new, innovative method of luggage distribution and I'll have to fess up anyway.

'Liam,' I begin.

'Don't worry. I'm not going to be interrogating anyone else. Even though I'm *positive* that guy on the boat was wearing my shirt.'

'Er, Liam, I have to tell you something.'

'U-huh?' Liam flashes a quizzical look in my direction, and my nerve almost abandons me.

I screw the greasy cake wrapper into a tight ball, not wanting to look at him.

'It was me.'

'What? What was you?'

'It's entirely possible that guy *was* wearing your lucky shirt, although for the life of me I don't know why, because I put it into a basket in the church, to hide the evidence.'

I chance a glance at Liam and see a pulse in his jaw.

'I panicked, I'm sorry. It was a stupid thing to do.' Liam is staring silently ahead, his fingers gripping the wheel.

I feel an overwhelming need to fill the silence, already regretting my confession.

'The maid, Maria, that first day. I left her alone in the apartment and when I got back, she had unpacked all my stuff into your room. I mean she obviously thought we were a couple. She'd even put my pyjamas on the pillow next to yours.' I give a nervous, high-pitched laugh. 'I thought you'd come back and think I was being difficult, making a point or something, so I scooped everything up quickly and stuffed it back in my case. It wasn't until the next morning I found your shirt in amongst my stuff, I must have grabbed it by mistake, but by then you'd been ranting like a mad man, and I hadn't owned up, so…' I trail off.

Liam finishes my sentence for me. 'So you decided rather than swallowing your pride, you would simply get rid of it.'

His tone has become cool and clipped. It's a very different side to the man who has been gentle, kind and funny today.

'Look, I'm truly sorry. I didn't think. But, you know, it *is* only a piece of clothing. Do you think you might be overreacting? I'll buy you another one. We'll go out to the shops tomorrow and find the most garish, flamboyant shirt to be had on the island. What do you say?'

Liam lets out a long breath through his nose, as though he's trying to calm himself.

Unsettled, I turn my gaze out of the window, wanting this journey to be over.

Eventually, he speaks, in a voice so quiet I have to strain to hear him.

'The shirt belonged to my little brother.'

An iciness trickles into my gut.

'Belonged?' I ask, already dreading his reply.

'Yeah. Belonged. He died four years ago. So, you know, not just a piece of clothing.'

'Fuck.'

The word leaves me in a whisper, and I close my eyes in the dark.

'Liam, I…'

'Please, Annie, do you mind if we don't talk about this.'

There is a flat weariness in his voice that makes my heart sink in regret.

'I'm so, so sorry.'

He runs a hand through his hair, doesn't look at me, just focuses steadfastly on the road ahead, then after an agonising stretch of silence, says softly, 'I need to not talk about this right now. Please.'

He turns the radio up and we drive the rest of the way back without speaking another word.

By the time we are coasting down the steep hill that leads into Kassiopi, I'm experiencing the unpleasantly mixed emotions of regret and shame. I understand Liam is upset and doesn't want to talk, but that does not align with my very selfish desire to try and make amends.

My phone buzzes in my bag in the footwell and I reach down for it.

There is a message from Jess.

*Gone full Shirley Valentine yet? Shagged the waiter? Remember he'll do it with Kelly from Cardiff next week, so I hope you used a johnny.*

I haven't ever seen the Shirley Valentine film but can imagine I am treading in her footsteps. Although I highly doubt the movie's romantic action played out over a fishing rod and a bucket of chum.

*No worries on that count*, I type. Then, because I'm feeling tired and rather shitty, I add, *Miss you guys.*

There is a swift, decisive response, as my friend interprets my shorthand.

*Wanna Facetime?*

Do I?

I check the time, still only eight o' clock back in Blighty. Perhaps that's exactly what I need, the kind of no-nonsense shake up that can only be delivered from my friend.

*Give me fifteen,* I reply, realising a walk and a rant before bed is exactly what I need. I'll leave Liam at the car hire place and walk down to the beach.

'Right,' says Liam, pulling up in almost exactly the same spot as my taxi driver had the night I arrived in Corfu. 'I'll drop you here so you can head back, as it's a bit of a walk from the car hire place, so…'

'Oh, OK,' I say, realising this is a polite cue for me to leave his company as soon as possible. Well at least I can chat to Jess in privacy on the balcony, which is the only place I've found with a signal. 'Thanks. See you later then, I guess.'

He nods and I step from the car awkwardly, like we've just parted after a disastrous date.

Back at the apartment, I turn on the air con to cool the stifling space down, then head onto the balcony and close the door behind me before dialling Jess's number.

I'm doubly delighted when it's not only Jess's face that appears on screen, but Vik's too and I see they're in the pub. Ash appears briefly in the background, crouching between them to wave hello and goodbye before shrugging on his coat and leaving.

'On location in Oxford tomorrow,' explains Vik. 'Early start.'

Jess rolls her eyes theatrically and picks up her drink, which looks suspiciously like an espresso martini. Blimey, looks like I've missed a good night.

'Why are you on here?' asks Jess, emphasising each word, 'you should be skinny dipping, then having scratchy beach sex.'

'Jess is a little bit pissed,' supplies Vik, helpfully.

'So I see. And to answer your question, I'm not having scratchy beach sex, partly because the beaches here are made of pebbles, not sand, and I've never really found the idea of a stoning even mildly erotic. And partly because I seem to have spent most of my holiday repelling all the hot guys.'

The words leave my mouth before I've even thought it through, and although an unconscious slip, it is still, I feel, an indisputable fact. Liam is hot. And actually, pretty decent – not at all the self-absorbed salesman I'd had him pegged as.

But Jess doesn't appear to notice my slip-up, because she's tugging on Vik's sleeve like a five-year-old demanding attention, stage-whispering something about sharing their gossip.

'What's that?' I ask, keen to distract my friends from my love life, or lack of it.

Vik takes on the appearance of a ventriloquist, smiling brightly at me whilst audibly muttering to Jess to shut up. The microphones on modern iPhones are insane. Now might not be the time to tell Vik I can hear him when he has a sneaky wee, even though he always sits down. I know that because he told me, not because it's ever been a spectator activity.

I sigh.

'Look. If it's about the bookshop, tell me something I don't know. It's fine. There are other jobs, other bookshops. There are even other towns, believe it or not.'

This provokes a dual, wide-eyed gasp.

'What? I'm quite capable of starting again somewhere new, you know. I've done it before.'

Jess is shaking her head vehemently and looks about to go off on a tangent, so I head her off at the pass, quickly.

'I don't mean the other side of the world, just, you know, Norwich, or something. I've always quite fancied Norwich. But anyway, what was the gossip you were going to tell me? Come on, spit it out!'

'Norwich is three hours away,' says Jess, becoming argumentative, 'it is totally the other side of the world. I'll tell you the gossip –*if* you promise not to move to Norwich.'

'Ok, Jess. I promise not to move to Norwich,' I say, but cross my fingers behind my back, because it is exactly the sort of place I could picture myself opening a bookshop one day, if I could ever wrench myself away from my friends and family, which is the part I can't picture at all. 'Now. Spill.'

'Well,' says Jess dramatically, before inching closer to the phone screen, which I presume is propped against a pint glass or something because it's at a really unflattering angle. 'Whilst Vik and me were in Franklyn's on Saturday, we got chatting to the assistant manager, nice girl, bit ethereal for my liking though, you know the sort – drag out all their vowels in a high-pitched whine in an effort to sound sincere but instead appear intellectually challenged.'

'It's fashionable these days,' chips in Vik. 'All the girls at school sound like that.'

'Excuse me?' I interject. 'Could we cut to the chase here?

Because I'm pretty sure the point of your story is not to comment on the affected accents of Generation Z.'

Jess blinks, visibly recentring her thought process – it's quite amusing to watch. Perhaps I should record it to play back to her when I'm bored one evening.

'So anyway,' she says, back in the game. 'Cherry, no, what was her name? I'm sure it was something fruity.'

Cue another side conversation with Vik.

'Damson? Peaches?' suggests Vik.

What the heck does a school register look like these days?

'Clementine!' roars Jess, slapping the table and making the glasses rattle. 'Maybe in her case she really did have a silver-plated serving spoon up her waify little arse. But I digress.'

'I hadn't noticed,' I smile, amused.

'Turns out dear Clemmie, has something of a crush on your mate. All I said was I'd heard on the grapevine the Franklyn's chain was in trouble and how sad I'd be to lose my favourite bookshop…'

Vik interrupts. 'She was digging for info on the branch closure.'

'Er, yeah, I got that. And?'

'And she opened up like a daffodil in spring. Told us it wasn't yet common knowledge, but a wealthy mogul was rescuing the chain, and wasn't it the loveliest thing that her manager, who just so happens to be the son of said business mogul, is *so* likeable, *so* down to earth and so thoroughly *normal*, not flashy at all, even though his father is a bona fide billionaire? Honestly, she was so busy gushing about our regular Playboy friend I don't even think she noticed I was dressed as Cyndi Lauper.'

I blink furiously, sifting through the information I've just been given to get to the nub of the matter. Liam Shaw. Son of a billionaire business mogul!

'I can't believe it,' I say, puzzled. 'Why on earth would Liam be working for a shitty high-street shop if that was the case?'

'Uh, *dur!*' says Jess, wide-eyed as though I'm a complete moron. 'Why do you think?'

Vik, bless his heart, attempts diplomacy, 'It does look rather as though Liam's job might have been strategic, don't you think? Gather information on the shop floor, feed it to his dad. Be ready to pounce? I don't know,' he shrugs, 'doesn't make much sense otherwise.'

'And just who is his dad?' I ask, feeling a little dumbfounded.

'None other than Crispin Kaufman-Shaw, CEO of Phoenix PLC, custodian of his own private jet, a skyscraper in Tampa, countless off-shore residences and a sprawling fuck-off mansion in—'

'Florida Keys?' I finish the sentence for her.

'Yeah!' she says, looking genuinely impressed. 'Have you heard of him then? I had to google him. Owns a string of low-end high street businesses in the US and across Europe.'

'No, I haven't. But I get the picture.'

'I think the best way forward,' she says, going deadly serious, 'would be to bone him asap. You've only got two nights left, so make them count. Worst-case scenario, it's a holiday shag, best case – as your BFF I get to hang out with you in Miami and help choose your new cheekbones from a surgeon's glossy catalogue. It's a win-win.'

'Hang on, what's all this BFF business?' asks Vik looking most put out. 'She can't choose just one BFF – you know that, right?'

'Woah. *Guys,*' I say firmly, palms extended in protest. 'First up. No one's going to be boning anyone, not unless taken in a literal context because I'm quite minded to extract that sly, entitled fuckwit's spine, one vertebra at a time, and reinsert it up through his anus. How *dare* they manipulate the system like that! This isn't a fucking Monopoly board, it's people's livelihoods.'

'Um,' says Vik, looking chastened. 'That's perhaps going a little far, don't you think, Annie?'

Jess looks on, mildly amused, her eyes darting frantically about.

'Oh, come on! This is an outrageous abuse of power and yet another example of the kind of masculine toxicity that ensures middle-aged, white dudes get to keep on controlling every goddamn last one of us. And to think I'd started to think he was actually a decent guy – what a lowlife, lying piece of scum. Let me tell you, I wouldn't bone Liam Shaw if he was the last man on earth, no matter how good-looking he is.'

Vik sucks in a breath, and it's only then I feel the gentle whisper of crisp, air-conditioned air cooling the back of my neck. Air drifting out through the open balcony doors.

I turn my head slowly, my friends uncharacteristically silent as they strain to hear every last intake of breath.

Liam is standing there with a bottle of ouzo and two shot glasses he has procured from somewhere and he is staring past my shoulder at my phone screen.

Without meeting my eye, he says, 'Thought I'd grab a bottle of the good stuff and try to make up for being a bit of a jerk earlier, explain myself and clear the air. I see that will probably no longer be necessary.'

He shifts his attention to me but doesn't quite look me in the eye.

'For what it's worth, I didn't know anything about my father's involvement. I haven't spoken to him for six years. But it's good to know I'm so completely repulsive to you, it's prevented me from making a potential tit of myself, so thank you for that. Oh, and I must say thanks also to your friends for keeping me on my toes. If it hadn't been for all the extra hours on the shopfloor putting my stock back where it belonged, I doubt I'd have such a good relationship with my staff. Clem's gay by the way, so er, wrong tree there.'

And with that, he turns around, walks back through the lounge, plonking the bottle and glasses down as he goes, then I hear the apartment door click shut.

# CHAPTER 17

## CORFU, DAY SEVEN

After ending the FaceTime call to my somewhat bemused friends and sinking two medicinal shots of ouzo, I had retired to my bedroom to google Crispin Kaufman-Shaw. Wikipedia provided me with the bare essentials:

*Crispin Charles Kaufman-Shaw (born 12th May 1951) is an American retail business magnate and CEO of Phoenix PLC. He entered the stationery industry in 2005 with the acquisition of ailing US store chain WriteUp and has continued to add to a bulging portfolio.*

### Personal Life
*Eldest son of James Kaufman, a businessman from Boston and Eleanor Mary Shaw, Crispin Kaufman-Shaw was born in 1951. He was educated at Harvard, and married Marianne McKay, a Scottish-born singer in 1990. The couple had a son in 1991 but divorced in 2007, citing irrevocable differences. Kaufman-Shaw remarried in 2009 to Portuguese heiress Sienna Mendes, with whom he has three children.*

*Kaufman-Shaw is protective of his private life, and known*

*for having an extensive security detail. He has properties
all over the world.*

It had gone on to list various boring details on Kaufman-
Shaw's sporting associations, the softball team he supported,
his part ownership of a low-league British football club and
personal achievements in the even duller field of golf. I had
skipped over much of the entry, because the only information
I was interested in was whether anything Liam had said was
true.

But apart from citing his divorce to his first wife, I could
find nothing linking Liam by name. I guess money really can
buy discretion.

I'd heard Liam come back a little after one o' clock,
although he barely made a sound. Hats off to him. If it had
been me, I'd have stomped, crashed, smashed and ranted
my way around the apartment in anger. Even now, sitting in
bed, wondering if I dare get up yet, I feel my cheeks burn at
remembering some of the things I said about him.

Part of me had wanted to go to him last night. To demand
we talk this through once and for all. I was still annoyed, of
course I was. Liam had deliberately omitted to tell me who he
was, even though we'd spent the day together and had even
talked about our hometowns. And I refuse to believe he knew
nothing about his father's potential acquisition of Franklyn's.
If bloody Clementine knew about it, then I'm damned sure
he did.

But a bigger part of me, the part cowering here and
squirming in discomfort because I haven't heard Liam leave
yet this morning, is totally ashamed of myself.

I had ranted and scorned and belittled, used personal
slurs and even resorted to evaluating his 'bone-worthiness',
as though I belonged to the same seedy camp as prejudiced,
sexist Garrett Delaney.

Delaney *was* those things. A confident, privileged white
man, secure in a position of power afforded by class, race and

education. But he had also been an abuser of that power. A serial lothario, using his looks and position at the newspaper to dangle promotions over vulnerable female colleagues.

It's funny how good looks and a bucketload of charm can so thoroughly override the warning signs. How many times had it happened, before it had become my turn? Maybe, for some, it had been a mutual arrangement. Maybe some women had believed they were the ones in control. I find it hard to believe. I find it even harder to accept my own colleagues were able to stand by and watch as it happened over and over again, but there you are. All's fair in love and career journalism.

The thing was, despite my outrage last night, I didn't really feel Liam was capable of the things I had accused him of. And long before I discovered he was the son of a billionaire, I'd unfairly cast him in the role of a smooth-talking salesman likely to flatter and flirt if it meant he'd make another few quid. *I* was the one with the problem.

Eventually, the sheer heat of the morning forces me from bed. The one drawback from having the bedroom has undoubtedly been the lack of ability to control the air conditioning unit which, unfathomably, is situated in the lounge. I presume when Clare and Richard used the apartment, they did not close the bedroom door and slow roast themselves.

A little nervous, I enter the lounge.

Liam's bed has been put away, his sheets neatly folded and his rucksack sits against the wall, packed and zipped up. Sunlight pours in from the balcony, where Liam sits with a notebook and pen, coffee cup in hand.

'Morning,' I say, sounding sheepish. Then, because I don't feel I can lead with, *Sorry for saying I wouldn't bone you if you were the last man on earth*, I ask, 'Another coffee?'

In answer, Liam closes the notebook.

'I'm glad I caught you. I was going to leave you a note.' He taps the notebook, not meeting my eye. 'I'm checking into a hotel for the last night. Thought it was for the best.'

'Oh, right.'

He pushes back his chair and I experience a mildly panicky sensation, as though I'm aware on a subliminal level that after this juncture, there will be no going back.

'Liam, I…'

He looks up at me then, and give me a small, kind smile. 'Let's just draw a line under it, shall we? I had a really nice time yesterday and I hope maybe you did too.'

I nod enthusiastically.

'I don't tell people who my father is because nine times out of ten, I get exactly the same reaction as you had last night. Admittedly, not usually so loquacious, but then you are a woman of words.'

'And one time out of ten?' I ask.

He side-eyes me. 'They think I might be useful. Until they work out I mean it when I say I have absolutely nothing to do with that man and no inclination to change that.'

'Is that why you go as Liam Shaw? Instead of Kaufman-Shaw?'

'Partly. I could change my name, I suppose, but my paternal grandmother was actually British. I have relatives here in the UK, on both sides. I see no need to change that part of my history.'

I process what he has said.

'And, do you think Franklyn's might be in that one out of ten bracket?'

He laughs, but there is no mirth in it.

'Well, let's just say I've been giving that some thought, and on reflection – the fact that I seem to be the first ever employee to win a holiday? A coincidence? I think not. At a guess, the board have been finding ways to flatter my father over tee-offs on the golf course, knowing how they work.'

Liam bends to pick up his rucksack, along with a small plastic bag beside it, which he now hands to me.

'You should go and check out the coves around the headland before you leave. They're pretty special.'

I open the bag and see he is giving me his snorkel and mask.

'But don't you need it? I thought you went swimming every day.'

He shrugs. 'You were a natural. Enjoy the rest of your stay, Annie. See you around.'

And then, just like that, he is striding towards the door and what I'd wished for back when I'd arrived is coming true. Liam is leaving me to enjoy the rest of my holiday-for-one in Corfu, completely alone.

# CHAPTER 18

After giving myself a stern talking to about the pitfalls of judgement and assumption, and a re-evaluation of my hitherto slightly misaligned quasi-feminist outlook, I assuage my misery with cake, pastries and coffee in a harbourside cafe, then take off to the beach.

It is my last full day in Corfu, and I intend to make the most of it, even though it feels like any residual shine has already worn off, just like with Gatsby.

Instead of invigorating me, the harsh sun is pounding my shoulders and sweat is pooling beneath my boobs. I no longer feel buoyant with optimism about returning home, yet I don't want to be here either.

Of the seven books I brought with me, I've read one solitary chapter of *Not My Life*. I've carried books with me on a daily basis, having imagined myself awash with joy at having all this time to read. In truth, the only book I've read is *My Family and Other Animals* and as absorbing as that was, the only words that have drawn me in since were those of my mysterious correspondent.

It occurs to me to wonder whether I've spent so long surrounding myself with books lately that I've forgotten to notice people. Let's face it, would I have bothered to engage with my pen pal on face value alone? Probably not. I'd have drawn my own conclusions based firstly on appearance, gender, age. Then I'd have scrutinised their motives. It's what I do. What I've always done since leaving the city. And here's the clincher. If Jess and Vik hadn't already been my friends, would I have bothered to make any new ones? I hadn't bothered since. My world is very small. I like it small. I like living close to my family and friends, and I love working in the bookshop. But maybe that's not all there is.

I pull Liam's snorkel and mask from my bag and tug it over my head, immediately reminded of the sensation of his fingers gently grazing mine as I struggled to fasten it properly.

Foolishly, I can't resist scanning the beach as I plod into the water, my sturdy swim shoes coming into their own at last, just in case Liam is here, somewhere. After almost a week of bumping into him everywhere I've gone, it's come to feel expected. Welcome.

But none of the bodies reclining on loungers are familiar, none of the heads cresting the water are his.

I decide, assessing the bay as I submerge into the water, savouring every cooling step, I will swim out to the rocky outcrop of the headland.

Liam was right. Beneath the translucent shallow waters, against a backdrop of perfect, smooth white pebbles, a magnified world of marine life abounds. With gentle kicks, I glide along, mesmerised by this vibrantly colourful world just below the surface. At one point, I dive to retrieve a shimmering purple object from the bottom and when I break through the surface and get my breath back, I see it's a sea urchin shell. A perfect, spherical shell, dotted with a complex pattern of raised bumps and streaked with shades of purple, as beautiful and fragile as though it had been blown from glass. I have nowhere to store it, so I hold it gently in my palm as I swim.

The tiny beach at the end of the headland is very pretty. Gently sloping shelves of smooth rock are dotted with the occasional sun worshipper in a secluded bay of turquoise shallows, so warm it might be bathwater. Did Liam find this place whilst exploring? It might have been fun to share the discovery. It might have been fun to share our holiday. I rest for a while on a ledge of rock to drink in the scenery, tilt my face to the sun in the hope endorphins will flush out thoughts of Liam.

On the swim back to Pipitos beach, where I had left my bag under a towel, I find another sea urchin shell; pink and smaller than the first, but just as beautiful.

Thankfully, I reach the shore with both shells intact, and then back to the apartment without dropping them.

Stepping inside, I scan for signs Liam failed to find a hotel and sloped back here, but everything is as I left it. I place the sea-urchin shells carefully in a dish on the table for safe-keeping, until I can find something to pack them in for the journey home.

In the shower, I find that Liam has left behind the purple plastic tub. I twist the lid off and bring it to my nose, flooding my senses with the familiar scent. I'm not thinking of the sensation of my entire body being on fire, but of the smell of Liam's clothes, many of which I've handled, thanks to Maria's meddlesome unpacking.

It makes me smile now, to think of a billionaire's son decanting from his bottle of laundry liquid at home to take on holiday. I had got this man so wrong.

Later, I decide as it is my last evening on the island before flying home tomorrow, I will blow the last of my cash on a nice dinner. Maybe treat a cat or two to scraps from my fine dining.

My flight isn't until tomorrow night, but I begin tidying my room, which has become like a scene from *War of the Worlds*, if aliens used bikini tops and hair scarves as cannon fodder. Whilst shuffling around on my hands and knees to locate an errant sandal, I spot something protruding from under the bed, a thin book of some description. Recognising that whatever it is does not belong to me prompts two reactions; trepidation, in case the object is something of a pornographic nature that I do not wish to see, and curiosity, because human beings are insatiably nosey and since when did anyone ignore a potentially interesting discovery, even if the results are something you wish you'd never seen?

I reach across and use one finger to slide the book toward me. It's a run-of-the-mill Pukka notepad. I saw Liam with one similar this morning, so this is probably his. Intrigued, I pick it up and sit on the bed, then turn the cover.

In green, underlined felt tip pen, the first page declares the book to be:

*Mikey's Bucket List Travel Diary*

Who on earth is Mikey?

On the next page, there is a numbered list that reads as follows:

1) *Waikiki, Hawaii*
2) *Gold Coast, Sydney*
3) *Fistral, Newquay*
4) *Bali*
5) *Lagos, Portugal*
6) *Hossegor, France*
7) *Woolacombe, Devon*
8) *Jeffreys Bay, South Africa*
9) *Malibu, California*
10) *Bundoran, Ireland*

An eclectic mix, by anyone's standard. Newquay *and* Hawaii?

Some of the place names are written in that same green pen, but some are written in blue biro, in a cursive, looping handwriting that looks vaguely familiar.

I turn the page.

*Our Awesome trip to Hawaii*

The word 'awesome' is an addition, squeezed in above in different handwriting. There are clearly two authors in this narrative and in the next paragraph, it all makes sense.

*Me and Liam arrived in Honolulu yesterday afternoon. The first thing we did was to get doughnuts then we went to Waikiki beach.*

*Today we are going to the zoo.*

My hand slides to cover my mouth, as I realise what I am reading. Mikey must be Liam's brother, his brother who died.

I scan the journal entry, which jumps between statements of fact written in a childish hand and more descriptive passages, clearly added by Liam.

In one section, my eyes prick painfully as Liam recounts a visit to a well-known Honolulu store where they both bought Aloha shirts as a souvenir of their trip.

After the Hawaii entry, the rest of the notebook is empty.

Whilst I'd love to think more of Mikey's bucket list got to be ticked off, I strongly suspect the reason Liam keeps this with him, is because, sadly, it didn't happen.

Only Liam doesn't have this with him now.

The good news is, that whilst I might not see him again in Corfu, I do know where to find him, once I get home.

I stare at the last page again. At the way all of the 'j's' and 'g's' loop lazily into their neighbouring letters. At the sacrilegious use of a lower case 'a' written larger in place of a capital A.

And I know exactly where I have seen this writing before.


Three minutes later, I find myself hovering impatiently behind a woman in a leopard print sarong as she imbues the choosing of a book with as much complexity and jeopardy as defusing a bomb. Her polished, red-tipped fingers reach out first in one direction, then stop abruptly, or graze lightly along the spines, before she lunges to a different shelf entirely. She hooks out a Jilly Cooper, before pushing it back into place and selecting a Jack Reacher. At this point, I feel confident the book about the Durrells will be safe, but it is then upended when she returns Reacher to the shelf, drops to the floor and makes a beeline for *The Girl on The Train*. Surely every single person on God's green earth has read that book already?

Finally, she plumps for the Victoria Hislop next to *The*

*Girl on the Train* and turns, with her prize in hand, feigning surprise at finding me behind her – as though she hasn't been perfectly aware of my shuffling and pacing. She gives me a wide lip-sticked smile and brandishes her book aloft.

'I always like to read something set where I'm visiting. It can really enhance your holiday, don't you think?'

I politely refrain from pointing out that Crete, where her book is set, is as far from Corfu as London is from Frankfurt and probably just as varied, and instead thank my lucky stars she didn't clock the book which *is* set just eight kilometres from this very spot.

In truth, I haven't paid much thought to it since realising I'd been stood up at Niko's Bar. The fantasy of putting a handsome face to the architect of those messages had been superseded firstly by a monstrous hangover and secondly by spending a day in Liam's not so irritating, as it turned out, company.

So, when I tug out *The Girl on the Train* and spot the book nestled in its hiding spot, I experience a rush of adrenalin.

The book has been returned.

Feeling more self-conscious than I have before, I reach for it and slip it into my bag. I don't know if there will be a new message; I don't know what any of this means. But I'm not about to stand here while I find out.

Back in the sanctity of the apartment, I race into the bedroom for the travel diary and drop onto the bed to compare them.

As I open the Durrells book, a postcard falls out. Not the postcard I left inside, with my invitation to meet, but a new one featuring the incredible view overlooking Paleokastritsa from the monastery atop the hill.

With quivering fingers, I turn it over.

*Sorry I couldn't make it on Saturday night. I think it would have been fun. I wish you an enjoyable rest of your holiday and the best of wishes for wherever life takes you next. X*

There is absolutely no doubt, even if the postcard were not

proof enough, that Liam is the author of these messages. The handwriting is identical. The only time Liam left me a brief note, it had been written in block capitals, so I would never have noticed before now.

Of course, the obvious question, and one that now fills me with a peculiar nervous panic, is – did Liam know it was me he was corresponding with?

The words right there on these pages answer a question I hadn't even known to ask.

*Holidays are difficult for me; this is my first in four years.*

Of course they are. They were meant to have been enjoyed with his brother.

I have to find him.

My heart breaks for his loss, and I hate myself for treating him so badly. I can't get the shirt back for him, but I *can* reunite him with the travel diary, and I can apologise, repeatedly, if he will hear it.

And although my discoveries today raise so many more questions, that's all that matters right now.

# CHAPTER 19

Even with my unrefined powers of deduction, I think I've guessed Liam has a penchant for the Pukka pad. He probably orders them in bulk, and I can see the attraction; lightweight, slim, spiral bound for the easy removal of unwanted pages, the journalist's weapon of choice… or a writer. Liam is a writer.

The signs were there, if I'd known what I was looking for. But then I didn't know I was meant to be looking under my very own nose.

Urgently, I scan back through our messages, reminding myself of our conversations and looking for clues. I'd revealed my disinclination to reread books, whilst Liam had confessed to eagerly diving back into them like old friends. He was interested in people, of observing them and studying them; this was what made him so good at his job, his friendliness and willingness to engage.

I place both the book and the travel diary in my bag, replace my flip-flops for sandals and leave the apartment, with a hunch about exactly where I might find Liam tonight.

It's still quite early for dinner, but as I approach the open gate to The Olive Grove terrace, I see plenty of tables are occupied. Nervously, I scan them for Liam, whilst trying to keep a low profile.

'Kalispera, Madam, it is nice to see you again. Table for one?'

I'm slightly taken aback at the elderly man's familiar

greeting, his kindly face glistening with perspiration, already reaching for a menu from a stack on a nearby table.

'Um, yes please,' I say, although I'm torn between wanting to stay here to see if Liam shows up and scouring every other taverna and bar in the resort, which could take all night.

I'm led to a cosy table tucked into a corner beside a small fountain, the gentle trickling of which I find only mildly soothing, as I sit fidgeting. I politely defer to order my food, in place of a small glass of wine and some olives, because at this rate I could end up having to repeat this performance at every establishment in Kassiopi, in a carefully executed rotation of tiny mezze plates.

After half an hour, just as my nerve is beginning to falter and I'm contemplating leaving, I see a familiar figure enter the taverna garden. I hold my breath, anticipating he will be shown to the vacant table nearby, but instead, he disappears from view.

When ten more minutes have passed and the waiter approaches to see if I would like my glass replenishing, I make a bold and improvised decision.

'A man arrived a little while ago, tall, wearing shorts and a shirt,' I falter, realising I've described fifty per cent of their patrons. 'I was wondering…'

The waiter gives me a twinkly smile. 'You mean Liam? Great guy.'

It seems Liam just can't help making a lasting impression on everyone he meets.

'Yes,' I reply, awkwardly, 'Liam. Could I please order a carafe of wine to be taken to his table? Could you tell him – it's a peace offering?'

'Of course. And shall I tell him who made the kind gesture?'

I smile weakly and reach into my bag for the Durrells book. 'Perhaps you could be so kind as to also give him this?' I wince.

The man shakes his head, muttering something in Greek I

don't understand, and from the amused expression on his face I'm sure that's for the best.

There follows a window of time where I seriously contemplate vaulting the fountain and lemon trees to make my escape onto the street, rather than having to walk round to the entrance. The only thing stopping me is the fact I haven't yet paid my bill and can't afford to book a new flight should I be unable to board tomorrow's, owing to being incarcerated.

Eventually, the waiter appears at the corner with a tea towel flung over his shoulder and a laden tray in hand. He catches my eye and jerks his head to the side, before taking the food to waiting customers. His message seems clear; *this is a busy restaurant full of paying customers and whilst I appreciate romantic gestures are afoot, time is money, dear, sort it out yourself.*

Well, whilst much of that is true, my gesture was not romantic, it was insurance.

Gathering up my bag and my dignity as best I can, I make my way around the garden, to where I see Liam sitting in an opposite corner, beneath an arbour of vines.

When his eyes find mine, I have the answer I wanted. Liam is in no way surprised to see me.

I approach, noting two glasses of red wine have been poured, so I take it as a sign to sit down. I also notice he is wearing the blue linen shirt I'd fingered appreciatively in the wardrobe a few days ago, the colour making his eyes pop like precious gems.

'So,' he says, interest lighting up his features.

'So,' I repeat.

My eyes seek out the book at the edge of the table. 'May I ask when you worked out the sex pest fixated on hunting down randy tortoises was actually yours truly?'

His lips twitch.

'Probably around the time I realised you'd brought your toys on vacation.'

At that, heat floods my cheeks, as well as some more southernly regions of my body.

'I'm kidding,' he says, mirth cracking his face. 'That was a total mystery, until you told me about Maria's over-zealous housekeeping. Then the penny dropped.'

I narrow my eyes. 'Are you saying you *didn't* know it was me writing in the book? You didn't look surprised to see me just now.'

Liam says, 'That would be because George told me a beautiful redhead wanted to buy me a drink. That's not a regular occurrence, contrary to what you might think. Not unless they know who my father is anyway.'

I try not to feel flattered at his use of the word 'beautiful'. Technically, they were George's words, but on balance, I'll take the compliment.

'But I'll confess, I guessed it was you quite early on. You write just how you speak, all forthright and militant, but kinda funny too.'

'Well, *you* don't,' I snap back churlishly. 'You write like Charles Bingley stuffed his cheeks with a punnet of plums. And the fact you used the word "holiday" repeatedly, when I know damned well you say 'vacation', that's active deception right there.'

Liam gives me a small smile. 'Maybe. At first, it was fun, you know – you were happily chatting with me without knowing who I was, when in reality I've been lucky to avoid frostbite just from being in your company. It meant I could get to know you, behind all those prickles.'

I give a mock gasp of outrage. He is, of course, right.

'I finished the book on the flight, discovered the shelves by the pool when I checked the place out that first night, swapped it for another one, like you're supposed to.'

'So, what made you pick it back up?' I ask, genuinely intrigued.

He shrugs. 'I didn't fancy the book I chose, went back to the shelves and noticed our book was gone. When it appeared back there the next day, I thought hmm, either someone loved it just as much as me, or they absolutely hated it. Either way, it was worth a look. But I could ask you the same thing.'

'Touché. I'm just incredibly nosey. It seemed like such a personal gesture, in a place where no one is connected beyond briefly staying at the same hotel, or swimming in the same pool. The physical space might stay the same, somewhere like this, but everything else is so temporary.'

'Not everything,' says Liam, indicating our surroundings. 'George and his brother Konstantinos have run this place for eighteen years. Lived on the island all their lives. How did you know I'd be here, by the way? And how did you work out it was me?'

'What, you mean beside the giant hint in the form of a postcard of Paleokastritsa? No, I had no intention of returning to the book after embarrassing myself with the suggestion of drinks, but then I found something.' I reach into my bag, and fold my fingers around Mikey's travel diary, before sliding it across the table. 'It was under the bed.'

I watch Liam's face change from bemusement to horror, to relief, as it dawns on him that he hadn't even spotted it was missing.

'I recognised your handwriting immediately. And I guessed I'd find you here because the clues had been there all along – you're a writer, you're fascinated by people, and you stop to drink everything in. I remembered that I saw you writing when you were here before, and how you chatted with the staff.'

I pause, wait for him to take the book. 'Liam, I'm so very sorry.'

I'm not sure which part, exactly, I'm most sorry for, I just know that I have not behaved well when it comes to this man and for that, I truly am sorry.

He doesn't look up for a while and my heart races as I prepare myself for him to politely, but firmly, dismiss me.

Eventually, he says, 'I ordered the beef stifado. It's good – shall I get them to make that two?'

'That depends.'

'On?' he asks, intrigued.

'Whether they'll like it,' I point toward the two bony cats bothering an unsympathetic couple.

'Beggars can't be choosers,' suggests Liam, reasonably, then he adds, 'I'm pretty confident they will, but we'll order a side dish of prawns, just in case it's not quite to taste.'

When the food is ordered, and George has finished giving his eyebrows a workout, Liam turns serious once more.

'Mikey was a surprise baby, Mom had him when I was fourteen. Dad was happy about it, until Mikey was born with Down's Syndrome.' A bitterness creeps into Liam's tone. 'The news was so unwelcome, it drove him into the arms of another woman, several, actually.'

'Oh, Liam. I'm so sorry.'

Liam shrugs. 'To be honest, Annie, he'd probably been having affairs the whole time. That's the sort of man my father is. But this time he didn't hide it. His disappointment was so absolute that he felt vindicated to do exactly as he pleased. So, when Mikey was four, Mom finally did what she should have done years before and divorced him. He was vile of course; his legal team did a full number on her. But we had Mikey to think about, so Mom gave up the fight, we moved to Edinburgh and that was that.'

I'm so taken aback by what Liam is telling me that I simply sit in stunned silence.

'Mikey was an absolute superstar,' he adds, with warmth. 'I could never have wished for a better brother; he was my everything and our father will never know the joy he brought to us. Clearly, he doesn't even care, because as far as I can tell, he's erased him from the history books. No mention that he ever had a son called Michael, anywhere that I can tell. Perhaps he intended to deny his paternity if ever he needed to. Money, *real* money, can buy you almost anything.'

As horrifying as it is, this makes sense, because my internet searches had only found reference to a son around Liam's age, no mention of a second. Not before he remarried, then fathered more children.

'Do you mind me asking what happened to Mikey?' I ask gently.

Liam raises sad eyes to mine. 'Childhood leukaemia happened.'

I reach across the table and brush Liam's fingertips. He doesn't flinch or move them.

'He was such a happy boy, Annie. He didn't need anyone's sympathy or pity, and certainly not their money, just the family time he craved. Probably it was because of the stories I used to tell him about growing up in Florida, but he was fascinated by the States – although strangely not by his absent dad, go figure. But anyway, he became totally obsessed with surfing. Spent hours watching YouTube videos; Kelly Slater was his absolute hero, he's a world surfing champion, if you haven't heard of him. We didn't live far from the Scottish coast, so sometimes we'd take off at weekends and I taught him to bodyboard. By the time he turned thirteen and the leukaemia was diagnosed, he'd created this massive list of places he wanted to visit.'

He taps the book, and the penny drops. What all those seemingly random places have in common. They are all world-famous surfing spots.

'He whittled it down to his top ten, even though with the best will in the world, an extended trip to Australia was never going to work with his medical needs, never mind the cost. Although, I'll say this for Daddy Dearest, he did send Mom a heap of cash when he learned about Mikey's prognosis. Couldn't risk the negative press, should the cold-hearted abandonment of his family be exposed, I guess. I'd had the bones of a relationship with him up to that point, visited occasionally when he'd sent for me. Met my new, younger siblings once or twice, but the fact he wouldn't even see his own son when he was diagnosed with a terminal illness? That was it for me. I haven't seen him since.'

'But you did manage one of them?' I ask, gently. 'The trip? I read the journal entry, sorry.'

He rubs his face, 'We knew he'd never manage the list, but we decided to do Hawaii, whilst he was still well enough to do it.'

Liam reaches into his pocket for his wallet and brings out a small photo which he passes for me to see. It is a picture of Liam, a surfboard in one arm, the other wrapped around the shoulders of a well-built teenager, hugging a bodyboard to him. Both are beaming at the camera, and both are wearing gaudy Aloha shirts, open above plain white t-shirts. Behind them, palm trees frame a skyline peppered with tower blocks.

'We had the most amazing time; I'll treasure those memories forever.'

My throat aches with the effort of keeping a hard lump of emotion in check.

'I'm so sorry, Liam. If I could get the shirt back, I would. I wish I could take back what I did.'

Liam frowns, then closes a hand over mine. 'Hey. It doesn't matter, not really. It was just a shirt. No one can ever take away the memory of my brother and the fun times we had together. I shouldn't have got so hung up on it.'

He sighs then and pulls his hand away, taking a sip of his wine. 'The truth is, I made a promise to Mikey that I'd visit all the places on his list and surf those beaches, even if he couldn't get there himself. I told him I'd go and see them all and carry on with his travel journal, finish our big adventure. But after he died, I couldn't face the idea of going anywhere, let alone somewhere I knew he wished he could have gone too. This is the first trip I've made in the four years since he passed away and that was only because it was handed to me on a plate. I thought it would be a good first step and maybe if I brought his shirt along, it would be as though a part of him was experiencing it with me. As it turns out, even if I wanted to, I can't escape his cheeky jabbering inside my head, commenting on everything I do. He encourages me to be a better person, through his sheer joyous outlook on life.' His face breaks into a wide grin. 'He'd have irritated the *fuck* out of you. Bullied you basically, until you gave him your full attention, not dissimilar to Marvin, now I think about it.'

Before I can respond to this fairly accurate, if damning perception of my inherently flawed character, George and another gentleman, who could only be his brother, given their similar appearance, arrive with armfuls of plates and dishes.

'Ela,' says George. 'Stifado for the lady, another stifado for Liam, green salad, potatoes, garlic prawns and lastly, bread. Can we get you anything else, more wine perhaps?'

'A bed to lie down on after polishing off this lot?' I ask, eyes bulging at the volume of delicious-looking food.

'Nonsense,' replies Konstantinos, 'in Greece, there is always the eating, the drinking and then the dancing. This is fuel for the dancing. After, maybe bed.'

With that, he winks at Liam and returns with his brother to the kitchen.

'*Slightly presumptuous,*' I say under my breath, more to fill the loaded silence that has been left in their wake.

'Totally. My dancing is almost as accomplished as my singing,' says Liam, deliberately being obtuse. 'But...' he says, twirling the stem of his glass, 'it's not an *awful* idea. Seeing as this is our last night, what do you say to leaving Corfu with a bang?'

I hold my glass aloft in response.

'I say, we party like Greek Titans who've been trying to kill each other for a week, only to find out they might just be on the same side, after all.'

'Amen to that,' he says, with a clink.

# CHAPTER 20

'So, what I want to know,' I say, pulling a cherry from a cocktail stick with my teeth, 'is why you stood me up on Saturday night. I mean, you saw the postcard, right? Inviting you, or whoever I thought "you" was, for a drink?'

'Ah,' replies Liam, looking as sheepish as one can with a rose tucked behind one's ear; I have one too, as the girl who harangued Liam with her basket in the restaurant earlier wasn't taking no for an answer, so I saved him some face and bought him one straight back. Later, a different girl came around with glow stick necklaces, so we bought those too and have them draped around our necks.

'I spent a lot of time thinking about what to do for the best,' he says, looking genuinely thoughtful. 'On the one hand, I could just come clean and tell you it was me, so you didn't waste an evening waiting for someone who was never going to show up. Or I could actually show up and admit it to you then. Best-case scenario, we'd laugh about it and enjoy a drink, worst-case scenario, you'd still hate me.'

'I didn't *hate* you,' I say, appalled.

'Oh, I think you did, a little bit.'

I sigh, 'OK, maybe just a little.' I use my thumb and forefinger to indicate the tiniest amount. 'But that was only because I resented you for potentially taking my job from me. Your shop's bigger, better, more successful, and you're a bloke, so obvs that makes you better—'

'Woah, back up there,' interrupts Liam. 'What backward logic is that? How on earth am I any better than you, or anyone else for that matter? Where did that come from?'

I take a steadying glug of my cosmopolitan. Bringing this up always makes me thirsty.

'Because, Liam, regretfully and unbelievably, that is the way this shitty little world still operates on a local and global scale. Guys with looks, swagger and the gift of the gab usually prosper. Guys with money bulldoze their way to success. Guys with looks, charm *and* money destroy everyone in their path. Take your own father as an example. But anyway, it doesn't matter anymore. Apparently, this time I should be grateful people like him exist, because for now, at least, it sounds like I might have my job to go back to, if Franklyn's are no longer having to resort to store closures.'

Liam is shaking his head. 'I don't know what happened to you, Annie, but that just isn't me.'

'I know,' I say, becoming serious. 'And I don't hate you. Newsflash, I might even like you, a bit.'

A wild expression darkens his eyes for a heartbeat, and I feel my pulse race.

'So, why didn't you?' I ask.

'Why didn't I what?'

'Why didn't you show up at Niko's bar that night and come clean?'

'I did,' he says with a small shrug. 'But after I left Taverna Diana in Corfu Town that day, which was a genuine coincidence, I swear, I discovered they'd cancelled the next two buses, so it was pretty late by the time I got back.'

I remember the moment I left Niko sitting at the bar, when I'd spotted Liam sitting with Marvin and Sue.

'You knew I was there; you saw me. Why didn't you come over?' My words come out all hushed, because I know exactly what he's going to say.

'It looked like you were having fun, and I didn't want to spoil that for you.'

I go to protest, but he beats me to it.

'Besides, if Marvin and Sue had spotted you sooner...' He holds up two hands in defence.

'God, they're not in here, are they?' I scan the patrons of Apollo Greek Music Bar, which has so far treated us to eighties gems such as Black Box and A-ha, not even a semi-quaver of anything Greek. 'Sorry,' I add hastily, 'it's just that now we're actually able to be in a room together and behave like civil members of society, I'm quite invested to see how it pans out.'

Liam's eyes narrow. 'How do you hope it pans out?'

'Well,' I say, inching closer to speak slowly and deliberately, 'if I'm not mistaken... that very much looks like a karaoke machine being set up in the corner. This is going to be your lucky night.'

His head whips around and I fall back against my seat in hysterics.

Inexplicably, the sound of many terrible songs being caterwauled into the night by punters draws more customers to the Apollo Greek Music Bar than when Yazz was singing her heart out. Believing you're rocking Mariah Carey while emboldened by booze I can accept. I have been that person many a time. But willingly flocking to hear these renditions, instead of actual enjoyable music, is unfathomable.

The atmosphere is buzzing. People are smiling, laughing, drinking, some are even dancing, and everyone claps at the end of each song.

I put in the request twenty minutes ago when I went to the bar for more cocktails and am finding it hilarious watching Liam's nervous face twitch every time a new song starts. Personally, I'm on holiday, I don't know anyone, or care what they think, and I'm pleasantly but not overly tipsy. Karaoke-schmokey, I could do it standing on my head. Clearly, Liam is feeling quite differently, because he's drained his second drink in record time.

Eventually, the iconic opening bars of the Spice Girls'

crowning glory floods the bar and the crowd whoops in appreciation.

'We're up!' I yelp, slamming down my glass and grasping for Liam's hand.

He looks up at me in relief. 'I thought you were going to make me do it on my own.'

'Don't be a wally,' I say, pulling him to his feet, 'this is a practice run. The next one's just for you.'

Even above the cheers and the intro beat, I hear him muttering under his breath as he follows me, hand in hand, to the stage, and it cheers my soul.

I sing out the opening lyrics, rocking my inner diva and turning to Liam, who is mumbling inaudibly into his microphone and I grin widely.

It takes a few bars, and some considerable cajoling and finger pointing from me, but by the time we get to the chorus, Liam is swaying his hips and throwing his arms around like the superstar we're singing about. A group of girlfriends get onto the dance floor and start swinging-it, shaking-it and moving-it for real and before the end of the song, the whole place is singing along.

The cheer at the end makes Liam blush with genuine pleasure and it might be the sweetest thing I've ever seen. I doubt anyone but me realised he was singing the words all wrong, despite them being on a screen in front of him.

I can't resist throwing my arms around him, as we arrive at the bar, whilst behind us the familiar strains of Dancing Queen play out.

'Well done, that was awesome.'

He moves two hands slowly to my lower back and returns the squeeze. I drink in the scent of him, now comfortingly familiar through my repeated handling of his clothes. 'It was awful, not awesome, but also kind of fun.'

'There you go then,' I say, pulling back to look him in the eye. 'I do know how it's done.'

Liam's gaze lowers to my lips as I speak, and a rush of adrenalin hits my belly.

'Oh, I don't doubt it,' he says.

Perhaps we've been skirting around it all week, in this silly battle of wills. Would I honestly have insisted upon staying put in the apartment if Liam was an overweight, uncouth guy with body odour? Has my determination not to be bested by him been driven by serious conviction, or because I've been intrigued by him? I can no longer tell.

All I know is that this is a man whose kindness and generosity shine through as much as his startlingly good looks, and that makes him truly attractive.

'Another drink?' I ask, to break the tension.

'That depends,'

'On?'

'Whether I really do have to go up there on my own and get through another song?'

His frightened boy expression is adorable.

'I'll leave that one entirely up to you. Either way, my work is done.'

'In that case, I could do with some air – mind if we take a walk?'

'Sure, let's go.'

# CHAPTER 21

We exit the bar onto the street, which hums with the sounds of neighbouring tavernas. Kassiopi is a working fishing village which possesses a charming mix of tourists and locals. Among the bars, restaurants and gelaterias, there are also elderly men playing dominoes over tumblers of brandy in the cool evening air outside an establishment with no name. A bar which only the locals use, not designed to attract tourists.

'What do you think they're talking about?' whispers Liam, as we pass the men, two of whom are in the midst of a heated debate.

'If I had to guess, the one with the hat's just announced he's done for the night, and the other one's calling him a pussy-whipped lightweight who'd rather go home to his Mrs and a cup of cocoa than finish the game like a man.'

Liam shakes his head in amazement.

'Wow. You really do have a low opinion of men, don't you? How do you know they're not arguing about whose round it is next, or contesting the last piece played?'

'Since you brought it up, yes, recent experience hasn't been great. But in this case, I came to that conclusion because matey just packed away his rolling tobacco, drained his glass and has a wedding ring on his left hand.'

Liam chuckles. 'Alright, Sherlock.'

We stroll down to the twinkling harbour; the sky bright and starlit, ships blinking at sea.

'Do you want to talk about it?' asks Liam, as we gravitate towards the water's edge, 'Recent experience? How did you put it, in your message? You've known a few chrome-plated men?'

I wince a little. 'Yeah, I don't know why I said that. I'm not a man-hater, you know. Some of my best friends are guys, my dad is loving and gentle. I guess I'm just bitter about a certain man.'

'Your ex? Who left you for the farmer's daughter?'

'Travis? No. I mean, yeah, that was upsetting. But it didn't gut-punch me. Not like it did when my boss tried to seduce me with the promise of promotion, and the implied career-ending alternative, should I not feel inclined. I know, I know, in the time of #Metoo, such accounts are neither surprising nor rare. But the thing is, I truly thought I could handle it, that as a modern, educated woman, I could manage the situation professionally.'

Liam has gone quiet beside me. I don't know why I'm telling him all this, but it feels necessary to get it out there. I owe him some kind of explanation, so why not the truth?

'After university, I got a place on a graduate scheme, an internship at *Sunday Living*, it's a magazine supplement for—'

'*The Daily Scoop*,' he supplies.

'Yeah. Well, back then I thought I'd like to get into publishing. I'd always loved everything book-related but thought magazines would be more of a fun career, more, I don't know, glitzy. Anyway, it turned out, predictably, my role was more about making tea and selling advertising space than anything remotely journalistic or editorial. My line manager was a woman called Shannay, who had been a graduate herself. She was a bit of a cold fish, unfriendly and unwilling to help me progress. After I'd been there a couple of years, Shannay was promoted, and suddenly I found myself with her job, team leader of telesales. I did well, hit all my targets and then was offered a slightly different position, as PA to Editor in Chief, Garrett Delaney.'

'I've heard that name,' says Liam.

'Possibly you have. He's the Oxbridge son of a peer, with friends in all the right places, like most print media bosses.'

'Hmm,' he agrees. 'Go on,' he adds gently.

'He was an attractive man, and he knew it. Everyone around him seemed to simply be waiting for him to turn his winning beam on them. But he turned his beam on me instead, and everything changed.'

I stop and inhale deeply. We wait for a couple walking hand in hand to pass us by, then Liam pulls me toward a bench.

'What happened?' he asks.

'Well, mainly my job turned into a vicious game of outsmarting backstabbers. It was as though everyone was out to get me, trying to slip me up, simply because Garrett liked me.'

'And I take it there wasn't anything going on, between you?' asks Liam, caution having crept into his tone.

I give a small, mirthless laugh. 'I wouldn't have touched that man with one of his own Oxford oars. Charm can be the most sinister form of flattery. It didn't take me long to discover that all the urgent summons to his office, were in fact, just excuses to get me alone. Doubtless everyone else knew it too.'

'Did he try anything?'

'Depends on what you class as anything. Does him brazenly asking if I liked the fact that my green silk blouse made him hard, and inviting me to see for myself, count as trying?'

I feel Liam tense beside me.

'At first, I tried all the classic self-preservation tactics – laughing it off, responding with a bit of light banter that indicated I was flattered but uninterested. And then, as is too often the case, he began to see me as a challenge. And when I still found ways to slip from his sometimes physical clutches, he began to dangle promotion and actual money before me, like a fucking gold carrot.'

'I'm so sorry this happened to you,' says Liam, softly. 'I can't even begin to imagine dealing with that.'

'It was pretty terrifying, especially when my colleagues closed ranks and decided I was bonking the boss for promotion, which was clearly a tried and tested blueprint for success. But do you know what was worse?'

I turn my head and find Liam watching me.

'When I reported him to HR, the magazine simply found a way to get rid of me, legally of course. You wouldn't have thought that was possible, would you, in this day and age?'

Liam shakes his head and looks down at his lap.

'I believe it, Annie, because my own father is just another Garrett Delaney. He buys, bribes and womanises his way through life, and nobody ever stops him. Do you know what he bought me for my eighteenth birthday present?'

'A Ferrari?' I hazard, only in semi-earnest.

Liam shakes his head, 'Uh-uh. A prostitute.'

'Fuck. No way.'

'Yes way. And, in case you were wondering, no, I did not. My own father honestly believed that would be the best way to celebrate my coming of age. I think that tells you everything you need to know about him. So, trust me, there's a *long* way to go before I'm shocked about anything much.'

We're both quiet, each of us processing the other's words, when a loud cheer roars up behind us, piercing the solemnity that has descended.

'Hold up,' says Liam, spinning around. 'Looks like we've got ourselves a bride and groom.'

We stand and watch as a group of well-wishers and a glowing couple file out of a taverna onto the street, followed by two musicians with stringed instruments, playing the instantly recognisable music from *Zorba the Greek*. The guests swiftly arrange themselves into a cheering, clapping semi-circle as the bride and groom attempt dance steps that would plunge Stavros Flatley into pits of despair.

As the tempo quickens, we find ourselves clapping along, caught up in the infectious joy of the happy crowd. Under the tutelage of the musicians, the wedding guests wrap their arms around each other's shoulders and kick their heels in time to the rhythm.

'Come on!' shouts a woman in a lilac halterneck dress, a bridesmaid, I suspect, and a pissed one at that, 'don't just stand there, join in!'

We look to each other and grin. 'Can't say Konstantinos didn't warn us, right?' laughs Liam, grabbing my hand and tugging me along.

I throw my arm around the bridesmaid's shoulders and Liam throws his around mine. We laugh when the bride gives up trying not to trip over her dress, kicks and flings her sandals across the pavement, and hoicks the flimsy satin up to her thighs so she can really give it some welly.

I'm intensely aware of the heat from Liam's upper body where it nestles firmly against mine and of my own fingers curling along his upper arm. The music gets faster and faster, the kicks get higher and the laughter louder. Eventually, the song reaches its crescendo, and the guests break apart, hot and breathless.

We stand and watch, Liam's arm still draped loosely around me, as a yacht strung with fairy lights and ribbons across its bow, pulls up in front of the jetty and a man in black trousers and a white shirt jumps out to secure its mooring.

The groom, to more clapping and cheering, gathers up his bride in one fell swoop and carries her across to the waiting yacht. It feels like we're just a tiny part of something special, something everyone here will remember for many years to come, though none of them will remember us.

'Well,' I comment, as the happy couple wave goodbye and the yacht begins to move. 'I think that was a fitting end to our last night, don't you?'

Liam's arm falls away and I instantly miss it. Already miss him, because now, after a week of squandered opportunity, *this* is almost over.

'It was a perfect ending,' he says. 'Let me walk you back to the apartment.'

'But where's your hotel, is it far?'

Liam shakes his head. 'It's fine, I need the exercise.'

'Really? You'd haul your arse all the way up that hill even when you don't have to? You must be mad.'

'You did see how much food I ate tonight didn't you? I doubt five minutes of dancing, *if* you could call it that, burned off so much as a lettuce leaf.'

I don't argue, glad to have his company, right up until we have to say goodnight.

When we reach the top of the hill, and before I've thought it through, I find myself saying, 'You could just stay. I mean I know you've paid for a hotel room, but as you're here...'

Liam looks briefly to the floor for an answer, and I think he's going to decline, but instead he says, 'If you're sure you don't mind? I'll be honest, it wasn't a four-star place. As bad as that sofa bed is, it will be more comfortable than what's on offer back there.'

'Cool,' I reply, whilst my stomach plunges into freefall, preventing a more articulate response. I busy myself with fishing around for the keys in my bag, then remember something I've been meaning to ask.

'Liam, how did you get the keys for this place? That first night? Because these were in there,' I point to the key safe on the wall, 'Clare gave me the code.'

'Oh, I'd never even noticed that before. Someone from head office brought them into the shop, along with the euros. I guess they must have been Richard's keys.'

I let us in and switch on the overhead kitchen light, which after the magical moonlit evening sky feels like an interrogation light, so I turn it straight back off.

'Sorry,' I say, using the light of my phone to find the wall light instead. 'Not sure my eyes are ready for a fluorescent strip.'

In truth, what I don't want is reality. I don't want this night to be over. I don't want to go back to monosyllabic exchanges with Liam, but I also don't know what comes next.

Perhaps Liam senses it too, because he hangs back like a visitor, rather than the paid-up occupant of this space that he is, and every part my equal.

When we go through to the lounge, I ask, 'Can I get you a drink? It'll have to be black coffee or water because that's all there is left.'

He smiles. 'No, thank you. I'm fine.'

There is an awkward pause, on a night where neither of us have stopped laughing or talking long enough to catch our breath.

'Right, well shall I just leave you to it then? Are you sure I can't get you anything?'

Liam smiles again, 'Honestly, I'm good.'

I nod, disappointment raining down on my smouldering insides as I turn to leave.

'Annie?'

'Yeah?' I halt.

'Thank you.'

'What for?'

'For being a good listener and for being so honest with me. And, also, for a fantastic evening. I've had fun tonight.'

'I've had fun too. Goodnight Liam,' I say, then head to my room and close the door.

I flop down onto the bed fully clothed and lie there on top of the sheets, my heart thudding and my mind whirling.

Had I imagined the heated looks, the brushes against skin, the glinting eyes? All signs Liam felt it just as keenly as I did. Did I imagine that all night, perhaps even long before tonight, there had been a building, bubbling, tension between us that had nothing to do with petty arguments and everything to do with raw physical and emotional attraction? No, I'm sure I haven't. I'm certain he felt it too.

Had telling him about Garrett scared him off? Did my prickles extend beyond my bolshy personality and create a giant impenetrable chastity belt no decent man would ever dare approach again?

Never have I felt as aware of another person's presence as I do right now. I hear the tell-tale sound of the sofa bed being pulled out. I can picture that just on the other side of that wall, Liam is removing his phone and wallet from his shorts pockets, placing them on the table.

Silence falls, broken only by the gentle hum of the aircon unit in the other room, and my own racing pulse.

Do I have anything to lose if I just walk out there right now and tell him I fancy the pants off him? Potentially only my dignity, and I'm going home tomorrow. I need never see him again, apart from at The Franks. I'll just make Tom go in my place – sorted.

Emboldened by the idea, I slip from the bed and creep to the door.

With a shaky hand, I turn the door handle and inch it open.

In the darkness a shape fills the doorway.

My breath hitches and I step forward.

'Annie…' Liam's voice is low and rough.

I take another tentative step and he doesn't move. His eyes blaze in the dim light, and I understand.

Another step brings me to within a foot of him, so close I can see the rapid rise and fall of his taut chest.

Our lips meet in a collision of hot, urgent need. His thumbs slide up to cup my face and I move closer, seeking him out. One of his hands slides down to rest on my lower back and he pulls me towards him, into him, against his toned, warm chest.

'You had to let me know,' he says, breaking the kiss and pulling his head back just enough to search my eyes. 'I had to know it's what you wanted; you understand?'

I nod eagerly, desperate to get back to the kiss.

'It's what I want,' I breath into his mouth. 'It's absolutely what I want.'

It's what he wants too, of that I have no doubt, because beneath the brushed cotton of his tailored chino shorts, his body is screaming it loud and clear.

He walks me backwards into the bedroom, but only as far as the wardrobe, where he pushes me gently against the louvred slats and begins trailing soft, delicate kisses along the length of my neck. I tilt my chin upwards, inviting him to explore me. Each brush of his lips as they graze my skin sets my blood on fire.

When he finds my mouth again, I reach for the buttons on his shirt. He stops me with fingers clasped over mine, then takes over the job himself.

I watch, pressed up against the wardrobe, until the garment is discarded, and he reaches down to kiss me again, my fingers finding the smooth skin of his broad shoulders and tangling in his hair, before tracing a path down his back. His sharp intake of breath between my lips sends giddy shivers shuddering through me.

If I'd ever doubted bringing laundry liquid on holiday was a sensible thing to do, tonight I'm paying for that foolhardiness. Beneath my dress are not mismatched undies, or even my oldest, frayed pants. No, because owing to the fact I ran out of clean underwear yesterday, beneath my dress is absolutely nothing.

At least, I conclude, it will remove a few steps, so I undo the side zip of my floral dress and unhook the shoulder straps, so it slips to the floor.

Liam lets out a murmur of surprise, and from the expression on his face I don't think it's the unwelcome kind.

'You went out commando tonight?' he asks gruffly.

'Looks like it.' I wince. 'Ran out of pants.'

His hungry eyes roam the contours of my body, and he tugs me toward him, grunting, 'Thank fuck I didn't know that earlier. I had a hard enough time keeping my hands off you in the karaoke bar.'

'Yeah, well, I think some of the wedding guests noticed, when the kicks got faster and higher. Didn't you notice the old guy across from us twitching as though he was having a stroke?'

'No,' he murmurs into my hair, trailing a fingertip delicately across my breast and sending ripples of delight to every nerve ending in my body, 'and I don't want to think about anyone else right now. Nobody, apart from you.'

# CHAPTER 22

## CORFU, DAY EIGHT

When I wake, the first thing I see is Liam's skin, golden from a week in the Corfiot sun, stark against the white sheet.

He really is a beautiful man, I muse, watching his chest rise and fall, appreciating the sculpted shape of his shoulder blades, and his bristled angular jaw glittering in the streaks of sunlight that pierce the window shutters.

'Good morning,' he says, lips twitching into a smile.

I grin, as his face rolls towards me on the pillow, eyes flicking open.

'How did you know I was awake?' I ask, my fingers wandering across to meet his skin. 'I might have been deeply involved in a very pleasurable dream.'

'Oh, I believe you were, judging by the sighs and whimpers.'

I hoist myself up onto an elbow. 'I do not sigh and whimper, how dare you?'

Liam laughs and pushes me back on the pillow, silencing me with a kiss. 'It's rather endearing,' he murmurs against my lips 'especially seeing as for nearly a week, I've been hearing it from the other side of this wall and had begun to assume you had an incredibly insatiable appetite.'

'For?' I ask, one eyebrow cocked.

He jerks his head towards the nightstand drawer, and I gasp, only to be silenced again, this time for the best part of an hour. That bloody drawer.

Last night, at a point when I was almost rent asunder with need, Liam had wrenched himself away from me, run his hands roughly through his hair and muttered, with the use of expletives, that he had nothing on him.

Once I'd deduced that meant he had no contraception, and not that he was checking for nits, I was able to play an, albeit sheepish, trump card and produce a Best Lover in Corfu condom from the bottom of my case.

'I wondered what happened to these,' he'd said, with confused delight. 'They were a joke gift for a mate, then they disappeared from my bag. Maria?' he'd asked.

'U-huh.'

And that, it seemed, had been sufficient explanation.

Afterwards, as I lie idly stroking Liam's firm stomach, we plan our day.

'What have you wanted to do ever since you've been here?' I ask.

'Oh, that's easy. You,' replies Liam, prompting a flick on the pectoral from me.

'Sorry,' he adds, turning serious and flipping over onto his side. 'I shouldn't have said that. I mean obviously, I find you incredibly attractive, but I don't want you to think I've been objectifying you. That's not who I am, I hope you know that.'

The earnestness in his voice touches me deep in my gut.

'I know that, Liam, you don't have to apologise. I *love* that you find me attractive. I'm not made of eggshell, I'm pretty tough and squishy.'

His brow crumples. 'I hate that you had to go through that, with that pathetic excuse for a human being. I do get it, you know. I would be cautious of men too if I were you.'

I reach up and press a finger to Liam's lips.

'I'm not. With you, it was all about the job – I was angry that, yet again, my career prospects were going to be squashed because of a good looking guy who everyone loved over transparent, disposable me. The thing is, what I didn't tell you last night, is that around the same time I filed my complaint against Garrett Delaney, Mum got diagnosed with breast cancer. And I know working in a small-town bookshop might not sound like a career to many, but for me it was like slipping on an old pair of comfortable shoes. When I moved back home, I was able to help Mum with hospital visits, spend time with her and Dad, I got my old job back in the bookshop where I'd worked before going to uni and after a while, after a long bloody while, gradually, I became happy again. Mum recovered and I put all that behind me. Also, because karma sometimes delivers, I later learned Delaney had an entire lawsuit of complaints against him. Seems I was far from the only one, although I guess I knew that at the time.'

Liam sinks back against the pillow, as he waits for me to continue.

I sigh, feeling the relief that comes with honesty. 'The truth is, I like being close to home, to my family, my friends. They helped me through a tough patch, and I'll be forever thankful for that. I love working in a bookshop and with Howard retiring in the next couple of months, I was told the management job would almost certainly be mine, which means, given the fact I'm being booted from my house at some point in the near future, I will be able to afford to rent my own place.'

Liam is quiet and I assume he is thinking about his own position.

'How about you? Are you happy working in the bookshop too or is it just to pay the bills? I assume writing for a living is what you'd rather be doing?'

He looks at me blankly, as though he hasn't heard the question, before finally coming to.

'Yes. Writing has always been my first love; I only came to be working for Franklyn's when I moved to Essex to be near a now ex-girlfriend. Before that I've worked all over, different jobs, always something flexible to allow time for my writing.'

'What sort of thing do you write?'

'Crime fiction, cosy mysteries – I suppose you'd call them. I've been shortlisted for awards, had a few short stories published, but never one of my novels.'

'And how is it going? Your writing? I've seen you making notes.'

'Good, thanks. I lost it for a bit after Mikey, but I'm getting there, and this trip's helped too. Perhaps you have a second career, Annabel, as a struggling writer's muse.'

Liam flings back the covers and swings his legs to the floor.

'Now then. To more pressing matters. It's…' he checks his phone 'nearly eleven o' clock on our last day in Greece and I demand we make the most of it. Up you get.'

He yanks the sheet from me, making me shriek, as though I'm a table adorned with crockery, and he's just performed a magic trick.

'Go and get in that shower before I ravish you again.'

We had calculated that despite there being two hours between my flight to Stansted and Liam's to Gatwick, we could share a taxi to the airport at seven o'clock. It would mean I had a few hours to kill after his flight left, but let's face it, I still had seven unread books.

We arranged to meet back at the pool, because he had to go and check out of his hotel room before twelve. A hotel room which had been a thoroughly pointless waste of energy and money, seeing as he'd barely used it for an hour. I took advantage of this time to finish packing, tidy up the apartment then take myself off for a nice relaxing swim.

As I float on an abandoned lilo, pondering the dramatic turn my holiday has taken, I can't quite decide if I am happy about it, or sad that it is coming to an end.

On the one hand, I've run out of money and need to get back to work, which now appears to be less of a bin fire and more of a gently flickering tea light. Owing to Liam's repugnant father, it looks as though Franklyn's is out of trouble, and although that leaves a bitter taste in my mouth, Liam must be practically gagging. But, depending on Crispin Kaufman-Shaw's level of involvement, the urgent need to find a new job has hopefully gone for now.

On the other hand, what happens next? Do Liam and I pick this up back at home? The thought brings a heated smile to my face, which is abruptly wiped off when a sudden jerk sends me faceplanting into the water.

'Bleurgh!' I gasp for breath, spitting out the water that shot up my nose, and wiping it from my eyes, only to see Liam bobbing about in fits of laughter.

'You arsehole!' I cry, immediately, diving for him.

Liam catches me before I reach him and spins me around, trapping me in his arms.

'What were you going to do? Splash me?' he taunts into my ear, before nipping my lobe with his teeth. 'Hate to tell you, but I'm already wet.'

I writhe around in his arms, until he lets me turn to face him.

'Just you wait. It might not be now, it might not be today, but you'd better be ready, 'cause I'm coming for you, and it won't be pretty.'

'Is that a promise?' he murmurs devilishly, making my tummy flip.

'Hey!' a voice cuts across the pool, which is far from empty. In fact, the whole resort has been getting noticeably busier in the last few days as June turned into July and the school holidays drew closer.

We both turn to the direction of the voice, to see Greta standing at the edge of the pool, a wicked grin on her face.

'No canoodling in the pool. Hotel rules!' she says, pointing to the small sign that only states, as far as I can tell, the pool depth.

'Is she serious?' I whisper, mortified.

'No,' says Liam, sounding amused, 'she's just smug.

Greta's been haranguing me since the day I arrived to ask you out on a date.'

I look from Liam to Greta, aghast.

'Whatever would give you the idea I'd want to go on a date? I've done nothing but moan about him.' I don't voice the fact I'd thought she had her eyes on him for herself.

'What was it your man of Shakespeare said? "The woman doth protest too much"?' snorts Greta. 'But, when you lovebirds are done swimming, if that's what you call it, there's someone who wants to see you.'

Liam and I glance at each other, bemused, as Greta slopes back to the bar.

'Come on then, we'd better get a move on anyway if we want to get everything done.' Liam turns to swim to the edge.

'What I want to know,' I ask, halting him at the steps, 'is whether you would have asked me out on a date?'

'I may have done,' he says, lips twitching, 'if you hadn't have said you wouldn't bang me if I was the last man on earth – that kind of sent out a signal, you know.'

'Yeah, well, I would have,' I say.

'What, said yes to a date?'

'Banged you if you were the last man on earth. Even when I thought you were a jerk, I still thought you were hot – a girl has needs, you know.'

I trail a finger from his bottom lip, all the way to the waistband of his shorts, before grabbing hold of the railings and hoisting myself up the steps, relishing the fact I've left Liam needing to do another quick length before also climbing from the pool.

When we are dried and dressed, we make our way to the bar area.

To our mutual astonishment, the slight woman seated at the bar sipping a cappuccino turns at our approach, jumps from her stool and commences a passionate, incomprehensible imploring.

'Maria? What's wrong?'

I'm hit by a horrible thought. Has something happened at home? As the only point of contact between Clare and myself, would she be the messenger of terrible news? I scrabble around for my phone, realising I haven't even looked at it since meeting Liam last night.

Oh God, what's happened? And *where* is my phone? It must still be in the apartment.

'Wait, this is Maria?' pipes up Liam, happily. 'Hello,' he says, thrusting out a hand. 'I'm Liam. Thanks so much for looking after us.'

This prompts another torrent of Greek from Maria, complemented by hand on heart, wiping of brow and at one point the signing of the cross upon her breast.

Mercifully, Greta reappears with a tray of empty glasses and takes matters into hand.

'Maria is very upset,' she says, stating the somewhat obvious.

'She has only today discovered, when I bumped into her at the fishmongers, that you,' she points at me 'are not Clare, and you,' she points at Liam, 'are not Clare's lover.'

'Lover?' we both say at the same time.

'Yeah,' says Greta, wincing. 'Apparently Clare regularly uses the apartment when she fancies a spot of extramarital fun.'

Liam and I look at each other in bewilderment.

'Maria has met Richard in person, but never Clare. And there have been many other male guests, so it did not seem unusual.'

The penny begins to drop.

'So, wait, she thought I was Clare, and Liam was my bit on the side?'

'I'm not sure what to think about that,' says Liam, amused. 'Other than it makes sense now that Richard's making life difficult for her.'

'Perhaps she was not as discreet as she thinks?' I offer.

'She is a complete idiot if she thinks the people who live here and work here don't notice what happens under our nose,' snorts Greta, leaving us in little doubt as to her feelings about the woman. 'There have been more men go in and out of that apartment than seats on an aeroplane to bring them here.'

I shoot Liam a scandalised grin. This was pretty much the ultimate office gossip and whilst it made my skin crawl to think of the goings-on in the place we'd just been, well, going *in*, it also goes some way to explain the decanting of what Maria thought to be Clare's case and the decanting of Liam's rucksack later in the week. Maria must have simply assumed another of Clare's 'guests' had arrived.

Greta continues, 'When I saw Maria this morning, she was quite upset about the situation, said she felt like she worked for a…' she searched around for the word, and settled, diplomatically on 'woman with bad morals.'

'*Disgusting* hooker!' Maria hisses passionately, having comprehended quite well.

'And she wanted to apologise for any inappropriate conclusions,' finished Greta.

'There is no apology necessary,' says Liam earnestly, making my heart contract as he drapes an arm around my shoulders, 'we've had a wonderful holiday and we're grateful for your hard work.'

Greta gives me a knowing smile, which I return, physically unable to keep my lips from tugging upwards.

Later, as we traipse in and out of the shops of Kassiopi buying last-minute souvenirs for friends, I'm struck by how attentive and friendly Liam is to literally everyone he meets. No wonder he's popular, I observe with a pang of guilt; he greets every single person with enthusiasm and genuine interest, almost to the point of nosiness. The Greek lady currently talking him through her wares appears rapt at his questions, possibly too enamoured, I think, scowling at a set of polished red nails that briefly settle on his forearm.

'What do you think of this? I've never seen one this big, have you?' he asks, breaking into my thoughts.

Given the stylishness of the olive wood kitchenware on the shelves around us, I'm quite shocked at what Liam is brandishing. That is, until I register the object is, in fact, a giant pestle to accompany the sizeable mortar in his other hand.

'My, that's a beast!' I enthuse, 'got a lot of pounding and grinding in mind back home, have you?'

Liam's lip curves, 'I was actually thinking of Mom, she makes a mean curry. This, on the other hand,' he says, plucking a colossal, polished pepper mill from a shelf, 'has your name written *all* over it. The bigger the tool, the spicier the result, right?'

'Excellent choice,' remarks the shopkeeper with delight, entirely missing the volley of childish smut batting between us.

'Absolutely,' I agree, nodding sagely. 'Although, as keepsakes go…' I point to a chess board on a table display at my right, and select the smallest piece on the board, pinching the tiny wooden pawn between my thumb and forefinger. 'There's just something about this that reminds me of the first night I got here.' I let my gaze drift into the middle distance as I pretend to ponder. 'Nope, can't put my finger on it.'

The woman beams and looks from Liam to me and back again.

Liam caves first, 'We'll take this please,' he says, handing his pestle and mortar over and flashing me a look of mock horror once her back is turned, followed by a stomach-flipping grin. 'I think you might need a lesson in geometry, dear. How long until we have to check out of the apartment?'

# CHAPTER 23

We head back to the apartment anyway, both weighed down with souvenirs. I was already regretting the matching phallus-shaped bottles of kumquat liqueur I'd bought for both Vik and Jess; the fairest way to avoid the inevitable squabbles if they didn't both get one. I just hoped I could find a way to tessellate the penises into my already rammed suitcase. I'd plumped for the far safer option of traditional tacky tea towels for my parents and Howard and planned to use them as padding.

It seemed only right we make full use of our pitstop and therefore use our remaining time and access to the bed, each other and the shower wisely, before finishing up the packing and leaving Villa Karina for the last time.

'I'm going to miss this place,' I say, shooting one last glance at the view before closing the balcony doors.

'Me too,' agrees Liam. 'Apart from the sofa bed. I won't miss that.'

I plant a kiss on his cheek. 'If you'd owned up to your mysterious alter ego sooner, you might have had the comfy bed.'

'Seriously? You'd sleep with someone on the basis they wrote nice messages in a book?'

I shoot him a meaningful look. 'Maybe, if they were also pretty cute.'

Liam flashes me a grin but seems distracted. He makes no further comment and picks up our bags from the floor.

We have booked a taxi to collect us in the village and take us somewhere we've both decided will be a truly fitting end to our holiday. However, as we approach the main square, hot, sticky and loaded down, a familiar sight emerges from a shop across the road and my internal body temperature slides up another notch.

'Hold that,' I hiss, thrusting the handle of my suitcase at Liam who, looks back at me, puzzled.

It wasn't so much the people that snagged in my peripheral vision, as what one of them was wearing – the garment that was seared into my memory banks with a guilty hot poker.

'Excuse me,' I say firmly, blocking the French couple's path. 'You might remember my friend over there from the boat trip the other day?'

The man glances across the road, catches sight of Liam, and visibly bristles.

Liam, to his credit, gives him a toothy, comedy wave.

I, on the other hand, feel nowhere near as ambivalent.

'Now, I know your fancy chemise was un *chapeau* from your girlfriend,' (at least *I hope* that is the word for gift). I also hope my sarcastic emphasis on the word and meaningful look at bikini-babe may have acted as a warning, which judging by her startled Jessica Rabbit-like face, it has. 'But I have *un proposition* for you.' I take a stab in the dark that our lexicons overlap here and pronounce everything as though auditioning for an *'Allo 'Allo* revival.

'My shirt is a hat? What are you talking about, you mad woman?' scoffs the Frenchman, looking at me most uncharitably.

Ah, *cadeau*, not chapeau, I remember belatedly.

I shake my head, keen to get to the point.

'Your English is clearly better than my French, so I'll cut to the chase. I would like to buy your shirt. I have...' I dip into my shoulder bag, the one I use for travel, fingers closing around a melted Twix from my outgoing flight, which I retrieve along with my purse. I unzip it and empty the contents into my hands to count. 'I have, er, thirty-seven euros and fifteen cents. And a Twix. Every penny I have to my name, more than enough to purchase yourself a perfectly decent replacement from any of these fine establishments.'

I sweep an arm to indicate the three or four gift shops within our vicinity.

The man looks from me to his girlfriend and back again, then laughs out loud.

'What is this? Are you con artists or something? What do you want from me? I should call the police.'

At this, his girlfriend's eyes widen.

I decide to take a different angle.

'No, sir, we are not criminals. Look,' I say, whipping my head around to make certain Liam hasn't crept up behind me. 'I believe you are a man of faith?' This is a punt, based entirely on my hope that the cross dangling from a silver chain nestled against his chest is there for more than just decoration. 'My friend has a terrible illness.' I lower my voice to a whisper. 'It has affected him badly. He's not quite himself, if you know what I mean. He's convinced that when he prayed in the Church of Panagia Kassopitra, the Holy Virgin appeared to him and told him he would only recover if he found his missing shirt.'

I see I have now not only got the attention of the Frenchman, but the silently pleading, startled eyes of his girlfriend.

'Now, I can't say as I remember if he had a shirt that looked like this one, but he is convinced of it. Believes he's sick because of that very shirt. Now, if I were a betting woman, I'd say a nice young couple like you would welcome the opportunity to help a fellow Christian.'

I pause, giving his girlfriend a stare to warn her that I *will* tell her boyfriend she stole his 'gift' from the church basket.

'And of course, there is the thirty-seven euros and fifteen cents, Luca,' she adds quickly, with a hand on his arm, the bitch.

'And the Twix,' I mumble, as though that might seal the deal.

Luca glances over to Liam and I pray he doesn't decide to go over there himself.

A silver saloon with radio blaring roars to a halt.

'That's our taxi, we have to leave now. What do you say?'

Then, he nods, and just like that, he slips his arms from the open shirt, revealing an incredibly taut, gym-honed physique and hands it to me.

In return, I hand him a fist full of loose change, banknotes and the chocolate, grin my thanks and bolt towards Liam and the waiting car.

'How the hell did you manage that?' asks Liam, gobsmacked, as he cradles Mikey's shirt as we sit in the back of the taxi.

'Pulled a few strings,' I reply, neglecting to admit I'd practically imbued the garment with a mythical mental leprosy, and Luca couldn't take it off fast enough. 'Although I'm afraid you're going to have to pay for dinner.'

'Fair swap,' he says, pulling me in to a hug. 'You know, in a way, it's like Mikey went on his own little Corfu adventure without me. Who knows where this has been?'

'From the smell of it,' I say, wrinkling my nose, 'up every mountain and into every brothel. Perhaps not quite the experience you had in mind.'

Liam laughs and I open my bag to stuff it in, his rucksack being in the boot. I spot the pilfered copy of *My Family and Other Animals*, which we'd unanimously agreed not to return to the shelves.

'First thing I'm going to do as manager,' I say, handling it fondly, 'is set up a travel section in our shop, whether Franklyn's approve or not. I'll order in copies of this book, and the rest of the trilogy. Our customers are always asking for holiday reads and it's so much more than that. Perhaps I'll come over to see how it's done in your shop, get some inspiration.'

Liam mumbles an acknowledgement, falling quiet to look out the window.

It only occurs to me then to wonder if Liam's expectations of where this goes between us, once we're back home in Essex, may wildly differ from mine.

What if this was just a holiday fling for him?

# CHAPTER 24

'So... this is it! The place where Gerald Durrell got most of his inspiration. The White House, Kalami.'

Liam pulls our luggage from the boot of the taxi, while I wait on the roadside.

'Yes,' I reply, 'although apparently, this was Gerry's brother Lawrence's house, rather than the family home in the TV show, but I gather he spent a lot of time here. Who'd have thought we'd finally bond over a dog-eared copy of a memoir from 1956?'

Liam smiles, crossing the road as the taxi drives away, but doesn't comment.

We are shown to an outside seating area overlooking a bay as beautiful as any I've seen so far on this island, azure blue sea gently lapping at an almost deserted beach as day turns into evening.

I open the menu. This is not a cheap restaurant – not outrageous, by any means, but considering I gave every last euro I owned to Luca, it makes me feel slightly awkward.

'This looks lovely,' says Liam, oohing as he reads through the dishes on offer.

I skim the menu quickly, looking for the cheaper salad options.

'The Octopus Carpaccio starter sounds delicious, so does the Lobster. Fancy sharing a few dishes, unless there's anything you particularly want?'

I chance a glance up at him, as he devours the options, and decide honesty is always the best policy.

'Liam,' I start.

He glances up, frowning at the seriousness in my tone.

'What is it?'

'Nothing. This is lovely. It's just that when I said I'd given all my money to Luca, I meant it – not just the last of my euros, I have no money left. I checked my banking app this morning, and I've got literally nothing until payday. I used all my savings, which were pitiful, even by my standards, to take this holiday.'

Liam nods, taking on board what I'm saying.

'It's ok, Annie, I said this would be my treat.'

'Yes, I know,' I hasten to assure him, 'and that's lovely, but I just wanted you to know. Because when we get back home,' a blush instantly warms my cheeks, 'that is, if you'd like for us to still see each other, then things are going to be tight for me for a while. Until I get my promotion at least. I'm just hoping the house will take a while to sell, give me chance to save up a bit.'

Liam shuffles in his seat, and gives me a tight smile.

'Of course I want us to see each other when we get home. I wouldn't care if you lived in a cardboard box. Well, obviously, that would be fucking horrible, but what I mean is, I don't care about things like that. I live frugally, in a one-bedroom apartment, on a salary that's frankly a bit of a joke. Maybe in the future I'll want more, but I've been focusing on healing for a while and having the head space to get back to my writing has been a big part of that.'

'Me too,' I confess. 'I fell apart after what happened at *Sunday Living*. Moved back in with my parents and let them and my friends take care of me for a while. Getting my old job back in the bookshop made me feel like myself again. I know I'm not setting the world on fire, but one day I want to open my own bookshop, one where I decide what to stock and where I can provide what the community wants. Until then, I'm happy.'

'Then that's all that matters.'

This felt like the frankest conversation I'd had with anyone for a long time. I rarely liked to voice the fact my experience at the magazine had shaken me. It had shattered my confidence, desecrated my trust and set fire to my ambitions. I'd talked to Jess at length about it, and once she'd got past the stage of wanting to go straight to Garrett's office and take out his spleen with a box-cutter stage, she'd been my rock. Gradually, she and Vik had coaxed me off the sofa and back into the world, albeit the sedentary Langtree version. But I had to face some uncomfortable truths; despite projecting a persona as spiky as a pineapple, inside I was just a Pina colada – totally kitsch, a little tangy and best enjoyed on a beach back in 1988 with a good old-fashioned paperback.

I might try to maintain an air of nonchalance, but I am simply not cut out for competition, or pretence – either from myself or those around me.

We order our food and I attempt to lighten the mood by telling Liam about Ash's foray into AC-12 territory, and Jess and Stu's upcoming beach-hopping extravaganza, but he seems distant. His eyes, which are normally so lively, seem almost shuttered. It's possible he's just extremely tired, given we got little sleep, although I wouldn't change that outcome for all the kumquats in Greece.

'I hope you won't hold it against them,' I add.

'Hmm?' he asks, dragging his attention back to me.

'Jess and Vik? I was just saying I hope you won't hold their futile attempts to screw with your Saturday trading against them. They were only looking out for me, albeit in an Austin Powers kind of way.'

He gives me a weak smile.

'And,' I continue, 'to be fair, Jess has long been a closet fan. "Immensely shaggable" was how I believe she referred to you once.'

'A nicer compliment was never received,' he remarks with an attempt at levity, taking a deep swig of his ice-cold beer.

'And yet...' I say, cocking an eyebrow. 'Why do I get the sense you're holding something back? Have I said something to upset you?'

Liam shakes his head fervently. 'Of course not. And I can't wait to meet your friends properly, minus their most unconvincing disguises.'

'You suspected?'

'Who am I to judge? You'd be surprised how many eccentric characters come into the shop. We once had a gentleman in the full Sherlock Holmes garb, cape, hat, the lot – and it wasn't even World Book Day.'

He's smiling, but it isn't reaching his eyes. I've spent enough time with him this week to see something has changed. I have no idea what and can only deduce that he is starting to regret this – us.

Our starters arrive, delivered not by blustery, red-faced brothers on mismatched crockery, but by smart, uniformed waiters who carefully place plain white dishes onto bright white linen. It's a beautiful setting, and the food looks divine, but I can't help longing for the rustic charm of The Olive Grove.

I muse out loud, 'I wonder if Franklyn's will stump up a holiday next year for "Employee of the Year", once Clare and Richard's apartment has sold, or do you think it really was just a ruse to impress your father?'

Liam has a forkful of seafood halfway to his mouth but pauses at my words. Places his fork back down.

He lets out a long sigh.

'Trust me, I highly doubt my father even knew I worked there. They were wasting their money if they thought that would sway him.'

I snort. 'Well, their loss is your gain. Mine too, I hope,' I add, tentatively.

Liam closes his eyes and drags a palm across his chin, and I feel the blood drain from my face.

'Annie,' he says, his tone quiet and serious.

'No,' I stutter, mortification settling over me, horror that I've read this all wrong. 'Please,' I'm embarrassed to hear the shake in my voice. 'Please.' I cough, then start again, 'Don't. You don't need to say anything. We'll just enjoy this last meal, get on our separate flights and return to our hometowns, as though nothing ever happened. It doesn't need to be a big deal. Please, don't make it a big deal.'

A flash of hurt passes across Liam's eyes.

'Is that honestly what you think?'

I force my voice to remain even. 'We wouldn't be the first to cross a professional line Liam, and we won't be the last. We're grown adults, it doesn't have to affect our working lives.'

His handsome face crinkles in confusion. 'I couldn't give a shit about professionalism; we sell fantasies for a living, not lifesaving drugs, although there might be a good argument for them being equally relevant.'

'So, what's the problem then?' I demand. 'Why are you looking at your expensive lobster as though you've just been served up your last meal on death row?'

Eventually, he raises doleful eyes from his lap to mine.

'There's something I haven't told you. Something important.'

Icy tendrils of unease tiptoe their way through my bloodstream, making me feel cold, despite the warm evening air.

'At first, I wasn't sure how to tell you, then as I've got to know you better it's become harder and harder to bring it up.'

'Right... ok, I'm getting a little nervous here. And I'm kind of struggling to see how anything can be worse than telling me the shirt I chucked away belonged to your cherished late brother. Is it worse?'

'That's just an object, Annie, I know how sorry you were.

I truly appreciate you getting it back, but I'd never have held it against you if you hadn't. This is different.'

I push my plate away and sit up straighter.

'You're going to have to help me out here, I'm afraid.'

Liam scratches his neck, visibly uncomfortable.

'You asked me how I got the keys for the apartment. I told you someone from head office brought them into the bookstore, but what I didn't tell you was that the area manager brought them to me two days before my flight, along with some rather unpalatable news.'

My first thought is relief, that whatever he's going to tell me has to do with work, rather than anything that has happened between us.

But then Liam speaks again, and I begin to understand where this is going.

'When your friends spoke with Clem the other day, she had some of the facts from an internal newsletter explaining about the Kaufman-Shaw investment, but she didn't have them all. Yes, the Franklyn's chain has been saved from possible collapse, but the Chelmsford store hasn't. When it came down to the economics of the situation, it seems the Langtree premises offer far greater value for money. Cheaper rates, cheaper rent, no immediate competition and the scope to expand up into two more storeys above it.'

'But that's residential, there are tenants in those flats,' I say, in disbelief.

Liam practically sneers. 'Franklyn's will always find a way to get what they want. Especially now my father is on board. If you think they've been a ruthless operation thus far, you've seen nothing yet.'

'And I'm guessing the reason you've not enlightened me on this turn of events, isn't because an enormous hike in salary to reflect my expanding place of work awaits me back home.'

Even I flinch at the coldness that's crept into my voice.

'No,' says Liam, looking as though he'd rather take a running jump into the deep blue sea beside us than explain himself. He chews the side of his mouth, then pulls the pin out of his grenade. 'Howard is being given gardening leave until his retirement date and I am to step into his shoes as manager of the Langtree store. I will be permitted to bring three members of my team to work alongside you and your existing staff. They have a working timescale of six weeks in mind, before the transition is complete.'

I open my mouth to speak but nothing comes out.

After a brief spell impersonating a goldfish, I finally utter, 'But Howard would have told me.'

'Really? If Howard is even aware of the plans, and I'm not sure he is, would he have risked ruining your holiday, rather than waiting for you to get back?'

I already knew the answer to that question. No, of course he would not have done that.

'But *you* knew,' I say, with a low, quiet anger that is almost overwhelming. 'You've known since before you even got here and yet you've said nothing. You've spent an entire week with me, knowing how important that bookshop is to me, how important my job is to me.' My voice cracks and my eyes burn, 'and after everything I told you about that... that *utter arsehole* in my last job, still you kept this from me?'

Liam looks away, unable, it seems, to tolerate my emotional reaction to his bombshell.

Well, tough. I AM emotional. I am hurt, angry and embarrassed. Feeling like I've been taken for a fool and ashamed of myself for letting another bloody man get one over on me.

'It wasn't like that,' he mutters. 'When we found ourselves double-booked in the apartment, I realised it could be a golden opportunity to get to know each other properly, especially if we were going to be working together. I thought you would be happy the Langtree store had been saved.'

I let out a hollow laugh.

'If you think I would be happy that perfectly innocent paying tenants are to be ejected from their homes to further line the pockets of a multinational conglomerate, just so they can save a few quid on business rates, then I'm afraid you have rather misunderstood who I am, Liam.'

I push back my chair and toss down my napkin, immediately wanting, needing to be away from here.

'Annie,' says Liam, jumping to his feet and causing an approaching waiter bearing our main courses to shrink back in alarm. 'I do understand. Really. And I hadn't appreciated until these last couple of days how much you needed that promotion. I would never have planned to undermine you like that; I didn't get a choice.'

At this my head buzzes with rage.

'A choice? Of course you had a choice. You're the son of a fucking billionaire, Liam, you don't even need a job. My career, my hometown, the shop, we're all just pieces on a Monopoly board to someone like that. And you're quite happy to just let him trample us underfoot, whilst you charm everyone you meet into thinking you're God's humble gift.'

By now I'm aware of several heads turned in our direction, as well as what I presume to be the head waiter, edging our way.

'It's not like that. I'm not like that. I thought I'd made that clear.'

'And I thought I'd made it Swarovski crystal clear I would never be an entitled man's disposable plaything, NEVER again. I should have trusted my instincts about you from the start. You know, if you'd just have been honest, held up your hands and admitted what Franklyn's had in store, this could have turned out very, very differently. But you've let me humiliate myself before you. Just another controlling guy who thought he could get what he wanted, on his own terms.'

'Sir, Madam?' ventures the waiter, having now approached the table.

'It's fine,' I retort, not meeting his eye. 'I'm going. He's picking up the bill.'

And with that, I stride over to the low wall where my

suitcase had been stowed, pull up the handle and drag it loudly away across the stone floor, back through the restaurant and out into the street.

Once outside, I check myself. Willing away the solid ball that has lodged in my throat and blinking at the hot tears already coating my lashes. Fleetingly, I wonder if Liam will follow me, but after a few minutes and no sign of him, I continue walking until I spot a bench, then I take out my phone and retrieve the card from my purse, given to me by the taxi driver on the day of my arrival, and begin to dial.

# CHAPTER 25

Hardly even registering the breakneck speed of my driver this time around, I arrive at the airport five hours early for my flight, approximately one hour, by my reckoning, ahead of Liam, who is doubtlessly working his way through our main courses back at the restaurant. This included a pitstop at a cashpoint to withdraw the taxi fare from a credit card I keep for emergencies – the fees will be eye-watering, but when needs must...

I silently will the lengthy security queue to hurry up and diminish so I can find a dark, lonely corner to curl up in until I'm safely aboard my flight. As though even through my own limited experience, a dark lonely corner has ever been commonplace in a small, but busy international airport.

Finally, after an embarrassing spot check of my suitcase, which bore two glass bottle penises, my vibrators and the surplus condoms, causing the female security clerk to eyeball me with something like admiration, I collapse onto a plastic seat at the furthest and emptiest gate. One unexpected bonus of the suitcase inspection was the discovery of a stray five euros rolling around with my knickers, so I have been able to procure a coffee and a small tub of Pringles, which apart from one mouthful of lobster will be all that sustains me until I get home.

I make many futile attempts to distract myself with a book, something I'm starting to doubt will ever be possible again, whilst around me the seats gradually fill up. My own gate won't be announced until much closer to my flight time of eleven fifteen and I'm loath to leave my seat even if it becomes standing room only. The only thing right now that would make me budge would be if Liam sat down beside me.

As I force myself to reread the same paragraph for a seventh time, I'm dimly aware of someone settling onto the adjoining seat which, linked as they are by a supporting bar, has a slight see-saw effect on mine. I glance sideways at the knees beside mine and immediately recognise the tanned, muscular legs and the washed-out cotton shorts.

Liam has sat down beside me.

'Annabel,' he says, quietly. 'Please let me explain.'

'Go and find somewhere else to sit. I don't want to talk to you.'

'This is my gate. I'll be boarding soon.'

In my keenness to find the furthest corner of the airport, it hadn't even occurred to me to check where Liam's flight was departing from.

I gather up my things and get up from my seat.

'Annie, wait. We need to talk.'

'Nothing more to say. Have a nice flight,' I say immaturely in a phoney American accent, before turning on my heel.

Then abruptly I do a U-turn, remembering I still have something of his.

'You'll be wanting this.' I say, tossing him Mikey's shirt.

There is a desolate sadness in his eyes as they flick from mine down to the balled-up garment in his lap and I just catch the way his hands curl around it, hugging it tight before I turn on my heel. As I walk away, an image plants itself in my mind, and I remember the beautiful sea-urchin shells, sitting forgotten in the dish on the kitchen table. My own treasure, gone.

By the time I emerge into the chilly, dawn gloom of the Stansted Airport Pick Up Point, I'm so tired I don't even spot

Jess waiting in her entirely obvious tangerine-orange Toyota. She honks her horn, startling me, then waves incredulous hands in the air as though I'm as thick as chips.

Jess had drawn the short straw in our game of airport taxi roulette. The three of us had always agreed a favour given was a favour owed rather than forking out for taxis. It helped of course that we only lived a mere half an hour from the airport, but middle of the night collections were never fun for anyone.

'Thanks so much for coming out, Jess,' I say, as my friend jumps out of the car to give me a quick hug.

'You're welcome. We've got a holiday booked too, remember?' she counters, as though any of us could forget.

'Put my name down,' I say.

'Oh, don't worry I have. Vik's already baggsied the pickup, so you've got the drop off. Heathrow five am.'

'Magic. Sleep is over-rated anyway,' I say, yawning.

'So,' prompts Jess, navigating her way out of the carpark, 'tell me what happened with the bonkable billionaire after he caught you slagging him off on FaceTime? No, wait don't tell me,' she says, holding up a palm. 'You discovered deep down he's a philanthropist, with a weak spot for outraged socialist bookworms and after a heated row, you tore each other's clothes off and had wild sex for the rest of your trip. Am I right?'

'And there was I believing you'd never read a Mills and Boon in your life.'

'Not since I was twelve and stayed at my Gran's. But that's not the point. You take the plot of every single romance novel and movie ever written from *Pride and Prejudice* to *You've Got Mail* and it will break down to two opinionated people flirting and sparring until one of them drops their hanky and bends down to find a hard-on in their face. You two have been flirting and sparring since you met. I was watching, remember, when you dropped your proverbial hanky. The sexual tension on that balcony was tighter than Darcy's breeches.'

Jess's reference to *You've Got Mail* sets my teeth on edge.

An unsuspecting bookseller falling in love with a mystery pen pal only to find he's the mogul running her bookshop out of town? If only she knew how close to the mark she'd just been.

'Trust me, Jess, there's way more to *Pride and Prejudice*. And Liam's no Mr Darcy. If you dropped your hanky around him, he'd blow his nose on it first then hand it back with a grin on his face.'

Jess side-eyes me, then after a beat, 'So what happened? Really? Because you don't look like someone in a state of post-holiday bliss.'

A brief memory of Liam's hot lips snaking an exploratory trail across my stomach flashes across my mind and I physically flinch at the memory. Bliss had been exactly my state of being for several long, luxurious hours, before the wool had been so cruelly wrenched from my eyes.

'I don't want to talk about it, if that's all right,' I say into the darkness of the car.

'OK,' she says, 'OK,' with a comforting squeeze to my knee.

It's almost two o'clock when Jess drops me home.

Exactly one week since I'd let myself into that Greek apartment with the excited anticipation of a summer holiday. It seems so long ago now — a lot can happen in a week.

Declining Jess's offers of help, I haul my bags from her boot and promise to meet her for coffee the following day, waving goodbye as she drives away, then I put my key into the lock.

Life, sometimes, has a nasty habit of parodying itself, and I often have the vague expectation the cast of Monty Python will spring from a cupboard singing 'Always Look on the Bright Side of Life.' Never is this better illustrated than when I switch on the hallway light and find Travis emerging from my downstairs toilet, one week after a similar scenario – although it feels like a lifetime ago.

I can't even be bothered to jump. Surprise is an emotion currently unavailable to me.

'What are you doing here, Travis?' I ask wearily, depositing my luggage on the floor and traipsing through to the kitchen to flip on the kettle.

'Waiting for you to get back. Did you have a nice time? Great tan.' He sounds uncharacteristically chipper for a man whom I've only ever seen get excited at triple word scores in Scrabble.

'Lovely, thanks. Look, I'm very tired and I know from experience you're normally in bed by ten-thirty, so can you just cut to the chase, seeing as whatever it is clearly won't wait until tomorrow?'

I watch the forced jollity slide from his lips and recognise the familiar folded arm stance that normally preceded news of a business trip, or meetings. Meetings that in all likelihood I would not have found in his work diary.

'Yes, sorry. Well, there's no easy way to say this, Annie, but rather unexpectedly, I received an offer on the house whilst you were away.' He says his next words with all the gravitas of a lottery winner, '*Cash buyer.*'

'I see,' I say, heart rate spiking, despite a severe lack of caffeine in the past twelve hours. 'And do I presume you have accepted this offer?'

Travis's eyes actually twinkle. I've never seen them twinkle.

'You bet I did. The gentleman wanted to be closer to his elderly mother, lives a few doors down...'

'Mrs Hadley?' I interrupt, mentally running though our neighbours.

'That's right. Her son's a—'

'Barrister.' I finish the sentence for him.

'Quite. Anyway, it doesn't sound as though money is an object, he just really wants this house. Said he'd been hoping it would come on the market.'

'How very fortunate for him,' I say, with barely concealed sarcasm.

To be fair, it was a lovely house. A detached Victorian former schoolmaster's lodge in red brick, with parking, which was a rarity in town.

'And how quickly does the agent envisage this sale will go through?' I have to forcibly bring myself to ask the question, dreading the response.

'Well, that's just it,' says Travis, treating me to a sympathetic half smile. 'We've already exchanged. Completion should be by the end of the week. I didn't want to start packing any of your belongings up, that would be far too inappropriate. But I have made a start on the furniture.'

It's only as he says it that I look towards the adjoining dining room. Inexplicably, I hadn't yet noticed the dining table and chairs had vanished.

'You're not serious?' Anger flashes through me, galvanising me to life.

Before he can say another word, I storm off down the corridor and fling open the lounge door, staring gobsmacked into the empty room. There are two large patches of sumptuous soft carpet where the sofas had been, stark against the remaining well-trodden weave.

'You can't do this!' I cry, rounding on him as he appears in the doorway. 'You can't dismantle my home whilst I'm on holiday and give me two days to find somewhere else to live!'

Travis merely sighs, unphased by my outburst.

'To be fair, Annie, you've had plenty of time to find somewhere to live. I moved out months ago, to give you the space and time to make arrangements.'

'You moved out,' I spit, 'to shack up with your horse-faced hussy. Don't do me the indignity of pretending it was for my own good. If little Miss-Many-Acres had been prepared to slum it for a bit whilst Daddy built a new west wing for you, you'd both have booted me out of here faster than you can say Harris Tweed.'

'I've left the television,' he says, ignoring my insults. 'And all the kitchenware, bedding and linen. I'm not heartless, I know you'll need to replace all those things wherever you move to next.'

I puff out my cheeks. 'How big of you. I'll be sure to throw up prayers of sincere thanks to the merciful benefactor that is Travis Goodman, that he gave me pots to piss in, when I have no cooker, no kitchen and no fucking bed to sleep in.'

'I've also left the bed,' he mutters, looking down at the floor.

'Hallelujah. I don't know what I'd have done if I'd had to sleep on the streets without a pocket-sprung mattress.'

'I know you're upset, Annie, but do you think there is any need to be quite so unreasonable? The house is mine, after all.'

I start to shake my head, slowly at first, in genuine disbelief. How could I have got things so wrong? Travis had seemed like such a gentleman, after my experience with that animal Delaney. And as for Liam…

'You need to leave. Now, Travis,' I say, desperate to fall into bed and for this day to be over.

He holds his hands up as though I've given him a narrow window to flee before opening both barrels of a shotgun into the back of his head.

'OK, I'm going.'

'For what it's worth,' I snarl, right before shutting the door in his face. 'When you invite someone to live with you, propose marriage to them, let them do the housework, the cooking, the shopping, the gardening, choose new worktops and colour schemes, don't be surprised when they treat it like their home too. Something you might want to bear in mind, as you take a turn about the estate and retire to the drawing room for a cigar. Because take it from me, you might well live there now, but it will never be yours. I'd cling for dear life to whatever killing you make on this place if I were you, you'll never know when you might need it.'

# CHAPTER 26

Sloping back to my mum and dad's with a car full of possessions and asking for my old room back was easier than having to go and see Howard.

I'd phoned in sick for the first few days after returning from Corfu, feigning stomach upset. Travis had left me in the uncompromising position of having to vacate my home immediately, and since there weren't enough hours in the day to do three full shifts at work, pack and move house, it felt easier than supplying the truth. Howard would understand, when I explained, but I couldn't face it right away.

Dad had seemed rather pleased to have me back, declaring it always my home no matter how old I was, whilst Mum became concerned.

'It's not like it was before,' I'd assured her, as she hovered by my door with a duster. 'I just need somewhere for a few weeks whilst I get the money together for a deposit on a flat.' Although the truth was that even outside of London as we were, I could likely only afford a room.

'You know you're always welcome, love, I'm just worried about you.'

'I know you are Mum. But you don't need to be. I'm not back there again. Promise.'

She'd enveloped me in a tight hug, and I'd breathed in her familiar scent, a mix of Herbal Essence shampoo and her favourite cheap Avon perfume. It didn't matter how many expensive brands we bought her as gifts, she always drifted back to this sweet, musky scent.

During these miserable few days, in which I sorted through clothes, shoes, bags, books, photos and everything else I owned, I also fielded multiple calls from Jess and Vik. The easiest thing seemed to be to maintain the 'something I ate' line and buy myself some time, although that did also require me to spin my mum into the yarn, so Jess wouldn't feel compelled to bang my door down with bowls of homemade chicken soup.

When mum asked me why I was hiding from my friends, I couldn't even give her an answer. The truth was, I didn't know. Perhaps it was pride, or perhaps it went deeper. Perhaps I felt if I started talking about everything that had happened in Corfu and since I got home, it might unravel something in me I wanted to remain safely spooled away. I had to regain control of my life, before I could even begin to dissect it.

On Monday morning, almost a week after arriving home, I finally steel myself to face Howard.

I don't work on Mondays, so with Tom there to hold the fort, I plan to abduct Howard for a cuppa and a chat. I will explain I simply cannot work for Liam, and I will be handing in my resignation. It seems likely Howard will be pushed into an earlier retirement than expected, so I'm not concerned my leaving will be in any way to his detriment.

I tug on my jeans and an ancient Supergrass t-shirt, because even though it's a pleasantly warm July day, I still haven't got around to doing any washing, despite Mum's best efforts to prise armfuls of it from my bedroom floor. It feels alien, encasing my toes in socks and trainers after nearly a fortnight of slopping around in my flip-flops and I experience a pang of loss for our apartment in Greece. With its panoramic view of Kassiopi, the clattering sounds of dishes, splashing, rapid-fire Greek from within the maze of buildings below and the faint beat from someone's Bluetooth speaker, it still managed to be peaceful, and I yearned to be back there. Whether that yearning was for the place, or for the often flummoxing, yet at the same time thrilling, company, I couldn't tell.

Armed with the speech I'd rehearsed in the shower and the tea towel I'd bought for Howard as a souvenir, I cover the length of Langtree High Street with purpose.

What I'm not prepared for, as I push on the door and stroll across the shop floor, is the sight of Howard and Theresa, our area manager, engaged in deep discussion at the sales desk, along with a third familiar face, Daphne. A heavy sadness settles in the pit of my stomach.

All three of them look up at me as I approach, and I register a startled expression on Howard's face. Today is going to be even more uncomfortable than I'd feared.

'Annie,' says Theresa, greeting me like an old friend. 'How lovely to see you, I do hope you're feeling better? Eat a dodgy prawn, did you? I got ill from a kebab once in Turkey, never eaten one since. Much better to stick to plain food when one's abroad, I always think, much safer.'

'Mm,' I agree, non-committal, thinking how well she and my dad would get along.

'It's great to see you love,' says Howard, with genuine warmth. I notice there are three steaming mugs of coffee on the counter, along with a stack of files and paperwork.

Daphne offers a thin-lipped smile, which I take to be indifference. Perhaps she has no qualms at all about making innocent people homeless if it means a slightly higher return on rent.

'Theresa is just running through some urgent head-office business,' explains Howard, widening his eyes to signal something to me, but in the absence of telepathic powers, I remain clueless.

'No worries at all. I only popped in for a chat.' I cradle the tea towel tightly to my chest, unwilling to present it with an audience. 'Is Tom out back? I'll say a quick hi before I go.'

Howard coughs as I start to make my way to the staff kitchenette and before I can puzzle through his code, I find myself walking straight into the path of Liam Shaw, a mug of hot coffee in hand.

I have a visceral response to seeing him again, every nerve ending in my body electrocharged at the shock of seeing him here. His sun-kissed skin and golden hair contrast strikingly with the deep navy of his Franklyn's polo shirt – it feels so out of context seeing him like this; faded shorts and bare feet replaced with smart trousers and tan brogues.

Despite my body's reaction to finding him here, it doesn't escape my notice he's carrying the Harry Potter mug I'd immediately claimed as my own when it arrived with some publisher freebies.

'Annie,' he says, recovering himself enough to make his mouth work, something I seem to be having trouble with. 'I didn't think you were rostered to work today.'

Seriously? He didn't consider there was even a slight chance I'd come by my place of work, in the very small town where I live? That, lo, I may even have wanted to purchase a book?

'So I gather. Well, it's nice to know you're wasting no time getting your feet under the table. Would you like me to go and buy you a nice cream cake to go with the coffee you're having in my mug, whilst you plan the detail of taking over my job?'

Liam blinks, looks down at the cup, then raises serious eyes to mine.

'It's not like that,' he says.

'Really? Because from where I'm standing, that's exactly what it looks like.'

From behind me, I hear Howard cough before launching into an obvious and futile attempt at distracting the others by starting a conversation about last night's women's singles match at Wimbledon.

'Please, can we not do this now,' says Liam, looking pained. 'Not here. Let me have the chance to explain properly. I think you might feel differently if you had the full picture. Can we meet later – this evening if you're free?'

Incredulous, I shake my head. How is it possible that after everything we talked about, after everything I told him, he could be this stupid or insensitive?

'Oh, believe me, I've got the picture. And you needn't trouble yourself with...'

I'm interrupted by the flinging open of the stockroom door and the emergence of Tom carrying a cardboard box.

'Annie!' Tom calls out cheerfully, 'I was starting to think you'd gone all Meryl Streep on us and shacked up in Greece with a string of sexy suitors.' He shimmies his hips and treats us both to a burst of Mamma Mia, as he heads to the children's section, completely oblivious to the frigid atmosphere he's lobbed his glitterball into.

A whisper of heat warms my cheeks as I'm briefly transported to an island paradise and one particularly sexy suitor. Perhaps Liam spots my blush. Perhaps he, too, is remembering because I watch his eyes darken.

'Liam,' I begin, dragging myself back to the present, to the fact our employer is at this moment finalising the details to promote this man to a job that was mine. 'There really isn't anything more to say.'

He opens his mouth as though he's going to speak, but I beat him to it.

'You know, it's possible you might actually have done me a favour.' I let out a small laugh, though there's nothing remotely funny about any of this. 'Who knows how long I might have stagnated here, in this — ' I flick a palm to indicate the beloved shop, where I spent a good deal of my formative years and much of the last five, 'smalltown, dead-end job.'

An uncomfortable noise from Howard alerts me that my voice has risen to audible levels, but I couldn't care less.

'You might want to ask Daddy to stump up for a new sign out front though, Franklyn's Boo Shop probably isn't the look you're going for, even if it does sum up this company.'

With that, I turn my back on Liam and march to the sales desk, where Theresa eyes me with caution and Howard is concentrating on a stapler as though it were a Krypton Factor challenge. Daphne merely raises her eyebrows, as I push past her and thrust my tea towel at Howard.

'This is for you,' I say, plonking it in front of him. Heat pricks at the back of my eyes. 'Thanks for everything.' My voice cracks with the effort of holding tears in check. 'Have a wonderful retirement.'

A watery film distorts my vision as I stride for the door, leaving a thick silence in my wake.

I make it about twenty metres down the road, before a loud gulp escapes me and the tears begin to fall.

# CHAPTER 27

## ESSEX

### (One Week Later)

Thirty years of age, with a literature degree, a career in bookselling and a truncated stint in journalism and the only job I could find with an immediate start was in the cafe at our local garden centre, which also boasts a farmyard animal petting zoo.

How lovely, you may think. What a happy environment to work in, you'll assume. Pensioners perusing leather gardening gloves and stopping for tea and scones. Green-fingered gardeners, selecting seeds and perennials, choosing fruit trees and pots. Families killing time at the weekend; Mum filling her basket with artisan coffee cake and overpriced bottles of apple press in the farm shop, whilst Dad shepherds toddlers between a donkey and three chickens.

Well, no. Because last Friday, most UK schools finished for their summer break and now every last primary-aged pupil in Essex is currently running around the restaurant of Langtree Nurseries, crayons clutched in one hand and iPad in the other. When the little bastards aren't drawing on the tabletops, or tipping over salt pots, their anthropomorphic digital characters are deafening everyone within a half-mile radius. This is my third shift, and I've sold more Fruit Shoots in this cafe than the entire garden centre has sold plants.

'Annabel, could you pop out back and get some more sauce sachets please,' asks Linda, my supervisor, swooping past me with two plates of sandwiches.

And why not – let's re-stock every bitter parent's weapon of choice. When your own life consists of sticky surfaces, snotty tissues, wet beds and crumbs, why not get revenge on the rest of society by leaving half squeezed packets of mayonnaise, ketchup and salad cream stuck to tabletops, chairs, floors and my personal favourite, the underside of plates, ripe for oozing over your fingers when you pick them up.

I return with the boxes of sachets and begin refilling the condiment baskets, when there is a tap to my shoulder.

I turn around to see Jess and Vik loitering behind me.

My throat goes tight.

It's not that I've been actively ignoring my friends. I mean I haven't exactly had the time for socialising, nor the money for drinks in bars.

I've also been aware of how painfully close I've come to crumbling, again.

If I just keep going, keep my head down and work hard, I can get through this without going back there.

'Hey,' says Vik, giving me a gentle smile.

Jess isn't smiling. Jess looks mad.

'Hey,' I reply.

'What are you doing here?' asks Jess eventually, looking around in distaste.

I scowl. 'What does it look like, Jess? What are you doing here?'

No idea at all why I'm acting like a teenager who found out her friends went to a party without her. If anyone went anywhere, it was me, but unfortunately, I haven't managed to quite make it back.

'Oh, I'm just looking for a – um, bay tree,' says Vik, his voice raising at the end in question, which immediately exposes him.

'Right. They grow pretty big. Ash all right with that, is he? Given you live in a flat?'

Jess rolls her eyes.

'Er, well, actually, your mum told us you were here,' Vik says, giving up on the pretence.

I nod.

'Yeah,' chips in Jess. 'Turns out that not only are you now living back with your parents, but you've jacked in your job. Two pretty major events, Annie, that you haven't even mentioned.'

I swallow down the rising lump, the hard knot of emotion I've been doing so well keeping at bay.

'I would have told you, when I saw you,' I say, wincing inwardly at the hard tone that comes out of my mouth.

'And when might that have been?' asks Jess, narrowing her eyes. 'Because you've not been returning either of our calls or replying to messages.'

'Annabel?' calls Linda from the counter where a queue some dozen or so deep has formed. 'Can I have a hand?'

'I've got to go,' I say, shoving handfuls of ketchup sachets into the already overflowing basket.

As I scoot back behind the counter and begin to take a customer's order, I pray my friends won't stay and eat. I'm not sure I can cope with keeping up a pretence of normality whilst cutting slices of cake and percolating coffee, all under Jess's X-ray scrutiny.

It's been a week since I walked away from the bookshop and, despite a few concerned texts from Howard, I've heard nothing from anyone.

Franklyn's emailed me with my P45, on the back of my perfunctory email to HR advising them of my termination of employment. There have been no calls from head office and no messages from Liam. I walked away, and they let me.

Instinctively, what I want more than anything is to collapse on the sofa with Jess and sink a bottle of wine, whilst I weep into a cushion. But an innate fear of mental collapse is preventing me from following this path. Instead, I am steeling myself. Training my brain to concentrate on the here and now, rather than what's done. I'm fortifying my soul with take-home cake instead of books (to be fair the lemon drizzle is immense) and focusing on getting through one day at a time, instead of daydreaming about the future. Daydreams that had begun to include Liam.

Besides, how could I ever go in there again? Have Liam serve me? No, thank you very much.

There will be no going back for me. Not to Franklyn's, or Braithwaite's Books, as was. Even the Langtree Tearooms feel out of bounds to me now; Daphne was complicit in feeding the machine that stole her own father's business.

I've decided it's time to move on. I'd barely been serious when I mentioned moving away to Jess and Vik on holiday, merely idly musing on the paths open to me. But there are no other paths. If I had to work here for the next thirty years, I'd either top myself, or commit infanticide.

My friends, cherished as they are, will be consigned to the Langtree chapter of my life. A chapter which is soon to end.

'Here you are. love,' says Mum later that evening, handing me a mug of tea and settling on the sofa beside me.

Dad's out for a pint with a friend, an extremely rare occurrence according to Mum, and I read between the lines it's only because I'm here to keep her company, otherwise he wouldn't leave her side. This adds another layer to the guilt already shrouding me, because as soon as I've found a job I'll enjoy and somewhere I can afford to live, I will be leaving this town, leaving Mum and Dad.

'Here, do you know what I've been watching?' she says, fiddling with the TV remote and scrolling through her recordings, 'I'd forgotten how good it was, The Durrell's. It's your fault going off to Corfu like that and getting me into it again. I've binged two whole series in a week.'

She presses play and the familiar theme tune plays out over the opening titles, before bursting into the topaz blue of Greek skies, creamy stone buildings draped in bougainvillea and the good-natured bickering of the Durrell family. The camera zooms in on young Gerry, as he tries to coax an unsuspecting creature into his specimen net and I think of Gerry in the book, and his tortoises.

A sensation of loss punches me in the gut so hard that it winds me.

Mum chatters away beside me, slurping her tea and cooing over Spiros, the handsome Greek love interest of Louisa, whilst I stare at the screen through hot, silent tears that spill down my cheeks and drip from my chin.

'I tell you, that man could drive me anywhere, even in that old claptrap of a car.'

Mum looks sidelong at me, and the smile slides from her face.

'Annie, love? Whatever is wrong?'

She takes my untouched tea from me and puts it on the coffee table along with her own, then twists in her seat beside me.

'Hey, come on love.'

She pulls me into her, wrapping an arm around my shoulder and stroking my head.

I submit to the tears, letting them leave me in great, heaving sobs, unable to stop now even if I wanted to.

Mum doesn't rush me, she just holds me tight, murmuring 'It's all right darling, let it all out.'

Eventually, when my chest has stopped spasming from each burning, wrenching sob, I pull away. Mum does what so many mums up and down the country do and produces a tissue from up her sleeve and assures me it's clean.

'I'm sorry,' I gulp, then blow my nose.

Mum frowns. 'You've nothing to be sorry for, love. You came back from a lovely holiday to find you had to move out, so it's completely understandable if you feel a bit down. And I don't know what's happened at the bookshop. I don't like to pry, but I'm sure you have your reasons for leaving.'

'I didn't though,' I say, voice choked and thick. 'Have a lovely holiday.'

Mum waits for me to continue.

'Most of the time I was lonely, even though the apartment was double-booked, and I had to share it with the worst man on earth.'

At this mum looks surprised. I'd never told her anything about Liam being there. There didn't seem much point.

'Liam. He's the manager of the Chelmsford branch.'

Mum nods in understanding. 'The anti-Christ who wins all the prizes?'

'How do you know about that?'

'Oh, I see Jess from time to time in town. She usually gives me the low-down.'

I nod, trying not to flinch at Mum using the phrase 'low-down'.

'Tight arseholes sent him to the rental apartment I booked, as his so-called luxury holiday prize.'

'O-kay,' Mum ventures, treading carefully. 'And so, I'm guessing you two didn't quite hit it off?'

Another wave of misery engulfs me. 'We didn't. And then there were the tortoises. And then we did. But he's just another Garrett Delaney, and now he's gone and taken my job.' The tears come again, drowning out my efforts to clarify, so that all I add is, 'He's using my mug.'

Mum waits patiently until my current volley of tears dries up, before patting my hand and saying, 'I'm going to make us both fresh mugs of tea, then when you're feeling up to it, I want you to start at the beginning.'

And so, in between sips of hot sweet tea and nibbles on a digestive biscuit, I do.

I tell her about encountering Liam at the conference, and how it already felt like a competition between us, about whose branch would survive. About arriving in Corfu to find him there, neither of us prepared to back down.

I tell her about finding the book with the message, and how

I had replied. I don't tell her it was Liam, but I explain how it became personal, how exciting it was.

I tell her about the shirt, but not about the vibrator. I tell her about the sunset cruise, and how everywhere I went he was there. I don't tell her about Niko, because she's my mother and doesn't need to know about my willingness to get into a fishing boat alone with a total stranger.

When I explain about finding Mikey's bucket list and recognising Liam's handwriting, that he was the mystery scribe, she surprises me by not being surprised at all.

'Of course he was,' she says.

'But why would I suspect it was Liam?' I ask, a little frustrated at Mum's blasé attitude. 'It could have been any of a hundred guests.'

'Annie, come on. Two total bookworms staying an arm's throw away from this bookshelf. You didn't think it odd that a stranger would be interested enough to keep messaging another stranger when they could be off meeting people on Tinder if they were that desperate?'

'But...'

'Didn't it occur to you that maybe Liam wanted the chance to get to know you, without being treated like a pariah?'

I must look wounded by this, because Mum softens her words with a kind smile.

'It's OK, love. I know more than anyone what that utter bastard Delaney did to your confidence. You struggle to let people in. You're wary, and with good reason. But at some point, you're going to have to try and let it go, or you'll push away everyone who ever tries to get close.'

'But Liam *is* a bastard, and I was right to be wary. He let me get close to him, let me care about him, and then he pulled out his ace.'

I fill Mum in on the rest, glossing over the night of rampant sex and jumping to the part where I found out his billionaire father had invested in Franklyn's and they would be closing the Chelmsford shop and instead installing the prodigal son in my job, until he'd penned enough poems and back-handed enough publishers to go ahead and leave anyway.

'But from what you've said, it doesn't sound as though Liam was gloating about Franklyn's plans,' says Mum, ever the diplomat. 'It doesn't sound as though he had any choice about it.'

'There's always a choice, Mum. He could have told me on the first day of our holiday – that would have been the fair thing to do, even if it didn't change anything.'

'And what does Jess say about all this?' she asks.

I play with the tassel on a cushion. 'I haven't spoken to her about any of it.'

'Vikram?'

I shake my head.

'Why ever not? They're your friends, Annie, they'll be worried about you. I thought it was odd when they showed up here the other day asking where you were. I assumed they meant which garden centre you were working in.'

'I'm scared.'

'Scared of what, darling?' asks Mum, coaxing me gently.

'That if I dwell on everything that's happened, with Travis, the house, the holiday, Liam, the bookshop – that it will be like before.'

That I'll once again take to my bed and remain there, curled into a foetal position, only surfacing to take infrequent, forced showers, eat when food is given to me, and chase sleep away every night.

PTSD, the doctor had said, which at the time had somewhat baffled me. Of course, I was familiar with the condition but associated it with tours of Basra and Vietnam veterans, survivors of rape, abuse, trauma, national disasters. It had been a shock to learn people like me could be affected too.

When I got the call to say Mum had been diagnosed with cancer, I'd literally just filed my complaint against Garrett. If I'd been armed with this information two days sooner, I would never have done it. I would have handed in my notice and left.

But instead, when I just wanted to go home, I was subjected to a string of gruelling, uncomfortable meetings, all of which ostensibly resulted in the termination of my employment and a burden of shame, embarrassment and fury which I would carry for quite some time.

There wasn't time to process these feelings. I understand this now. Once home, I developed an iron-clad determination to support my parents in every way I could. I took Mum to appointments, I talked with Macmillan nurses, I geed up Dad when he got so low that he was practically horizontal. I watched TV with Mum, cooked them both nutritious dinners. When my parents couldn't parent me, I parented them.

And then, Mum recovered. It wasn't an instant miraculous event, but gradual. So gradual, I didn't notice the roles begin to reverse again.

When I should have been joyously celebrating my mother's remission, instead I retreated to my room.

Purpose had sustained me for almost a year, until it ebbed away and left me bereft.

'Oh, darling,' Mum says, hugging me to her and rocking me. 'If anyone is going to understand, it's going to be your friends. They were here for you then and they're here for you now. Sometimes, in order to unburden yourself, you have to do the exact opposite of what feels right. Losing control, feeling your emotions, giving in and giving up, they're all part of finding your solid ground, so you can start building your way back up.'

'But what if I don't find solid ground? What if I just keep falling?' I mumble into Mum's jumper.

'I wish I could promise everything will always be all right. It's what any mother wants their child to believe. But the truth is, sometimes everything goes to shit.'

I laugh-snort. I've never been able to handle it when my sweet mother swears.

'And when that happens, you have to trust in those who

love you. You have to trust they've got your back. Like you've got theirs.'

I pull away and sit back, clutching at my sodden tissue.

'It feels like home isn't home anymore. And I don't mean this house, or you and Dad. I mean this place.' I wave an arm to indicate the wider community of Langtree. 'Home was also the bookshop, it's where I've been happy. And now it's gone. What if I can't be happy here anymore?'

Mum studies me for a moment, then says, 'Well, the way I see it, is the bookshop is just a building. A building, that from the sounds of it, will be pretty unrecognisable soon. Maybe home *is* the books, the customers, your friends, new and old. Maybe you don't need a physical space to enjoy those things. Maybe you, I don't know, start up a book club or something, find new ways to carry on enjoying what you love.'

I look down. 'I've been wondering if it's time to move on. Perhaps it's time I tried to build a new life for myself, without relying on familiar faces and places. Maybe, I don't know, maybe I could go back to college, train as a librarian?'

Mum smiles warmly and strokes my arm.

'You'll be great at anything you put your mind to, Annie, and I think you'd be an amazing librarian. There's nowhere you could go that wouldn't be home, just try keeping your father and me away, Jess and Stu, Vik and Ash. I tell you, within months, you'd be sick of the endless visits.'

# CHAPTER 28

Dad came home an hour ago, nicely merry after three pints of Adnams with Geoff, so he didn't notice my red-rimmed eyes, or at least, if he did, he thought better than to ask. I left him and Mum reminiscing over old Glastonbury footage on TV and sloped off to bed, yawning.

Physically, I'm exhausted. My rib cage aches from sobbing and my eyelids are puffy. Emotionally, I'm wrung out; the chat with Mum has helped me to see how irrational my thoughts have become. How terrified I am of finding myself engulfed once more by a debilitating, lonely fear.

But I'm not back there.

I'd known I'd be moving out of Travis's house sooner rather than later, and if I'm honest, I'd expected to have to move back home for a bit, if only to regroup. It was the timing that sucked.

I'd also known for at least four months the Langtree shop might close. I'd already mentally prepared myself for having to find a new job.

The reality was nothing had changed, and unless I was prepared to work for Liam, I still needed to find a new job.

And so there it was – the real reason for my emotional PPE failing whilst I was already balancing on a ladder, my metaphysical hard hat tumbling to the ground below.

Liam.

Liam was unlike Travis in every way possible. But he was also unlike Garrett Delaney.

Yes, he was confident, unpredictable, charismatic – and I'd seen him as a threat because of it, but despite keeping his bombshell from me until the last day of our holiday, I'd known deep down, it hadn't been out of spite. It hadn't been him trying to control me.

My single bed is freshly made with the new cream bedding my mum bought in an effort to make my room feel more adult and less as it had when adorned with Westlife posters – don't judge me, there was also one of Joni Mitchell, my tastes are nothing if not eclectic. And a neat pile of freshly laundered clothing sits on top.

Resting on top of the small bookcase which still bears some of my GCSE texts (*Much Ado About Nothing*, *An Inspector Calls* and my personal favourite, *To Kill a Mockingbird*) is the now familiar cover of *My Family and Other Animals*.

I'd left it in my bag, not wanting to even look at it, but at some point over the past few days my mother has liberated it, along with my dirty washing, despite my protests.

My mother and I both share a habit of flicking to somewhere near the middle of a book to read a random sentence. As though within those few words we can appraise an entire book's potential, a habit I need to kick, so I'd say the chances of her having had a quick nose are high.

I collapse onto my bed with the book and shuffle backwards, propping my pillows behind me.

They say hindsight is a wonderful thing, but in this case I disagree. I'd read all Liam's messages entirely without judgement; curiosity – of course, scepticism, possibly, but with interest – definitely. Would I have given him the same benefit of the doubt, otherwise?

I already know the answer to that. I'd decided what Liam was or wasn't based entirely on my own pessimism.

How would I have reacted if Liam had collared me one morning in those early days of the holiday and said, *Hey,*

*Annabel. You know what? We should hang out and get to know one another better, because it looks like I'm going to be your boss when we get back to old Blighty?*

I shudder at the thought. Booting him headfirst from the balcony may have been my first response and Liam knew it.

*Of course* he was going to bide his time, wait for the right moment. Except when the right moment finally came, when I eventually stopped accusing him of everything from favouritism to nepotism and started to actually listen, that moment turned rapidly to something else. To something urgent and fragile.

I open the book and the postcard of Paleokastritsa falls out, along with a heart-spiking sense of loss. Yes, for the brilliant blue skies and spectacular scenery, but also for the contented joy of that day. For the ease with which Liam and I fell into step, once I'd stopped chewing his ear off. For his dreadful singing voice and his schoolboy enthusiasm, for the gentle way he'd shown me how to snorkel, for carrying my bag up to the monastery when I complained I was hot and tired and for opening up to me on the beach under a blood-red sky.

If I thought I'd cried all the tears I could today I was wrong, because another great fat one begins its journey down my cheek as I flick through the pages and land on Liam's words:

*...before you know it, you no longer remember the first impression they made, because that space has since been occupied.*

Through my tears, the words make me smile. I'm smiling because despite all recent evidence to the contrary, my first impression of Liam when I'd first clapped eyes on him at the Franklyn's conference two years ago, before humiliating myself last year, had been, 'Hell yeah, I would.'

Since then, I've existed in varying states of frustration when it comes to this man, from downright murderous to lustful longing. But in this he is right. Liam Shaw has occupied a space inside of me so large, that all the small things seem irrelevant. I've also committed the cardinal sin of letting a man get under my skin so completely, I've hit pause on my life.

The image of Jess, stern and concerned when she and Vik came to see me today, sends a ripple of shame through me. I know I've hurt her by pushing her away. She did not deserve that. I snatch up my phone. It's late and it's a work night, so instead of calling, I send a text.

*So sorry. I'm a self-absorbed dick, who went and got hung up on a guy when I should have known better. X*

The ticks turn blue immediately. I see she is typing, but then after a few seconds, my phone rings, startling me. Its Jess.

'I couldn't find the right emoji,' she says in a stage whisper. 'But I agree with you, you're a total dick. If you ever thought you were going to spend a glorious week with a genuinely lovely, hot guy who is clearly as into you as you are him, and not fall for him then you're more than a dick, you're a romance-deprived moron.'

I hear the running of a tap in the background and guess she's sneaked into the ensuite bathroom to avoid waking Stu.

She continues, 'I know about the bookshop, Howard told me. And I'm guessing that's why you've run off to serve sandwiches in a kindergarten café.'

It isn't a question. And Jess isn't leaving me room to reply.

'I get it. I do. I know what that place means to you, and why. But it's time, Annie. Time to grow and to take risks, with your life as well as your heart. And that doesn't mean drifting into the arms of the nearest safe option. Travis was nice enough but nice doesn't cut it, does it? Nice doesn't fill your soul up so completely you feel you can take on the world. Because that's what it means, to love someone – to feel invincible, so long as they're by your side.'

She finishes her monologue and draws in a deep breath. 'Sorry. I needed to say that. You're my best friend and I love you, but I want so much more for you than a second-rate boyfriend whose sole credentials are sensible, solid and safe.

And clearly, he wanted more than that too – if the chemistry isn't there from the start, you can't simply wish it into being.'

She's right. Everything she said is right. Well, apart from the bit about falling for Liam, of course. You don't fall for someone in a week. Do you?

'Is that what it's like for you and Stu?' I ask, instead. 'Do you feel... invincible?'

I've always admired Jess's resilience, for always seeing opportunity where I would see disaster.

I can't see my friend, but as she replies I can hear the smile.

'When he leaves his pants on the bathroom floor, I could kill him with the power of thought alone. But the rest of the time, it's as though there could be no burden so big, we wouldn't be OK. If that's invincible, then I guess so.'

'Yes,' I reply, 'I think it must be. I've never had that. Apart from with you and Vik of course, and no offence, but I think there could be limits to the giving and receiving parts of our friendship, as beautiful as it is.'

Jess tuts, then takes me by surprise with her next words. 'So, I'm guessing you banged him then? You know, if a colleague pisses me off at work, I don't go around declaring them to be the most unshaggable person on the planet. You might as well have waved a banner from your balcony declaring I HEART LIAM.'

I supress a snigger. This is what I've needed. Some high-quality straight talk, served up by my best mate. Why did I think I could just brush everything under a threadbare carpet as though it never happened?

'Yeah,' I reply, choosing not to address the banging part of her question. 'Well, it doesn't matter anymore. He chose to make a fool out of me, so I'm drawing a line under it. Like you said, it's time to take some risks. I've decided I'm going back to college. I'm going to do a postgraduate degree and become a librarian. I should have gone down that route from the start.'

There is a long silence and I begin to wonder if the line's gone dead.

'Jess?'

'Mmm, I'm still here, sorry. That sounds great, Annie. Look, better go, I've got an early meeting tomorrow. Are you around on Wednesday?'

'Yes.'

'Great. I have the day off too, meet me at the teashop?'

I hesitate, not particularly wanting to give Daphne my patronage given the current circumstances.

'School's finished so I'll see if Vik's free too?' suggests Jess and my resolve crumbles.

I'm not going to let my feelings about a stupid commercial building lease get in the way of a tradition my friends and I have enjoyed for many years.

'Sure.' I say, 'I'd love to. And Jess?'

'U-huh?'

'Thank you. You're fabulous.'

'Er, I know,' she says, as though I'd stated a blatantly obvious fact, and then she's gone.

# CHAPTER 29

The following day, when I finish my shift at the garden centre, I pull my phone from my bag and am surprised to see a missed call from Travis.

It will be another dull reminder to have my post redirected or cancel the window cleaner. Whatever it is can wait until I get home.

'See you Thursday, love,' says Linda cheerfully, as I call goodbye and exit the café.

She's a nice lady, Linda. Grown-up kids, widowed. This job has been a godsend, she's told me, for getting her out of the house and meeting people.

I understand that, and on the days when there has been time to chat with customers, especially the elderly ones, to help them choose between cakes and scones and assure them they deserve a treat, I've enjoyed myself. Just as I always enjoyed chatting with customers at the bookshop. I reflect again on the ruthless environment of the newspaper, and how it's a good job we're all different. A good job we don't all want to be CEOs and Executive Editors, or the employment landscape would be like a scene from *Braveheart;* stilettos protruding from eye sockets, heads caved in with MacBooks, the ground littered with half-drunk macchiatos and bloodied stumps, someone reciting lines from their Power Point presentation, whilst the victor does laps in an Aston Martin.

It's not that I don't have ambitions, just that I'm taking

my time to fine tune them. Maybe I'll have my dusty old bookshop one day, but in the meantime, I have a plan. And it's a damned good one.

When I get in, I chuck my bag on the kitchen table and flick the kettle on. I have the house to myself for an hour before anyone else gets home. Mum went back to work part-time after she recovered, and Dad still works every day at the same local shipping firm, as he has for the past thirty years.

I plod upstairs for my laptop, then bring my mug of tea to the table and settle down to research the postgrad course.

But first, I brace myself to confront the nuclear wasteland of my finances and log in to my online banking.

Expecting this month's salary to have been deposited, and hoping it's brought me back into the black, I gaze at the balance of my current account in confusion.

The figure makes no sense.

There are too many zeros for one thing. Two of them. And then some.

I click into my transactions, scanning the debits and credits.

There is the Franklyn's payment, exactly as expected.

But there, too, is a deposit into my account of thirty thousand pounds.

THIRTY THOUSAND POUNDS.

Transferred today, the 22nd of July by T. Buckley with the simple reference 'House'.

Travis.

What the heck?

This *has* to be a mistake. He's mixed me up with the solicitor or something and will be banging down my door any minute in panic.

Then I remember he called me earlier, so I yank my bag across the table and rummage inside for my phone, and find I have an unread message.

*Annie,*

*You will receive a deposit into your account today;*

*proceeds from the sale of the house after completion. I'll be honest, the house fetched a king's ransom.*

*I sought advice on the figure, to reflect our years of cohabitation and your contribution to the household. I hope you find it fair. Please use it to set yourself up somewhere and accept my good wishes to you and your family for whatever the future brings.*

*Travis*

*P.S. Confirmation of the above will follow in writing, to fulfil tax obligations.*

I stare at my phone screen for so long, the screen locks.

Bloody hell.

When my coffee date with Jess comes round the next day, I'm still in a state of shock.

I haven't mentioned the payment to my parents yet, wanting a little time to absorb this change in circumstances and properly think about my options. I don't think I'll mention it to Jess and Vik either, not yet.

I did reply to Travis though and thanked him courteously and sincerely.

This was not something he had to do. He *chose* to, because deep down he is still the sensible, solid and safe man he was when we first met. Just because we stopped loving each other, if ever we truly did, doesn't mean he became an arsehole overnight. If anything, I'm the arsehole. I wasted our time by mistaking fondness for love, and I know it.

At three o clock, I push open the door to the teashop and spot Jess, not at our usual table but a larger one, which seems odd because other than for her, the place is empty.

'Vik not coming?' I ask, when Jess releases me from a brief, yet lung-crushing hug.

'He's running a bit late,' says Jess.

I notice she hasn't pre-ordered, so I glance about for Daphne, who is nowhere to be seen.

'It's like the Mary Celeste in here. Where is everyone?' I ask.

Jess makes a 'beats me' face whilst seeming to find the laminated menu a source of fascination, despite the fact, that to our knowledge, it hasn't changed in at least five years.

Just as I'm starting to feel slightly uneasy and wondering what's up with my friend, the door opens and Daphne strides in, switching the sign on the door from open to closed before sliding the bolt across.

'Oh, sorry, we didn't know you were closing early. We'll go somewhere else,' I offer.

'No,' replies Daphne abruptly. 'You're fine. Usual, is it? One latte, one cappuccino?' she asks, without waiting for a reply.

I try to catch Jess's eye, hoping she'll agree this feels a bit weird. How are we meant to have a frank conversation in this stony silence? But she's typing quickly into her phone.

'How are the plans going?' I ask Jess, as the coffee machine gurgles into life.

'Mm?' she asks, distractedly.

'The big trip? The one you've been planning for the past year, which is now mere months away?'

'Oh, yeah. We've had some more ideas.'

'Ideas? I thought it was booked.'

Jess simply makes a non-committal noise as there comes a tap at the door.

Daphne delivers our drinks to our table, then moves to the door, unbolts it, and ushers someone in.

'Howard?' I look up in surprise.

The sudden presence of my old boss and friend fills me with both joy and shame. I have not treated him well. Not even had the decency to go and talk to him in person, since walking out of the shop and quitting my job.

'Hello Annie, love. How are you?'

He pulls up a chair at our table and I feel instantly on edge. What is this? Some kind of intervention? Are Jess and Howard conspiring to convince me to return to my old job? Well, they can save their breath. My mind is made up and no amount of sweet talking will change it.

'I'm fine,' I reply, a little coolly, feeling like a rabbit in the headlights, then because this is Howard, whom I love, add 'I'm sorry I've not had chance to see you yet, and for leaving you in the lurch.'

He shakes his head vigorously, resembling a good-natured Saint Bernard.

'Nothing to apologise for.'

I smile, then wait for him to continue. It's obvious he expected to find me here, so he clearly has something he wants to say. But an awkward silence follows, where all three of us sit there, waiting, for something, for someone, to speak.

'I never said thank you for the souvenir,' Howard finally says. 'Tea towels are always, er, handy.'

At this Jess shoots me a look.

'Souvenir? Why haven't I got a souvenir?'

Blast. I do, in fact have both Jess and Vik's souvenirs in my bag, where they clunked together noisily the whole walk here. But I sense now is not the moment to pull a large glass cock filled with booze from my bag.

'I'll give you yours later,' I say.

'Is it a tea towel too? Why can't I have it now?'

'It isn't a tea towel.'

'Ooh, I bet it's sweets. I love sweets from foreign countries, they have way better names than ours, like Twinkies and Pinkies. Am I right?' she asks, eagerly.

'Well, it's definitely something you can suck,' I retort, half tempted to thrust it at her just to shut her up.

Daphne reappears with a tray bearing a teapot, a cafetiere, five cups and a plate of millionaire shortbread, which she places on our table.

There is some kind of intervention in play, and I don't like it. Not one bit.

'What's going on here?' I demand, choosing to direct my

question at Jess, but an urgent rap on the door prevents her from replying.

Next, when Daphne opens the door, a flustered Vik files in, closely followed by another man.

Liam.

'Sorry everyone,' says Vik, hurrying over to the table and snatching up a shortbread from the plate. 'You didn't start without us, did you?'

Liam holds back a little, loitering behind Vik and in the week that has passed since I saw him last, he seems to have lost that holiday glow. He's dressed casually in jeans and a blue t-shirt that makes his sun-lightened hair pop, with a grey messenger bag slung across his shoulder. He looks tired, possibly even uptight.

His gaze slides to mine and he gives me a small, perfunctory nod.

The mere sight of him has butterflies tangoing in my tummy, but still my sceptical mind fills with panic. Surely to goodness he's not staged this, whatever *this* is? Surely, he isn't using my friends and colleague to bully me into working with him, *for* him? As though he knows what's best for me.

'What is this?' I ask again, this time a lot more forcefully. 'Will someone please tell me what the hell is going on?'

It's Howard who looks to the others first, and then delivers the news.

'Franklyn's have had a change of heart, Annie. The Langtree shop no longer presents a viable option for expansion, so they have decided to keep the Chelmsford branch open instead.'

He looks thrilled to impart this information, although considering the man was about to be consigned to gardening leave on full pay, God knows why.

'But I thought Langtree was so much cheaper, that was what it was all about wasn't it, cost-cutting? Why would they change their mind?'

'Couldn't say,' he says, shaking his head, in a tone implying he could.

Unable to keep the grin from her face, I see Jess's eyes slide towards Daphne, who merely shrugs, cool as a cucumber.

'What's going on?' I ask, again. 'I mean, really?'

'There may have been a few choice words bandied around in the lease renewal, signs of subsidence and damp, expensive forthcoming renovations, as reflected in the significantly increased rent,' explains Daphne.

'Oh, I see,' I say, not seeing at all. 'I'm sorry to hear that.'

Daphne rolls her eyes exaggeratedly.

'Fuck me. Of course, there ain't any subsidence. Not that I know of anyway.'

I frown, confused. 'I'm sorry, I don't get it. I thought you would have wanted Franklyn's to keep the shop open. I thought you were letting them expand into the flats above too.'

At this Daphne's serene composure visibly cracks.

'You think I intended to kick out a family of three and an elderly widower from their homes to line *their* pockets? Not bleedin' likely, which is exactly what I told the bigwig who came here with his flash car. They thought some legal jargon and a few magic numbers would be enough to bulldoze me, just like they did with my father. Well, I've been biding my time and September marks seven years since my father made a deal with the devil. Seven long years until the first break clause in their lease contract, which I will not be renewing, under any circumstances.'

Shocked at Daphne's impassioned speech and realising how little I've really known her all these years, I'm then further surprised when Liam steps forward and speaks.

'When dealing with large corporations like this... especially,' he stresses with ill-concealed distaste, 'if my father is involved, it can be better for everyone to let them feel like they've made their own decision. Even though Daphne would not be renewing, Franklyn's are the ones who have stepped away.'

Vik chips in. 'It was all above board, we took advice. From an old university friend of mine who went on to specialise in property law. That's why we're a bit late,' he adds, addressing the others, 'sorry – Nick's meeting overran.'

I stare blankly at my friend, then back at Liam, who has his hands hooked into his pockets, not at all his usual confident self. If I didn't know better, I'd say he looked nervous.

'But last week?' I ask, looking to Howard. 'In the bookshop—'

He gives me a kind smile, but it's Daphne who speaks.

'That was me delivering the good news,' she says triumphantly. 'And it's a bloody good job this young man came to see me a few days before,' she adds, looking at Liam.

'And that we happened to be in here at the time,' says Jess, with a mischievous, wild-eyed grin.

'You're lucky I even recognised you,' quips Liam. 'Without your comedy glasses.'

Jess feigns mock horror. 'I thought they rather suited me. I was thinking of getting some on prescription.'

'Takes all sorts, the Jeffrey Dahmer look's not one I'd have gone for myself.'

Jess sticks out her tongue.

I stare blankly at my friend and the man whom I've come to care for, yet hadn't expected to see again, sparring like old pals.

'OK, OK,' says Daphne, taking control. 'When you've quite finished dishing out sartorial advice, Liam, shall we get to the point of all this?'

'Yes, sorry,' he says, looking like a chastened schoolboy. Although to be fair, this is the effect Daphne has on all of us, so it's no wonder he's immediately in her thrall. 'I've got the paperwork here.'

He reaches into the messenger bag at his hip and pulls a wad of papers out, before passing them to Daphne.

She takes them from him and turns the pages, skimming and nodding, then she looks directly at me.

'Franklyn's are due to vacate the premises by the 13th of

September when their lease expires. This, is, a new lease, that I am hoping you will consider, Annie.'

'Me?' I ask, in shock. 'Why on earth would I need a lease?'

'Because I want you to restore Braithwaite's Books back to what it once was. It doesn't have to be called Braithwaite's of course, it can be anything you like, within reason. Vik's mate has drawn up a proposal, which I think you'll agree is fair. First three months will be rent free, give you chance to get established. I'll cover the business rates too. The lease is for five years, with a break clause after two, should the business be struggling. But I think you'll make it successful, just as it always was. Dad should never have given it away.'

My mouth falls open as Daphne slides the documents across the table to me and my brain stalls as I struggle to process what she's said.

'It's what you've always wanted,' says Howard, taking over from Daphne. 'Here is your opportunity. You know you can do it; you could run that place standing on your head.'

'But how?' I splutter, still feeling dazed. 'Where on earth would I get that kind of money? To set up accounts with publishers and suppliers, buy in stock and fittings and pay staff?'

In the back of my mind, a small voice pipes up and reminds me I am now the custodian of thirty thousand pounds, but I push that voice aside. This is ridiculous. You don't just wake up one day and set up a bookshop, with no planning or preparation.

'Whilst I would never take a penny from my father,' says Liam, his voice quiet and unsure, 'I don't draw the line at using his name to pull in favours. Setting up accounts won't be a problem. He's a powerful man in the retail world.'

'And I may be able to help with a small loan,' offers Daphne, 'to get you going. It would mean a lot to me to see you making a success of it. But I'll be completely straight with you if you don't want to take this opportunity, Annie, I will be looking for a manager anyway, but I'd rather it was you.'

At this I give a tight laugh and face Liam. 'Don't tell me. You're waiting in the wings after I've been given first refusal? Is that what you meant by using your connections?'

I sense all the oxygen being sucked from the room the second the words leave my mouth. Beside me, Jess shifts in her seat.

Liam's face darkens, hurt lancing across his eyes.

'Trust me, Annie. I'm done in the bookselling trade. I've handed in my notice at Franklyn's. I'm thinking of heading back to Scotland actually, once I've worked my notice.'

I feel the blood draining from my face.

'Liam never wanted to take this from you, Annie,' says Howard, gently. 'He came straight in the day he got back from Greece to see if there was anything that could be done to stop it. I told him to come next door and see Daphne.'

I struggle to swallow, look down at the paperwork. See my name in black and white.

'Well, I'd better get back,' says Liam. 'I'll leave you guys to it.'

I hear a few mumbled goodbyes and when I finally find the courage to look up, it is to see the door to the teashop closing.

Liam has gone.

# CHAPTER 30

There is a long, awkward silence that is finally punctuated by Howard announcing he needs to get back to the shop and lock up so Tom can go home.

He gives my shoulder a squeeze. 'Whatever you decide will be for the best, love,' he says, kindly, before departing.

Then Daphne, with all the subtlety of a sledgehammer, gathers and stacks the cups and plates and suggests we move across the road to the pub so she can go home to watch *The Chase*.

I move robotically, following Jess as she pushes back her chair, still unable to process what has just happened.

'You coming for a pint, Vik?' asks Jess.

'Can't. Ash is taking me out. Filming wrapped today so we're celebrating with a meal at The Thai Light.'

'Ooh, enjoy. Say hi to Ash.'

I barely manage a nod to my friend as he leaves, let alone acknowledge the effort he must have gone to on my behalf, with all the legal help.

'Have a good think about it, Annie, before you make any snap decisions,' says Daphne as she sees us out. She pauses, before shutting the door. 'One more thing, though it might not be my place to say so, that fella of yours clearly cares about you. I'd think on that too.'

I gawp and make to correct her, tell her he's not my fella, but Jess yanks me away.

'Thanks Daphne, see you soon,' calls Jess, before the door snaps shut.

I shake her off and turn to face her.

'Why is everyone treating me like a naughty kid you make allowances for? I don't deserve it! I've been unprofessional, jacking in my job like that, not to mention completely ungrateful to my mates – who for some reason keep on scooping me back off the floor and as for Liam...'

I drag my hands down my face, wishing I could unsee the look of hurt that flashed across Liam's face when I'd hurled yet another utterly unfounded accusation at him.

'Come on,' sings Jess, tugging at my sleeve. 'Pub.'

I don't even bother to argue.

Minutes later, we are tucked into our favourite spot in a booth near the back and Jess is pouring two glasses from a bottle of prosecco. She places it back in the ice bucket and pushes a glass towards me.

'Drink,' she says, so I do.

I take a large gulp of the ice-cold liquid and relish the bursting of bubbles on my tongue. It's the first drink I've had since arriving home from Corfu and it goes immediately to my head.

'So, what will you call it? "Annabel's", sounds quite nice. Although that does also sound like it could be a nail salon, or a children's clothing shop, how about "Baines' Books?"'

I shake my head. 'Jess, I can't do it.'

'And why ever not? You've been waffling on about having your own independent bookshop since you were about nine years of age and then when the opportunity literally falls into your lap, you're going to pass it up because, what? You're scared? Because you suddenly have a burning desire to be a librarian, which I don't believe for a minute? Or... is it because Liam had something to do with it, which counts in your head as some kind of powerplay? Because if that's true – I'm telling you, as your best mate, you need to sort your shit out.'

This makes me look up in surprise.

'I mean it, Annie. And I get it, I really do. Nobody wishes that arsehole Delaney a serious dose of dick-rot more than I do, but you have got to accept there are guys out there who will do things for you because they actually care. Not because they want or expect anything in return.'

Travis pops into my mind. Despite everything, he's shown me a genuine kindness, when he really didn't need to.

But Liam. How can I have got things so wrong?

'I said some terrible things to him,' I say, running a finger through the condensation on my glass.

'Yeah, I know, I was there, remember.'

'Not today. Before, in Corfu. On our last day.'

Jess watches me, her startling blue eyes blinking slowly, whilst she waits for me to continue.

And so, I tell her everything. Starting from the minute I arrived and found him in the apartment. I tell her about finding the book by the pool and reading that first message, how I'd been compelled to write one back and how they had continued, each one drawing me in to conversations with an enigmatic stranger. I tell Jess, when she can stop chortling long enough to let me speak, about Maria and the suitcases and the vibrator and the petals. About the lucky shirt. She tuts when I tell her how I got rid of it, then clamps her hand over her mouth in horror when I tell her about his brother Mikey. My eyes fill as I describe his pain, and the bucket list he carries around with him of the places they were meant to go.

I tell her about him rescuing me after my disastrous date with Niko, and the day we spent in Paleokastritsa, and how despite knowing he was my work rival, how I couldn't stop being drawn to him. How, even though I vowed to the contrary, it felt inevitable we'd find ourselves in bed together.

And then I tell her what he told me, as our dinner arrived on that last night.

'I didn't even let him explain,' I say, as Jess tops up my glass. 'Just outright accused him of manipulating, lying and generally being a self-serving bastard. And then, even after all that, he still went out of his way to try and help me. Well, this time, I've really blown it. I doubt he'll ever speak to me again.'

Jess is quiet for a moment, and I expect her to agree.

'Do you know what I think?' she says eventually.

'Hmm,' I reply, miserably. It might be the two glasses of fizz, but I'm suddenly painfully aware of how much I miss him.

'I think you've been a twat, there's no denying it. A stubborn, insecure twat who hasn't wanted to believe the truth when it was happening in front of her. You said yourself Liam guessed it was you he was chatting to in the book messages. And yet he continued. He still cared enough to want to get to know the real you beneath those frigging spiky prickles.'

Jess lets out a great sigh of frustration.

'He wasn't paving the way for a good working relationship, you moron. He fancied you and wanted to get closer.'

'And now I've ruined it and he's leaving. Going back to Scotland.'

'From where I was sitting, he looked like someone who was looking for a reason *not* to go back to Scotland,' says Jess.

'It's too late, Jess.'

'Is it? Why don't you talk to him, tell him how you feel?'

A fizz of adrenalin spikes through my veins. Could I?

'Not over the phone. We've never talked on the phone.' I give a small laugh, 'And anyway, I don't even have his number! Nor do I know where he lives, other than a flat in Chelmsford.'

'But you know where he works,' she says, eyes twinkling as she tips her glass in salute. 'Perhaps it's time *you* visited the competition. Made the grand gesture.'

As I process this thought, I become aware of Jess still smirking away like the cat who got the cream.

'What are you smiling about?' I ask.

'Nothing, I'm just happy. I want you to be happy too.'

'But you never smile. You say it gives you wrinkles.'

Jess twirls the stem of her glass, seeming to be considering what to say.

'I'd planned to wait until we were all together, but I don't think I can keep it to myself any longer.'

'Tell me! What is it?' I urge, curiosity spiking me to attention.

'Well, me and Stu's trip,' she pauses for dramatic effect, 'is going to be our honeymoon!'

I gasp, wide-eyed, at my friend.

'Stu proposed whilst you were away, and we decided — why wait? We're getting married at his parents' house in Cornwall in September. Fancy being my bridesmaid?'

# CHAPTER 31

As I cross the threshold of Franklyn's, Chelmsford, I am practically shaking with nerves.

I already know Liam's shift doesn't start until twelve o'clock, thanks to a reconnaissance phone call I made this morning. The woman I spoke to was friendly and squeaky, possibly Clem, and she assured me the manager would be in at twelve, should I wish to call back.

As I approach the sales desk, I almost chicken out. What am I doing? I should have just got his number and sent a text like any normal person would. But nothing between me and Liam has ever been normal, so why start now?

'Hi, how can I help?' asks the young brunette on the cash desk. Not the woman I spoke to earlier, I don't think, and I see her eying the yellow jiffy bag in my hand.

'Hello,' I enthuse, flashing her my widest smile. 'I wonder if you could please pass this on to your manager. It's a book he requested quite urgently.'

The woman glances at the package, which I have marked up for MR L. SHAW in a black marker pen.

'Sure,' she says, taking it from me and placing it under the desk. 'I'll make sure he gets it. Anything else I can help with today?'

'No. Thank you,' I say, disappointed. I'd hoped she'd take it straight out back to the staff room. What if he doesn't see it in time? What if he never sees it? How will I even know.

This was a terrible idea, I think, as I thank the bookseller and leave the shop.

I drive home and somehow get through my shift at the garden centre, although it feels like I'm existing outside of my body, going through the motions. If I'm not thinking about Liam and lambasting myself for ruining a good thing before it had even started, I'm mulling over the bookshop and everything Daphne said.

Eventually, five o'clock comes around and I practically trip over myself in my haste to leave.

'Everything alright?' asks Linda, as I double back for my forgotten bag.

'Yeah.' I reply on my way out, 'I really hope so!'

At home I shimmy past Mum on the stairs, calling over my shoulder that I won't be in for dinner tonight, prompting flashbacks to being sixteen. I shower, blow-dry my hair and slip into the silk Max Mara dress I'd worn the night I drank cocktails with Niko, whilst waiting for a man who never arrived. Then I walk to Langtree's tiny train station and wait for the seven fifteen to Chelmsford.

Twenty minutes later, I step from the train into a British July evening that, whilst clement, certainly isn't warm enough for this dress and curse myself for forgetting a cardigan. It's Thursday, which in some quarters is virtually the weekend, as evidenced by the many office workers weaving their way in and out of bars as I make my way to my destination.

I get there fifteen minutes early.

Fifteen whole minutes to ruminate on the fool I've made of myself, how I've offered too little, too late.

If it hadn't been for Stu going out of his way to collect the book on his commute home from London, I wouldn't have been able to make the gesture. The irony isn't lost on me either, that after telephoning around, I found the book in stock in a London branch of Franklyn's – *Birds, Beasts and Relatives*, the second in Gerald Durrell's trilogy.

I thought long and hard about what to write. In the end, I went for brevity.

*I gift this sequel to you because I'm not ready for our story to end.*

*Meet me, tonight. Eight o clock. Do you know Theo's Greek Taverna on London Street?*

Ok, so I borrowed some of it from the last time I invited Liam on a date. Before I'd known who he was. And just like before, there's no guarantee he'll come, or if he'll have even seen the message.

History repeating itself, I think, as a dark, handsome waiter approaches the bar where I'm perched upon a stool.

'Evening, Madam, what can I get you?' he asks, sounding as Essex as you can get.

I'm disarmed for a moment, having almost expected a Greek accent with thickly spoken s's and z's.

Alas, with this not being Corfu, a cocktail will likely set me back a small fortune, so I order a bottle of beer.

'Did you want to see a food menu? It's our special mezze platter night.' He pronounces mezze, 'mezzie' and if he enunciates the 't's in platter, I don't detect them.

'No thanks,' I say, taking my beer, 'I'll just sit here if that's all right?' It feels less conspicuous sitting here than alone at a table among couples and groups of friends, waiting. Because I'm not at all sure he will come.

'Knock yourself out,' he says, heading off to serve another customer. Corfu, it is not.

In the universal language for appearing occupied enough not to care you're waiting for someone; I reread old emails on my phone and pretend to type new ones.

At five to eight, my heart's beating so hard I'm certain it can be seen through my flimsy dress, and my hands are cold and clammy. I've barely sipped my beer, afraid the alcohol will blunt my senses. Nerves are what will see me through.

When my phone tells me its ten past eight, I begin to regret not leaving my number. Maybe he couldn't make it tonight, maybe if it had been another time, another day? But, in my heart of hearts, I know he could get hold of me if he wanted to. He's managed to become buddies with my mates in the last fortnight, after all.

I pick up my beer and take a long, deep glug, then fumble in my bag for my purse. This is pointless. I may as well go home.

'Hold up. Hope you've got your Jackie Os on there, love,' says the bartender muttering under his breath as the door goes behind me. 'What the fuck is he wearing?'

I don't turn around but have trouble keeping my face in check as a smile threatens the corners of my lips.

When a shadow falls across the counter beside me, I instead focus on the bartender's bemused expression as he asks the customer what he can get him.

'I'll have what she's having, in fact make it two,' says Liam.

'Dude, it's been a nice day, but it ain't bleedin' Barbados.'

'Life is what you make it, Theo.'

I turn my gaze on him, surprised to find the two men grinning at each other.

In truth, the vibrant turquoise, red, orange and green shirt does emphasise Liam's blonde hair and striking eyes and the fabric pulls taut across the broadest part of his chest, emphasising his trim physique. But the shirt is still ridiculous, especially in a fake Greek bar in the middle of Chelmsford High Street.

'Felt in need of some luck, did you?' I ask, tilting my head.

Liam fixes me with a look. 'Do I need it?'

I don't reply, but feeling the bartender's eyes upon us as he places two fresh beers on the counter, I suggest we go and sit down.

'Sorry – there were leaving drinks after work, that's why I'm late,' explains Liam. 'To be honest, I'd half expected to find you planning a boat trip with Theo. I was already plotting another dramatic rescue.'

'Wait. He has a boat?' I ask, suggestively, pretending to push back my chair, before leaning forward on my elbows. 'Too bad I've gone off them. But I *am* interested to know what your rescue plans were?'

'Oh, I was just going to walk alongside the river with a bulging picnic basket and an armful of books – guaranteed to turn your head. We go kayaking together sometimes,' he adds with a twinkle, nodding towards the bar.

Excellent. I suggest a totally random venue in this busy city centre, based on nothing but its link to Greece and hit upon one owned by one of Liam's mates.

Then I pick up on something else he said. 'Leaving drinks. Not *your* leaving drinks?'

'Uh-huh. Clem's been promoted, so today was my last day. It's for the best. Ever since I got back everyone's been weird, treading on eggshells around me. Which is exactly why I never tell anyone who my father is, as it always ends up the same.'

My heart twists at the bitterness in his words. I can't imagine what that's like, to live in someone's shadow like that, never able to escape their reach.

'Liam,' I begin, my practised words deserting me and leaving me feeling panicked.

He's leaving already. I've left it too late.

He looks up at me and offers a weak smile. 'Thank you for the book, Annie. That was thoughtful.'

I nod. Look down at my clasped hands.

'So that's it, you're leaving Essex now?' I ask.

He's quiet for a long moment.

'Well, that kind of depends,' is all he says, and a crackle of hope floods my veins.

'On?' I ask, breath held.

'On whether there's any reason I should stay.'

I gulp, suck in a breath and raise my eyes to meet his loaded gaze.

'I'm so sorry,' I say quickly, wanting, needing to get my

words out. 'I treated you so badly, when all you've ever shown me was kindness. You didn't deserve any of the things I said or accused you of. You're a good man, Liam. It's me with the issues and I'm working on them. I know I don't deserve another chance, but...'

A hand shoots across the table and encases mine.

'You didn't deserve what happened to you and I'm so sorry it did. I get it, Annie. Never apologise for trying to protect yourself. But you do need to recognise when saying no isn't in your best interest. Sometimes taking risks and trusting yourself is the only way to be happy.'

'Are you talking about the bookshop... or us?' I ask, tentatively, eyes inexplicably stinging.

Liam squeezes my hand.

'You went on holiday by yourself and invited a stranger to meet you for a drink. You felt in control of all those things, didn't you? Until a giant curveball showed up in your plans, in the shape of me.'

'I quite like the shape of you,' I blurt, pulling one of my hands free to swipe away moisture from my lashes.

Liam takes on a thoughtful expression. 'Why do I feel like I've heard that somewhere before?'

I splutter. 'You probably think Ed Sheeran has been singing about being in love with the shape of glue all this time.'

He grins, but I'm left feeling self-conscious at having needlessly brought the word 'love' into the conversation.

When Liam speaks again, it's softly and with complete earnestness. 'I have no desire to take an iota of control out of your hands, Annie. You're a strong, capable, passionate woman who should be following her dreams. If there's room in your life for a talented karaoke partner, I'd love to be that guy. But if now's not the right time, then that's fine too. You have to do what's right for you.'

I nod slowly, then tell him.

'I've decided to take on the shop. You're right, it has been my dream, no matter how small – ever since I was a kid. A bookshop of my own, shelves to fill with books I choose and which my customers want. I've got so many ideas for events and clubs; my head feels like it's bursting.'

A warm, slow grin breaks across Liam's face.

'I'm meeting with Daphne tomorrow to start planning timescales and what's more, I have the funding. Travis came through with a share from the sale of the house. I was going to use it to go back to college, but I know in my heart, this is the right thing to do. It feels like the right thing to do.'

'That's amazing. I'm so pleased for you, Annie. Really, I am.'

I take a nerve-wracking breath, then continue.

'The thing is though; you feel right too. I know we haven't known each other long and we've spent most of that time bickering, but I want to get to know you properly. I want to see what happens, if we pick up where we left off, before the bit where I ran off half-way through a lobster dinner.'

'Well, in that case,' says Liam, trailing a finger along my wrist which sends shockwaves through to my toes, 'it's a good job I've just signed the renewal contract on my flat for the next six months. It was the deadline today, so when I got your message, I thought I'd take a punt. Like I told you, this is my lucky shirt.'

I gasp aloud.

'It's not the only thing I've signed today, as a matter of fact. A proposal came through from a publishing house the day after we got back. They're offering me a three-book deal.'

I shove my chair back, ignoring the collective winces at the ear-piercing scraping of metal on ceramic tile, and circle the table in a nanosecond.

Liam pulls me into his lap, and I loop my arms around his shoulders.

'That's incredible, I'm so happy for you,' I cry, genuinely thrilled.

'Yeah, it's pretty cool. But I'll have to find another job, something part-time so I can concentrate on the books.

They're scheduled for quick release with the potential for more in a series if they are well received. I've been in touch with a Down's Syndrome charity too. Apparently, there are activity groups you can get involved in locally, water sports, kayaking, that kind of thing. I think Mikey would approve.'

I lean forwards and plant a kiss on his lips.

'Which reminds me of something else I want to ask you. How do you fancy being my plus one for a wedding in September?'

Liam laughs. "I'm not sure how that relates to kayaking, unless the bride's got a particularly unconventional entrance in mind. But, sure, I'd love to."

'Good. Because we're going to tick another two places off Mikey's list. Jess and Stu are getting married in Cornwall, near Stu's childhood home. We can visit Newquay whilst we're there, and Woolacombe Bay on our way home. Then, when you're feeling up to it, I've always fancied Bali. I think we should finish the bucket list.'

Liam grins. 'That might take a few years on a part-time wage as a struggling writer – but what are dreams for?'

'Speaking of which, shouldn't we be celebrating? It's not every day you sign a book deal.'

'Well,' says Liam, running a hand along my back. 'We could order one of Theo's dirty, beige, deep-fried platters which are about as Greek as I am, or there's a frozen pizza and a bottle of plonk back at mine. I might even have a bar of Galaxy. Which is it to be?'

I slip from Liam's lap, take his hand in mine, pull him to standing.

As we walk from the bar, I turn around and catch Theo's eye, before shooting him a wink.

There's being in control, and then there's enjoying yourself.

'You know what you need?' I say to Liam as he pulls me into his arms the minute we step outside.

'Yes, yes, I do,' he murmurs into my neck, flooding my

core with heat. 'I need lots of things, Annabel, and pizza and wine are nowhere near the top of that list.'

I gasp at the feel of his lips by my ear lobe and the whisper of warm breath.

'Someone like you, with a publishing deal, you could – really, ah,' I suck in a shuddering breath as his palm slides down to the top of my thigh, '– you could really use someone in the bookseller trade, someone passionate about books. To truly champion your work, make sure every last copy flies out the door.'

'Uh-huh,' he says, sliding a thumb across my lips. 'Know anyone like that?'

'Maybe,' I moan. 'But do you know what the real secret to success is? When it comes to selling books?'

'Tell me.'

We're nose to nose now and I'm watching his mouth as it inches closer to mine.

'The answer, Liam, to any question, is *always* to bribe with chocolate. You said you had Galaxy at home, right?'

# EPILOGUE

## CORFU

### (The Following June)

*The Bucket List Murders*, as the series has affectionately been coined, was released into the wild on the first of November with the publication of Liam's debut novel *Death in Dundee* – on the same day, coincidentally, that Braithwaithe & Baines Books opened its doors for the first time.

It's been a rollercoaster ride, this last twelve months and I would not change a minute of it, but if ever we'd needed a holiday, it was now.

Panting and breathless, I wait as Liam unlocks the door, then file past him into the cool, dim apartment.

'Oh, that is heaven!' I moan, baring my face to the air conditioning, whilst Liam grabs our luggage.

I reach for the light switch and snap it on. Nothing much has changed, but the fridge looks new and there is a visitor information booklet lying on the kitchen table. My breath catches when my eyes alight on the objects in a dish. The sea-urchin shells I'd left behind are inexplicably still here, precious and fragile, but safe. It makes me smile.

'Let's check out the bedroom,' says Liam mischievously, taking my hand in his.

'Seriously? That hill has killed me. I'd forgotten how brutal it is.'

I trail after Liam along the corridor, past the bathroom until we reach the bedroom.

'Ta-da!' he announces, flinging the door wide open.

'Maria?' I enquire, taking in the murderous looking towel swans perched among their carnage of blood red petals.

'The very same. Greta mentioned on the email that she works for Hotel Electra now, since they bought up these apartments.'

'And to think I vowed never to visit the same place twice,' I say, shaking my head, but happy to be back here.

'Yeah, I thought we might try and recreate the events that inspired me. You're all right with the sofa-bed tonight, right?'

I poke Liam in the chest, and he grabs hold of me and draws me tightly to him, laughing.

'As if I'd subject you to such torture,' he says. 'However, I have booked us a table at The Olive Grove, if that's OK? I rang ahead to let George and Konstantinos know we were coming.'

Liam has almost finished the third book in his Bucket List Murders series, a series that has been so successful that not only have the first two been in the UK bestseller charts for nearly six months, but there have also been whisperings of TV rights among certain publishing quarters.

The hugely successful books follow the plight of retired chemistry teacher Bernard and his friend Mavis, as they embark on a mission to complete Bernard's late wife's bucket list. Naturally, as the title suggests, all doesn't quite go to plan for Cosy Crime's newest septuagenarian sleuths.

*Havoc in Hawaii* did particularly well, which is amazing considering he wrote most of it during the four frantic weeks we spent renovating the bookshop between the departure of Franklyn's and our grand opening.

Looking back on that day, I still feel the huge swell of pride rise in my throat. I can remember the nervous jangling in my veins as Tom reported on the gathering queue in the street whilst I stuffed branded paper bags with goodies, bookmarks and promotional materials – naturally there was confectionary involved.

Tom had used the downtime to visit family in America and was almost as excited as me about our new venture. I'd stressed that we would have to see how things went, as to how permanent his new role would be, but was quietly optimistic. And I was right to be. Milly went off to university, so it's just the two of us now, with more than enough work to keep us busy.

Liam had been there by my side, flashing me a reassuring grin whenever he caught me quietly fretting.

'Are you ready to greet your adoring public, Mr Shaw?' I'd said, moving from behind the sales desk to where he stood near a small table bearing a towering display of *Death in Dundee* paperbacks.

He'd pulled me towards him and answered with a question. 'Are you ready to greet your eager customers, Ms Baines?'

'Course she is,' Daphne had affirmed, 'she could do it standin' on her head. Now, where am I putting these?' She held a tray of freshly baked miniature brownies and flapjacks. More shameless bribery, but hopefully to benefit us both. In a flash of inspiration during our early discussions, I'd suggested opening up the old, sealed, internal door that separated the bookshop from the tearooms to integrate the two spaces. To my surprise, Daphne had loved the idea. 'Bloody genius', she'd said. Praise indeed.

So now the old wooden door, which is painted a warm shade of teal to match the rest of the shop's interior, always sits open with a small sign above it which reads, 'through to the Langtree Tea Rooms' with a reciprocal sign on her side, which reads 'through to Braithwaite & Baines.' I'd decided from the off that I wanted to honour the original bookshop that had inspired my passion for reading as a girl. Plus, it made sense to include Daphne's name in the venture, since it wouldn't have been possible without her. I think it has a nice ring to it, traditional and bookish.

Jess and Vik had been there for the opening too of course, my stalwart supporters and wielders of paintbrushes, selflessly giving up their evenings and weekends to help with the cleaning, sanding, painting and endless shelf-fitting over the previous few weeks.

'Ready?' Vik had asked, and I'd noticed Jess was hiding something behind her back.

'What've you got there?' I'd asked, trying to peer around her.

Jess had rolled her eyes at my suspicious mind and produced a magnum of champagne. 'The shop's got to be christened, right?'

'You aren't seriously suggesting we smash it over one of my beautifully painted bookshelves?' I'd asked, horror-struck.

'No, Annabel. I'm suggesting Vik fetches the tray of glasses we've got ready back there and we drink it like normal people do,' she'd replied, smirking.

I'd peeked through the window as Jess popped and poured the champagne. Howard was standing in the queue, chatting to my parents. Mum had looked up and caught my eye, then elbowed Dad, who gave me the thumbs-up.

'Come on, quick, gather round,' chimed Jess behind me as I flashed them a wish me luck smile and went to join the others.

As Liam and I were handed a champagne flute each, I'd been reminded of the last time we'd made a toast, just six weeks before, in a hotel on a clifftop in Cornwall, to newlyweds Jess and Stu. It was the most incredible few days; a picture-perfect wedding in a stunning location, with my favourite people at my side. Liam and I left the following day and began our pilgrimage to the surfing capitals of Cornwall and Devon before making our way back home. Four of Mikey's ten locations have now been ticked off and I'm more than happy to play the role of surf-chick girlfriend, if only because Liam in a wetsuit is something I won't ever get tired of seeing.

'Speech,' Vik had demanded once we all had a glass in hand.

I'd glanced around at their expectant faces and felt enveloped in joy.

'Get a wriggle on,' said Daphne, 'we haven't got all day.'

'OK, OK.' I'd laughed, determined to relish the moment. 'This might be a business, but I'd like to think that here at Braithwaite & Baines...' I'd paused for the small cheer that erupted, then repeated, 'I'd like to think that its more than a shop. When people come here, I hope they will experience the wonder and possibility that all books possess. That they feel part of the community, welcomed and valued. That it can be a place of refuge to while away time, a million worlds to escape to when it all gets too much. I'd like them to spend lots of money because believe me, at thirty years of age, taking your boyfriend up to your bedroom whilst your parents are watching the telly is the opposite of cool.'

Everyone had laughed, and Liam snaked an arm around me.

'I'll be saying thank you until the end of time to you guys for helping me get this far, and as soon as I can afford it, dinner will be on me. Tom, thanks for sticking with me, I hope we make it a success, and lastly... Liam,' I looked up at him, beside me, adoration in his eyes, 'who is annoyingly good at most things, with the exception of singing, something tells me you're going to knock it out of the park with your writing career and I couldn't be prouder. So, let's raise a toast to all of us – and then go sell some books!'

'To selling books!' echoed the others, knocking back their fizz.

I handed my empty glass to Jess, turned and planted the lightest kiss on Liam's lips, then crossed the shopfloor to the front door and turned the key.

It was a day I will never forget, for as long as I live, and in the six months since, I have worked tirelessly to make my little shop a haven of bookish joy.

Liam is also taking a well-earned break from edits on his current book, a story partly inspired by last year's holiday in Kassiopi, although instead of a double-booking, Bernard and Mavis have something far less palatable to contend with. The working title is *A Corpse in Corfu* and I found it endlessly entertaining when Liam admitted to me once over dinner, that the idea had come to him when he found himself lying in what he'd thought to be blood-streaked sheets. Coupled with a tale George had told him in The Olive Grove one evening, about a creepy island legend; the idea was born for another Bucket List murder.

'Annie?' he asks, and I register that he'd asked me a question, before my mind had wandered into the fuzzy warmth of recent memories.

'The Olive Grove? Yeah sure. Sounds great. Do I have time for a shower first?'

'Oh yeah,' he says, nuzzling my neck, 'possibly even two.'

'You do realise we're here for a whole week, don't you?' I laugh at my boyfriend, extricating myself from his clutches. 'Anyone would think you were a sex starved teenager.'

Howard has generously dragged himself out of retirement to reprise his role of bookseller, allowing me and Liam some precious time out from our increasingly busy lives. Not that I'm complaining, the bookshop is booming and I'm loving every single minute of it. Liam gave up his flat in Chelmsford and we got a place together, just down the road from the shop. Its small but cosy and I can be either in the shop or in the pub in under ninety seconds. Yes, I've actually timed it.

Liam flops back on the bed and watches me, an amused expression on his face as I fetch my case and unzip it. I rifle through layers of fabric, tossing shoes behind me as I go and root around for my washbag, my packing style as chaotic as ever.

'That's weird,' I frown, scooping everything out onto the floor. 'I could have sworn I packed my washbag; I must have left it in the bathroom at home. Damn.' I scratch my head, annoyed with myself. 'Can I use your shower gel?' I ask Liam.

'Of course. Help yourself.'

I locate Liam's trusty backpack and unzip it, finding his familiar black wash bag with his equally trusty travel-sized tubs and bottles.

'It's probably best if you just tell me which one isn't laundry detergent, washing up liquid, boot polish, beeswax or whatever other cleaning products you've needlessly brought on holiday,' I say, sarcastically. Although there's only non-bio to be found in our house now.

'Sure. Try the orange one, I think you'll like that one.'

'Cool,' I say, before bending to plant a kiss on his lips and seductively shedding my clothes as I head to the bathroom with a towel.

I leave the door open and turn on the shower, suspecting Liam may decide to join me.

Under the water, I reach for the orange tub and spot Liam standing in the doorway. He runs a hand through his hair but doesn't move, so I gather maybe he wants to enjoy the show. I smile at him, then twist the lid of the tub for a scoop of soap, then stare down in confusion.

There is no soap in this pot, but another smaller one instead.

I place the lid on the shelf and take out the next one, twist the lid off that too.

This time, a shiny object glitters back at me and I gasp aloud in surprise.

'Liam,' I whisper, raising my eyes to his. 'This isn't soap.'

'Is it better than a head-to-toe rash?'

A giggle splutters out of me, and possibly also tears, but under the shower it's impossible to tell.

'Room for another one in there?' he asks, more sheepish than I've ever seen him.

I reach across and tug him into the shower cubicle, fully dressed.

Water plasters his hair to his forehead and welds his t-shirt to his chest. I run a hand up to cup his jaw and think to myself that his might be the loveliest, kindest, sexiest face I've ever known in my life. Jess was so right, a year ago. She knew it then and I know it now. Being in love makes me invincible.

'Is that a yes?' he asks, tentatively.

'It's an ask me and you'll find out.' I reply, passing him the tub.

Liam smiles, then teases the ring from where it is securely fastened inside a velvet cushion and reaches for my hand.

'Annabel Baines – bookseller, bucket-list adventurer, best friend and love of my life, will you do me the honour of becoming my wife?'

Only Liam could propose marriage to me whilst I'm standing naked in the shower, but then Liam rarely conforms to type. Reaching up on tiptoes, I kiss him slowly, muttering 'yes, yes, a thousand times yes,' into his lips, and then I offer my hand, fingers outstretched.

I wrinkle my nose. 'Alliteration *and* rhyme in a marriage proposal. You and I clearly spend far too much time around books.'

'Speaking of that,' he says, pushing the elegant, white gold band onto my fourth finger. 'I forgot to pack any. Fancy a trip to the book exchange in the morning?'

I wrap my arms around his neck, and he scoops me off the floor.

'Sure, but promise me something?'

'Anything,' he says, eyes glittering.

'Skip the cutesy messages on the ones you put back. I hear it can land you in all sorts of bother.'

# ACKNOWLEDGEMENTS

I'd like to thank everyone at Legend Times and Serendipity Fiction for their hard work in bringing *Double Booked in Corfu* to publication: Production Manager Ditte Løkkegaard, Head of Sales Liza Paderes, Managing Director Tom Chalmers and Data Manager Sam Rennie. Special thanks to Commissioning and Marketing Manager Olivia Le Maistre for her enthusiasm and insight.

Huge thanks also to Alice Greenway for designing the most gorgeous cover I could have imagined for this book. Each time I look at it, I want to go on holiday. This could prove problematic.

Thank you to Heloise Murdoch for her thorough copy edit, and thanks, as always, to my literary agent Kate Nash, and to the wider team for all their hard work and cheerleading.

Thank you to all the wonderful reviewers and bloggers out there for taking the time to read and shout about the book, and to all readers everywhere who pick up a copy. Thanks also to the RNA reader who was the first to read this book!

The beautiful village of Kassiopi, in the northeast of Corfu, is a real place, as are the church of Panagia Kassopitra and the stunning beaches and harbour. The hotels, villas, restaurants and bars mentioned are entirely fictional, as are all the characters. Also fictional, are the village of Langtree in Essex, and the Franklyn's bookshop chain.

Printed in Great Britain
by Amazon

44758563R00158